"Look, Olivia, I would like to tell you I love you. I think I do. I mean, I surely haven't felt this way in a long time about any woman at all. I guess I'm just, well, I'm afraid I might . . ."

"Yes?" Olivia asked softly.

His words came out rapidly. "I don't want to jinx anything."

Olivia looked up and saw the sincerity in his expression, and she quite suddenly felt a mirthful chortle surface to her lips.

"That's just about the silliest thing I ever heard," she said, smiling gently. "And the most believable."

Her next words brought his gaze up to meet hers.

"I suppose," she said, still smiling, "I suppose that if we don't know one another well enough at this point, we'll have plenty of opportunity to do so in the future. I accept your offer of marriage, Doctor."

Also by Nancy A. Hermann
Published by Ballantine Books:

OF SIMPLE DREAMS

THE
HOMESTEAD

Nancy A. Hermann

BALLANTINE BOOKS • NEW YORK

Copyright © 1993 by Nancy A. Hermann

All rights reserved under International and Pan-American Copyright Conventions. Published in the United States of America by Ballantine Books, a division of Random House, Inc., New York, and simultaneously in Canada by Random House of Canada Limited, Toronto.

Library of Congress Catalog Card Number: 92-97259

ISBN 0-345-36506-2

Manufactured in the United States of America

First Edition: May 1993

This book is for my nephew, Russell Edward Bell, who taught us all that persistence and determination really do pay off. Cheers!

PROLOGUE

Topeka, Kansas
1921

"And so," the old woman said, peering through the crepey slits of her eyelids at the middle-aged woman seated in a wooden chair near her bed, "where do you want me to start?"

Leah Rice tapped the end of her sharpened pencil, one of the many she had carried with her today, against the notepad on her knee. She smiled softly at the old woman, trying to stifle the impatience she'd been fighting all day. Surely she had not come all this way, had not spent all these years looking and searching and praying, for naught. She absently pushed back an errant strand of dark auburn hair, and then thought for a moment.

"I would like to hear everything. So . . . just start at the beginning."

"Which beginning? There were so many, you know. A woman didn't come to Kansas back in those days and just think that was it for the rest of her life. A woman in Kansas sometimes had lots and lots of beginnings."

"Well, why don't you start when you first came to

1

Kansas?'' Leah said. ''That would certainly be of interest to our study.''

Olivia Sands Burton shifted her gaze slowly, and as she looked out the window, sunlight illuminated the irises of her eyes. Leah was startled by their color, a deep, dark grass-green. Her breath caught unexpectedly in her throat. Her own eyes were that color. She conjured up an image, suddenly, of herself in the future. She waited, almost breathlessly, watching the old woman stare out the window, thinking perhaps she may have dozed off. Just as she glanced downward at the blank notepad, the woman spoke, her voice raspy, grating.

''I was beautiful once.'' The almost nonexistent line that was her mouth lifted at one corner, and a slightly trembling hand reached upward, stiff fingers combing a jagged line through the sparse yellow-gray hair.

''Had lots of hair. Too much, my mother used to say. Wouldn't stay put in the braids I did up every day. Thick, too. Real thick. And almost black, it was so dark. Ma used to worry on our trip overland that the Indians would think I was one of 'em, I'd get so dark from the sun. She was afraid they'd take off with me.'' Her hand dropped to the arm of the chair. ''Never did, of course. No. Indians never did me any harm at all.'' She pursed her lips together, and the green irises disappeared as her eyes squinted thoughtfully. ''Can't say that was the case for my entire family, though. No . . . can't say that at all. . . .''

Leah waited a moment and then prompted, ''Your family? The nursing supervisor said you had no living relatives now.''

''That's correct. No living relatives.'' She paused, appeared lost in thought, and then spoke again. ''I had a mother and father, of course, and a brother. Aaron was his name.''

Leah Rice was barely aware of holding her breath. Her gaze was riveted on the old woman.

Olivia's mouth worked soundlessly for a few seconds. "Aaron." She breathed the word through her lips, and her eyes opened wide as they gazed once more out the window, as if she could see something in the far distance. She was silent so long, it seemed to the younger woman as though she would never speak.

Finally Olivia let out a slow sigh and gave an almost imperceptible shake of her head. "Don't think there's been a day in my life I haven't thought of that boy." She uttered a small laugh. "*Boy*. It's a shame to call him that, isn't it? But that's what he was, seemed like, most of his life." Gradually she remembered her visitor and turned to look at her, a curious expression on her withered features. "Course, you don't have any idea of what I'm talking about. It's rude of me to go on so."

Leah spoke carefully. "Did something happen to your brother?"

Suddenly the older woman winced, her green eyes scrutinizing Leah Rice. "You sound as though you might know something about Aaron."

"Did I give that impression? I only meant that you sounded so . . . so . . . Look, if you don't care to talk about certain things, that's perfectly all right."

The old woman gave a wave of one hand. "Oh, no. I'll tell you whatever you want to know." She paused. "But as I said, there's so much to tell, I can't hardly think where to begin."

"I've got plenty of time." Leah Rice smiled. "I'd like to hear it all. Every single detail of your life—starting with your life in Ohio. Or when you first came to Kansas . . . whatever you like."

Olivia slumped back in her chair, feeling a sort of peacefulness washing over her. The unending solitude of the nursing home was depressing, and after all this time, here was someone actually wanting to share her company, to hear her talk. *Talk*. Lord, she hadn't talked in so long, she wondered how rusty her voice would be.

But rusty or no, she would do it. She'd never believed when she was younger that the older you got, the more you remembered all the little things about earlier years, details you thought had vanished. What was the point? she used to think when listening to older folk reminiscing, tiring of all their stories about the "old days." There was so much to do just making it through each day in order to get to the next. But now she understood. Oh, how she understood! Now life was nothing but waiting and thinking back on things you could never have back again. And it was so strange, the clarity of it all! Each memory seemed more real, somehow, than the actual event itself. And now here was this woman wanting to record her life story for some historical foundation she'd never heard of.

She glanced up at the sound of the wooden chair the younger woman was sitting in as it scraped against the floor. Leah Rice was standing up.

"Are you leaving now?"

Mrs. Rice smiled. "Perhaps I should. I've taken up so much of your time already."

"Oh, no, no, you haven't taken up too much of anything. I'm ready to start." She folded her gnarled hands in her lap and gave a definitive nod of her head.

"Are you certain?"

"Yes, I am. I'll start with the early years, about the time we came out West."

"All right." Leah Rice reached for her chair, pulled it toward the bed, and sat down again. The excitement she'd felt since first entering the building had now reached a crescendo. Perhaps now, she thought. Perhaps now I might find the answers.

CHAPTER I

Spring 1859

In the end, the leave-taking was much harder than Olivia had expected, despite the intensity of excitement she had lived with for two months straight, ever since February when her father had declared they were leaving Ohio to travel into Kansas territory.

Her brother, Aaron, was in much the same frame of mind. At sixteen years of age, he was two years younger than his sister, and the both of them were as close as two siblings could ever hope to be. They talked constantly about the upcoming journey, sharing their fears, their excitement. Neither of them slept much at night; both were busy planning their futures, wondering what they held, dreaming about the life that awaited them on the plains.

It had all begun, the decision to move, with their mother's intractable illness: consumption. The only thing for it, they'd been told by the army of doctors Claude Sands had consulted, was to place her in a sanitarium, a suggestion absolutely unthinkable to all of them. The only option left, then, Doc George Montague had told them, was to head west—west to where there was land for the taking, west where the air was drier and kinder to those who fell victim to the devastating disease.

Claude Sands had made inquiries immediately, and after much haggling with a land agent in Cincinnati, had purchased a tract of property in the central section of Kansas—sight unseen. One hundred eighty acres of land that Olivia could only dream about, wonder about.

Olivia tossed and turned every night that late spring, pulled by a strange mixture of emotions: anguish that she would be leaving behind the first and only man she had ever loved, the man who was to have been her husband, Silas Crawford; guilt that she could so easily decide to go with her parents rather than remain behind with the man who loved her and was counting on spending the rest of his life with her; but also elation that her life was taking such an unexpected turn, the most exciting one she could have ever imagined.

She was already seventeen years old—eighteen in another two months—and she had seen *nothing* of the world! Nothing other than the few dozen acres of farmland she lived on now with her parents, had been born on, and raised on all of her life! And if she stayed behind, she knew in her heart she would grapple forever with regret, regret that she would not have followed the three people she loved most in the world. Unfortunately, to reach this conclusion, she'd had to admit her feelings for Silas were not what she had thought they should be. Mostly, though, she would forever regret it if she did not take the chance to do something different with her life, something other than what had always been expected of her.

And so it was with a great deal of pain that she had spoken to Silas, guilty yet dismayed by his disbelief, the tears he'd shed. She had never seen him cry before, and though she had often seen Aaron do so, he was her brother, and brothers were allowed to behave differently with their sisters than with other women. She was being horribly unfair to Silas and she knew it, but there was no turning back in her mind now, no going back on the promise to herself and to her parents and brother.

She'd spoken only once more to Silas after breaking their unofficial betrothal, but it was a mere exchange of recognition, hardly a greeting. Olivia had driven the mule wagon into town for supplies and had seen him standing in front of the feed store, one scuffed-up boot aimlessly shifting back and forth in the dirt. Looking up, he saw her and nodded, uttering a curt "Hello."

"Hello, Silas," Olivia answered, wanting to stop, wanting to stand before him and look him in the eye and tell him she wished it didn't have to be that way, wished they could have gone together. But of course, that would have been more rhetoric, for Silas was going to inherit his father's farm, which he loved and cherished. And Olivia really, in her heart, did not want him to come along on the journey west. It was a harsh truth, so she bowed her head slightly, her bonnet shading her face as she walked past him into the building to place her own order for the oats and hay her father had asked her to purchase. It was a small order, one that would easily fit in the wagon, and one she could unload herself when she got back to the farm.

In fact, she had been doing most of the chores around the barn for the past week while her father and brother were busy in the fields, harvesting what would be the last of the early crops before they left. There was so much to do in preparing for the journey, and to Olivia it seemed as though they would never be done with it all. How in the world they would get all the possessions they planned to take with them loaded up in the brand-new Conestoga her father had paid hard-earned cash for in the next few weeks, Olivia had no idea. She only knew that each day, though she was busy from sunup to well past sundown, nevertheless seemed to drag on forever. She could not yet envision the day they would actually set forth.

Silas was gone when she emerged from the store, and she realized, as she jumped up onto the hardwood seat and took the traces in hand, that she most likely would never see Silas again. Sadness swept over her, and she grappled with it on the ride home.

When she arrived at the farm, she found her mother near the back of the house, bent over a huge wooden tub filled with soapy water, her arms wet to her elbows, the front of her apron almost soaked. Olivia reined in the mule and hurried over to her mother, letting out an exasperated sigh.

"Mother, what are you doing? You know you aren't supposed to be doing anything so strenuous! Here, give me that paddle."

Amelia Sands looked up at her daughter, and the starkness of her wan, wilted features made Olivia's heartbeat quicken. Taking the paddle from her mother's hand, she became further alarmed when Amelia swayed slightly on her feet.

"Mother!"

Placing an arm around her mother's back, she led her to a bench beneath a nearby shade tree, a mere plank of wood, actually, that Aaron had nailed into the trunk.

"Stay here until I bring you some water," Olivia instructed her mother, backing away slowly to make sure her command was complied with.

Hurrying to the well, she worked the pump as fast as her arm could manage, bringing up cold spring water into a ladle. She returned to where her mother now sat, her head leaned against the rough bark of the ancient oak, eyes closed. Olivia noted with dread the pasty complexion, the beads of perspiration that limned her narrow lips and dotted her brow line.

"Here, Mother," Olivia said quietly, moving the ladle close to her mother's mouth.

Amelia opened her eyes and smiled wanly at her daughter. So different they were, she mused to herself. Olivia so brown, so strong, so . . . eager for life, so full of life. And she herself so weary of it, so indifferent, really. There were days, of course, when she did not feel so, but those days, the ones when she felt almost normal, were becoming fewer and farther between. The last doctor had convinced Claude that moving west would be the best thing for her. The drier climate was supposed to help her lungs, help her get back the strength she hadn't had for years, but Amelia doubted this seriously. She could not envision ever feeling the way she used to feel, having the strength she had before the children were born, or even, for that matter, a mere year or two ago. And because she could no longer remember feeling well, she was not so sure any longer that it was a state of being she even longed for. She had adapted her life to the illness that had gradually invaded her entire being for the past three years.

As she watched her daughter bustling about, a worried expression on her smooth, unlined face, collecting more water for her to drink, Amelia felt as if she were looking into a mirror. It was strange; on one hand she felt as though it were only yesterday that she herself had been so young, so full of life and all of its promises. Olivia had her own looks, that was certain: her leanness, her angular face, eyes large and as clear a green as dew-misted grass. Aaron, however, had received his father's looks; he was every bit as handsome as Claude had been at his age, possibly more so. Amelia didn't know if it was a blessing or a curse for a man, for surely he would attract many, many females as he became more mature. She hoped that Aaron, like his father, would remain unaware of his unusual attractiveness, would give a deserving young woman the attention Claude had always showered on her, for he was a kind and gentle person.

She was thirty-seven years old now, and it seemed old, so very old. She could not live much longer; this she knew in her mind as well as her heart. Despite what the doctors said, despite what Claude or the children told her, she intuited they were all wrong. She would not tell them, of course. She would keep it to herself, for she alone could deal with the fate she had been given, she alone would be able to cope with the knowledge she could not, would not, live much longer in this world.

"Thank you, Olivia," she whispered to her daughter, lifting her hand to wipe the moisture from her upper lip.

"Mother," Olivia said earnestly, "please promise me you won't do anything for the rest of the day. You are too stubborn for your own good. There is no need for you to do *anything*."

Amelia looked at her daughter lovingly. "All right. If it will make you happy."

Olivia sighed. "What will make me happy is to see you well again. It seems forever until we will actually be leaving. But the sooner the better."

"But it is only a month now."

"A month too long." Olivia gave her mother a direct, assessing glance. "The sooner we get away from here, the better."

Amelia sighed and looked off in the distance. "I'm not so certain of that."

"How can you say so? The doctors have all said the same thing. You need dry air to help your illness. You *will* be better when we get there, Mother, I know you will."

Suppressing the ever-present urge to cough, Amelia remembered that she was careless in speaking aloud her thoughts. Here was her daughter, her beautiful, loving daughter, who truly believed that anything was possible, if you just set your mind to it. She could not destroy those illusions. Narrowing her eyes a bit, she asked Olivia, "Won't you miss Silas?"

"Of course I'll miss him; I already do."

"What do you mean?"

Olivia shrugged one shoulder lightly. "I saw him at the feed store today. He just ignored me."

"Well, what do you really expect? That boy is hurt pretty bad, I'm sure. He really loves you. Perhaps you should stay, Olivia."

They had covered this ground often enough, and Olivia was loath to get into another such discussion with her mother.

"Mother, you just stay here for a while, and if you need help getting back to the house, just call me. I'll be getting supper ready."

Amelia watched her daughter walking back toward the house with an odd mixture of regret and satisfaction. Regret that she could not share the chores she had trained and prepared Olivia for during her growing years, yet satisfaction that she had learned them so well. She was now quite a self-sufficient young woman.

No, she could not blame Silas for feeling anger or sadness. Olivia was not only beautiful, she was a strong, caring young woman. It was a terrible loss for him. When Olivia walked inside the house, some thirty feet from where she herself sat, Amelia leaned forward and gave in to a spell of coughing that lasted a full two minutes, and which left her shaking and pale and incapable of moving.

Aaron shook his head forcefully, sending a spray of water cascading through the air and sprinkling the glassy surface of the creek. The girl standing on the bank gasped and squealed as her smock was spattered by the water.

"Aaron!"

"Come on in," the young boy taunted her. "You're already wet, so you might as well."

"You made me wet on purpose."

"Don't you want to try it again?"

"What? Try what?"

Aaron grinned, the smile opening his clear green eyes even wider. His naked chest was taut and sun-browned, as were his wide shoulders. He had been a beautiful child, and now he was a handsome young man, and the girl waiting for him on the banks of the creek felt a pang of remorse like none she'd felt in her life. He was leaving; the boy she was in love with, would be in love with for the rest of her life. Tears puddled in her eyes, tears that brought anger to the surface of her fragile emotional state. She turned her back on him and made her way up the grassy embankment.

"Hey, where are you going?"

"Home," she answered, shoving the back of her wrist across her face, hastily ridding it of the tears that had spilled onto her cheeks.

"Why?"

"I have to get back to my chores."

"Thought you said your ma wouldn't mind if you were late this afternoon."

The girl shrugged.

"Come on, Sally, don't be that way."

She started to respond, then thought better of it. What good would it do to say anything at this point? He was going; there was no changing the situation. She'd be better off just staying away from him from here on out. She started to walk off, and after three steps, felt a wet hand on her shoulder. She turned and saw Aaron looking at her with a familiar intensity in his eyes, and suddenly she knew it was hopeless; as long as he was around, as long as he was so near to her, she would not be able to resist.

He pulled her close, and she felt the front of her smock dampening rapidly. Her mother would comment on it, no doubt scold her. But she didn't care now. For the moment, she was captivated by Aaron Sands's kiss, the wonderful, tingling feelings that he could summon forth inside her. Oh, how she would miss him! How very, very much! She opened her eyes, certain that she would see something on his face, a longing, a mirror of the regret that they would so soon be parted. But his eyes were closed, and with a sinking heart, Sally knew that she was but the first for him. The first of many more girls to come to him, openly, willing, as she did.

Olivia bustled around the table, setting pots of steaming vegetables and a platter of roast pork in the center of it, then a basket of cornbread squares on the sideboard. Her father waited patiently, but she watched her mother all the while, noting the gauntness, the slight sheen to her skin, and the telltale waxiness of her complexion. They could leave none too soon as far as Olivia was concerned. She was becoming more nervous by the day. It was as if, if they didn't hurry up and go, things would change and they would never leave at all. And they would be stuck here, on the farm her father had inherited from his father, and she would end up marrying Silas anyway, having his children and maybe ending up looking just like her mother did right now.

In her agitated state, she bumped a chair, scraping it across the polished oak floor.

"Sorry," Olivia muttered, seeing the vague expression of dissatisfaction on her mother's face. The solid oak floors were Amelia's pride. Even now, ill as she was, Amelia would sit down on the floor and rub a dampened square of oilcloth over a portion at a time. She'd lost track of the number of times she'd interrupted her mother during the day, demanding that she sit down in a chair.

"Biscuits are delicious, daughter."

Olivia looked across the table at her father, Claude Sands. In his early forties, he looked much older, though it was still quite apparent where Aaron's good looks had come from. Claude was a tall man with a slim yet muscular build, but his face had taken the brunt of his years working the farm, the wind and sun having baked and creased his skin until his clear green eyes were the only youthful aspect remaining.

"Thanks, Papa," Olivia answered, smiling brightly at her father. As important as it was to her that her mother regain her strength, she tried to keep her father in good spirits. He was an easygoing man, but he had a melancholy side to his nature, made worse of late by his wife's illness.

"What is keeping your brother?" Claude asked, dishing up a serving of stewed tomatoes onto his plate.

"I suppose still washing up. You two must have worked awful hard today. And in this heat." Olivia shook her head, cast a glance at her mother, and said, "Now, Mother, at least try some of it."

Amelia dutifully did as she was told, the child to her own now in almost every way. She obeyed all of them, mostly for Claude's sake. She couldn't bear to see the pained expression on his face every time he looked at her. It was worse than looking in a mirror, and probably more accurate.

"That boy hardly worked at all," Claude said. "Ran off some time after noon, and I haven't seen him since."

Olivia cocked an eyebrow. "Oh really?" She didn't bother to add that she wondered where he might have been instead of helping out their father in the fields. Aaron had done that often enough of late; he was forever saying he would help out with something or be somewhere in particular and then not follow through. But who could blame him? He was sixteen years old, and he was about to set out on the biggest adventure of his life. He was excited, and there were many things he needed to do before they left the place that he might never see again.

Just then the back door banged open and heavy footsteps were heard treading across the kitchen toward the dining room. Aaron entered the room with a slight duck of his head under the doorframe; he had grown so tall—taller than his father—over the past year.

He pulled out his chair and took a seat, immediately reaching for the bowl of mashed potatoes. "Sorry I'm late."

"What did you do, fall into the well?" Olivia asked, her eyebrows raised quizzically. "Your hair is dripping."

Aaron glanced quickly at both parents and ran a hand across his head. "No it's not."

"Where were you, son?" Claude asked quietly.

"Uh, well, I know I was supposed to be clearing that pen out, and I will, Papa, don't worry, I will tomorrow. I . . . well, I guess I forgot about it."

"Well, take care that you don't forget too much else," said Claude. "I'll not have us leaving the place in disrepair for the Shultzes."

"Yes, Father," Aaron replied.

The Shultz family, which consisted of husband, wife, and four children, would be taking over the farm in about a month. Immigrants from New York, they'd paid cash for the farm, and Claude was intent on doing right by them.

Amelia Sands smiled lovingly at her son and asked, "Did you see Sally?"

Aaron blushed and his arm jutted out so quickly across the table for the platter of roast that he almost upset the glass of milk in front of his plate. He mumbled an unintelligible reply, and Olivia said, "What was that?"

"I said, yes, I saw her." He thrust his jaw out defiantly.

"All right," said Claude. "It's not an issue what Aaron did or did not do today. Let's all eat and then we'll have a discussion. I'm thinking about a change in our plans."

Olivia looked up in alarm. Not now! she thought anxiously. Just when Amelia was looking the worst she ever had.

"Papa, what . . ." she began, but he shook his head and lowered it, applying himself to the plate full of food before him with complete concentration.

Olivia seemed to be the only one concerned about what her father might say. Her mother was conversing softly with her brother, who apparently had not heard his father, or if he had, assigned it no importance.

At last Claude looked up from his plate, wiped his mouth, and drank the remainder of his cider. He waited until his wife and son gave him their full attention, and then said, "Aaron and I will be leaving with the wagon alone."

Amelia raised her eyebrows in interest, Olivia frowned in alarm, and Aaron stared in wide-eyed surprise at his father.

"What do you mean, you and Aaron alone, Papa?" Olivia burst out. "We're all going to Kansas."

"Didn't say we weren't. I just have been thinking things over and decided that it would be best if you and your mother took the train to St. Joseph. Aaron and I will meet you there. From there we'll travel to Atchison and then join together with another party for the trip overland."

Olivia breathed a sigh of relief; her father's words sounded like a good suggestion. Especially now, seeing her mother deteriorating so rapidly.

"Claude," Amelia said in her delicate, melodic voice, "that sounds to be a lot of trouble. Why would we spend the money on train fare when we just purchased a new wagon? It's plenty big to hold all of us and—''

"No, Mother," Olivia interjected. "Papa's right. You aren't up to such a long journey. Anything we can do to lessen the time you will have to spend in that wagon, the better.''

"I won't have a problem in the wagon. I think—''

"My mind is made up, Amelia," Claude said. "We have the money, and Olivia is right. You need to preserve as much of your strength as possible. The journey overland from Atchison will be hard enough on you.''

"When would we have to leave, Papa?" Aaron spoke up, his mouth still full from the last bite of his biscuit.

"Well, I've done some calculating on it. I think it will take us a good three weeks to reach Atchison, which means we should be ready to leave here in no more than two weeks. Your mother and sister will leave next week.''

Aaron's eyes widened, and as he swallowed, his Adam's apple bobbed up and down a couple of times.

"I know it's sooner than we had planned on, son, but I think it's the best way.''

"Well . . . sure, Papa.''

Olivia grinned. "I've never seen such a look of surprise on your face, Aaron. I do believe you might be a little bit scared.''

"Horsefeathers. I'm not afraid of going west.''

"Then I wonder what else could account for that strange look in your eyes.''

Aaron's thoughts were focused on visions of Sally, her hair wet, her dress soaked, clinging to her bosom provocatively, but he wasn't about to let on to anyone at the table, least of all his nosy sister.

"You'll do all right, son," his mother said, reaching over and laying one slender, almost bony hand on his arm. Seeing that hand was enough to erase any doubts that may have lingered in Aaron's mind about leaving, doubts he'd barely admitted to himself, let alone discussed with his sister or parents. For despite what they all thought about him, he did care about this place, his home; he loved it here, more than he had ever admitted to himself, until his father had decided they would leave. Nevertheless, it pained him to watch his mother's illness progress to the point that she was a mere shell of the woman she had once been. He missed her the way she had been before, wanted her back again, just that way.

"I know, Mother. And you will, too."

Watching the looks exchanged between her brother and mother, Olivia felt a stab of envy for the love she felt she'd somehow missed out on. It wasn't that she doubted her mother's love, it was just that she could not help but notice the special feeling Amelia showed her son, her youngest. She wished, just once, her mother would look at her with the same longing, the same pure affection. But she never did. Though she treated Olivia with the same fair hand with which she treated her son, it seemed as though Amelia was always assessing her in some way. Judging her by her own standards. Olivia felt certain that she measured up, for her mother praised her, if infrequently. But Aaron was treated simply as Aaron. What he was, he was. Aside from occasional discipline, he was left to be, and it was always obvious that whomever he chose to be was perfectly fine with Amelia. But then, Olivia reminded herself, it was because he was a boy, and boys were always treated differently from girls. She supposed her mother was no different from any other mother.

Actually, she'd always treated him differently herself. Most girls she had known had always taken their siblings for granted, and had found nothing much in common with their brothers. Olivia had always been totally the opposite. From the time her baby brother was born—

she was only a little under two—she had been extremely possessive of him. To this day, she had clear memories of fretting her mother continually; why wasn't she allowed to hold the baby more often, to feed him, to bathe him? Her mother had told her she was too little, but she never thought she was at all. After all, she was a great deal bigger than her baby brother!

As they grew, her attachment to Aaron intensified. She saw to his every need and played endlessly with him— which Amelia had no objection to since it freed up more of her time. When he fell down, it was Olivia who bandaged his scrapes; when he cried, it was Olivia who wiped his tears away and hugged him. When he laughed, it was generally Olivia who had provoked him to do so. They shared secrets as they grew into their early teens, but conflict grew, too. They bickered over silly things, argued about chores, and Olivia could not help but notice their mother's attachment to her younger child. She felt no small measure of envy about this. Amelia simply loved her son with a love that knew no bounds. But Olivia's love was much the same, and so she could never find any good reason for resentment.

"Then it's settled," Claude said. "We'll discuss the details out on the front porch with our coffee."

"Aaron?" Olivia nodded to her brother, her pointed glance at the table an indication that she needed his help.

Silently the two of them cleared the table, washed and dried the dishes, then joined Claude and Amelia out on the front porch. A cool northwesterly breeze had picked up, and Claude had draped Amelia's shoulders with her woolen shawl.

Aaron and Olivia took seats across from their father behind the small wooden table he'd positioned in front of him and upon which was a stack of scribbled notes. Alongside this was a large unfolded map.

As Olivia looked at the wealth of information her

father began spreading out before them, she felt a jolt of reality. No longer were they just talking. They really were going to be leaving! She recognized an unusual sensation deep inside: anticipation laced with more than a good measure of fear.

She looked at the three people sitting close to her and felt a pang of dread, an inexplicable, ominous premonition. Maybe they *weren't* doing the right thing; maybe it was wrong to be giving up all they had ever known, all that was safe and sure in their lives. How could they be certain the doctors were right? How could they know that moving farther west, to Kansas, would help Amelia?

But when she studied her mother's face, so gaunt and pasty, the storm of anxiety began to quiet. There really was no choice in the matter. Everything that could have helped her here had been tried.

CHAPTER II

At the railway depot, the heavy summer air throbbed with noise, as human shouts mingled with the neighing of horses, braying of mules and the hissing and chugging of the coal-fire engines. But even through all of it, Olivia could hear her heart, beating with sheer excitement.

Her father and brother were seeing to the luggage that she and her mother were taking along aboard the train. They were carrying plenty of personal possessions, for their stay in Atchison would be at least ten days. Certain that Amelia would be exhausted from the journey, Claude wanted her to be as rested as possible for the trip overland into Kansas.

Olivia could not keep her eyes off her father and brother; she watched their every move hungrily, absorbing the details of how they looked, and trying to memorize every single word they said, as if she might never see them again.

Aaron appeared not at all like the carefree boy he had been a mere few weeks ago. He had a strained look about his eyes, a frown on his forehead, and the drawn-down corners of his mouth were all too familiar to Olivia. How many times had she seen that expression when they were younger; then, inevitably, tears would follow. Only he was supposed to be a man now, and tears would be most unseemly. His Adam's apple bobbed up and down, up and down, and she could see he was having a devil of a time holding in his emotions. His eyes were glued to their mother, and Olivia ached for him.

Instinctively she did as she always had, taking up slack where it was needed, relieving him of the need to show his own emotions by exposing her own.

Reaching up, she held his beautiful, handsome face in her hands, caught and held his gaze with her own. "Aaron, everything will be fine. I'll take perfect care of our mother."

He swallowed and blinked hard. "I know."

"And you and Father will be fine. You're not afraid, are you?"

Aaron frowned. "Of course not. What's to be afraid of? There aren't any Indians on this part of the trip."

Olivia smiled. "I don't think we'll have to worry about Indians at all."

"I don't know about that." Aaron sounded doubtful. He had recited almost daily the various stories he'd heard circulating about, stories of ambushes and slaughters of bands of traveling pioneers.

"At least you have your new Winchester. And you're a good shot if anyone is."

"I know." His expression lightened considerably, and finally he returned his sister's caring expression. "Guess I'll miss you. It won't be long before we're all together again. Don't forget that."

Olivia smiled. "I'll miss you, too. More than you know." She swallowed the tears gathering in the back of her throat. Then she turned to her father, and his eyes met hers.

Olivia nodded. "I'll take care of her for you, Father. You have nothing to worry about."

"I know you will, Olivia." His dust-covered hat was in his hand and he crumpled it unconsciously with rough, nervous fingers. He glanced down for a moment, frowned, and then looked back at her. So like her mother, she was, he thought, and yet so different. She was as lovely as Amelia had been as a girl, and yet there was something unique about his daughter. Something he could not define, for he did not know her as well as he would have wished to. Of course, that was the way it was supposed to be; a father could love and cherish his daughter as much as a son, but it was different. The daughter would be gone one day, giving over her life to another person entirely, another man. All this he understood and accepted, yet it pained him sometimes.

Impulsively he reached for her, placing his large hands on the sides of her head. When he saw the tears brimming over her lower lashes, he drew her to him, and they hugged silently for several moments.

"Please be careful, Father," Olivia whispered as she pulled back, wiping her cheeks brusquely with the back of one hand.

He nodded and then turned away, facing his wife. Silently he pulled Amelia into his arms and simply held her, cradling her head against his deep chest. Olivia and Aaron watched them until, with torturous reluctance, they pulled away from each other.

Deep evening shadows were blanketing the countryside through which the train was traveling. Olivia's head nodded against the window, and her eyelids opened and closed in hypnotic trance as the landscape whisked past. Her mother slept fitfully in her berth, her breathing disturbingly loud; Olivia could hear it over the ever-present sounds of the long train of moving passenger and cargo cars.

It had been a scant ten hours since they'd left Ohio,

and already Olivia was doubting whether her father's plan had been the best one.

The berth that he had secured for them wasn't exactly as elegant as he had hoped for. Though private—indeed, there were only two others like it on this train—it was extremely close and tight, requiring the utmost caution in moving about. Olivia's seat reclined, but not so comfortably that she didn't awaken frequently and with many physical aches and pains, and Amelia was afforded the relative comfort of a narrow bed that pulled down from the wall above the window. Though her mother moved about as little as possible, her fragile state was deteriorating further.

There was something about the odor in the private car that was strange, an odor of mildew or paint—Olivia wasn't certain what it was—that she had noticed immediately upon entering it. The fumes at each station they stopped at appeared to worsen her mother's symptoms, until now, less than a half day into the journey, Amelia seemed hardly able to breathe.

Olivia tried to reassure herself that as soon as they were in Kansas City, she would take her mother immediately to a physician. Meanwhile, all she could do was see to it that her mother did as little as possible, indeed, nothing more than remaining abed.

The evening light diminished into darkness, but the full moon illuminated the landscape clearly. Olivia changed into her nightgown and robe and pulled down her own berth. At the small sink she washed her face, drying it with the small, fluffy towel on the wooden stand next to it. She looked at the image staring back at her in the gilt-framed mirror above the sink, her features aglow in the light of the oil lamp that flickered on the wall.

She looked weary, much older than her nearly eighteen years of age. Then, in the mirror, she saw the slender shape of her mother's reclining figure behind her in the berth. Things would get better, Olivia told herself firmly. They would all be together again, a family, once they all reached Atchison. By the time her father and Aaron arrived, her mother would be recovered substantially, ready for the trip overland to their new home. And she herself would feel better just knowing her father and brother were there to help her with the responsibility of caring for her mother.

She sighed and moved away from the sink. She climbed into her berth and pulled the blanket up to her shoulders, then turned to face the window. She'd left the curtain pulled back slightly so that she could look out, and the moonlight flickered through tree branches hypnotically. Stars, bright in the clear sky above, rushed by in long, silver streaks. Soon her eyes blinked more and more slowly, and she fell deeply asleep.

The train stopped early the next morning, and since there would be a few hours wait until it departed again, most of the passengers disembarked, eager for some fresh air and breakfast in one of the hotel restaurants.

Amelia longed to walk around in the open herself, but after she had helped her mother down from the bed and assisted her in washing up and dressing, the older woman was so exhausted, it was all she could do to stay seated upright.

"Perhaps I should get a doctor," Olivia said, brushing her mother's hair with a tortoiseshell bristle brush.

"No," Amelia said, her voice raspy and breathless. "Not necessary."

"But, Mother, you're so pale. I'm worried about you."

"Be fine." As soon as the words were uttered, up came a thin hand to stifle the phlegmy cough that grew and grew until Amelia's entire body shook from it.

Olivia stood up quickly. "I'll be back shortly."

"Where—"

"Just rest, Mother. Here, take this pillow and push it against your chest." She turned, opened the door, and stepped into the hallway. She looked both ways and decided to take the exit that was to her right. There was no one in the car, it appeared, and she was able to make her way hastily down the narrow corridor.

A blast of cool air hit her square in the face as soon as she stepped onto the platform, and for a moment she hesitated, relishing the feel of it as it enveloped her. Only a few more days, she thought. Everything would be all right.

The stationmaster approached and asked if he could help, and Olivia explained that she would like to ask directions to the nearest doctor's office.

"My mother's ill," she said. "I would like someone to attend her while we are waiting."

"Of course, of course," the burly man replied. "I'll send the boy over with a message. Burness! Get on over here, son."

A young boy of twelve or so came running over, his face and hands covered with grime. "Yessir?"

"Run and fetch Doc Stratton."

The boy nodded and turned on his heel, then raced off in the opposite direction.

"Thank you," Olivia said, grateful that she would not be faced with traipsing all over a town with which she was wholly unfamiliar.

"Why don't you step inside the station, miss?" the stationmaster suggested. "Have a seat while you wait."

Olivia placed her hands at the small of her back and arched slightly. "Thank you, but I'm so exhausted from sitting, I think I'll just walk around a bit."

"Sure, sure, I understand. The doc will be along real soon."

Olivia strolled around the outside of the small, square building, her appetite whetted by the smells emanating from the hotel restaurant down the road.

"Miss?"

She glanced up to see a tall, dark-haired man of perhaps thirty years of age, his hat in his hand as he gave her a brief nod.

"Yes?"

"Excuse me for appearing forward, but I just overheard your conversation with the stationmaster. I am also a passenger on the train." He gave a brief nod. "My name is Francis Burton. I'm a physician."

"I see. Thank you, but the stationmaster sent word for the doctor here in town."

"I heard as much. But it may take a while. I would be more than happy to see to your mother in the interim."

"Thank you very much; I would really appreciate your looking at her, if you don't mind."

"No, not at all."

Olivia started for the platform, the doctor stepping in beside her. As they mounted the steps and entered the train, Olivia briefly explained her mother's condition.

Amelia appeared startled when they entered the tiny sleeper room. Her eyelids were heavy; she had apparently been dozing again.

"Mother," said Olivia, "this is Dr. Francis Burton. I want him to examine you." She moved closer and put her hand on her mother's forehead.

Amelia attempted to sit forward, but the motion set off a spasm of violent coughing, which after almost a full minute, left her weak and perspiring.

Olivia glanced worriedly at the doctor. "Should I give her some medicine? It's in the—"

"No, wait," said the doctor, one hand held outward. "If you don't mind, I'll just have a look and talk to your mother for a moment."

"Yes, of course. Should . . . would you like me to leave?"

"No, that won't be necessary." Taking a seat next to

Amelia, Francis Burton began speaking, his voice gentle and soothing, asking questions that Olivia had heard many, many times before. And yet her mother was more responsive to this man, more willing to discuss herself and her symptoms.

After several minutes, Burton stood up and cleared his throat. "I've some other medications that you might find useful until you reach your destination. They're in my bag. It will take me a few minutes to fetch them. I'm in the next car over."

Amelia actually smiled, which was astonishing to her daughter, who had not seen such an expression on her face in a long, long while. "Thank you very much, Dr. Burton."

Olivia followed the man out into the corridor and said, "And I thank you, too. I don't think I've seen my mother ever respond so well to anyone offering her care."

Burton grinned and gave a brief nod. "I'm pleased to be of help to you. I'll return in a few minutes then."

"All right. And thank you again."

Taking a few steps, Francis hesitated and then turned back to her. "You could repay me the favor, as a matter of fact."

"But of course, I had every intention of—"

"Of joining me for supper this evening in the dining car."

"Oh. I see." Olivia frowned lightly. "I was speaking of payment for your services."

"None is required. Will you? Join me for supper, that is."

Olivia raised her eyebrows and shoulders simultaneously. "I can't think of a reason not to, I suppose." She felt the corners of her mouth lift as her mother's had a few moments ago.

"Good. I'll be back in a few minutes."

Olivia watched the man's retreating figure for a few

seconds, still not quite knowing how such an invitation should be taken. But her mother's voice calling out for her gave her no chance to dwell on it further.

"Here I am," Olivia said, closing the door behind her.

Her mother was still slumped on her side on the plush velvet bench, her head tilted forward over the pillow braced against her chest. She looked up slowly and spoke, her voice barely more than a whisper. "He's a very nice man. A gentleman. I'm pleased you agreed to dine with him tonight."

Olivia flushed. "Mother . . . I didn't know you were listening."

"Couldn't be avoided. You were standing right outside the door."

Olivia moved toward the mirror, suddenly, inexplicably, drawn to it. One hand went up, fingers smoothing the sides of her swept-back dark hair.

"There's no cause for concern in that regard. You are beautiful."

Olivia laughed slightly and turned to face her mother. "Don't be silly, Mother. I have no intentions of anything more than supper with him. I don't even know why he asked me, to be honest."

"I'm sure you'll find out soon enough."

"What do you mean?"

"Never mind. Adjust the pillow for me, will you, darling?"

Olivia did not press her mother further. She bustled about, tidying up the small sleeping compartment. A few minutes later there was a tap on the door. She opened it, and Francis stood in the corridor, black bag in hand.

"Please, come in," Olivia said, stepping back as he entered.

Francis paused, studying Olivia briefly, and then turned his attention to Amelia. "Now then," he said, "let's see if I've something else that could help ease that cough of yours."

The dining car swayed rhythmically as the train sped along; Olivia clutched one hand protectively around the long-stemmed glass of claret. In front of her was a steaming bowl of soup; she ate it slowly, carefully, afraid that it might spill.

Francis looked at her with slight amusement in his dark brown eyes. "Have you not eaten in the dining car before?"

Olivia shook her head.

"Why on earth not? What sort of nourishment have you had since the journey began?"

"Only what we brought with us. I couldn't just leave Mother alone by herself."

Francis lifted his wineglass, took a sip, swallowed, and set it down. "You are obviously very fond of your mother."

"Oh yes, of course. We all are."

"We?"

"My family; my father and brother, Aaron."

"And where are they?"

Olivia frowned slightly. "I'm not sure right now. Somewhere between here and Ohio. They'll be meeting us in St. Joseph. We're headed for Kansas."

Francis cocked an eyebrow. "Are you now? That's where I'm going, also."

"Really? Where? What part?"

"I haven't really decided where I'll be staking out my claim. I'm really just going to see what it's like, I suppose you could say. Might even decide to continue on to Colorado. See if there is anything to the tall tales of gold and silver—something I certainly haven't seen much of back in Ohio." He paused. "However, I've arrangements for as far west as Salina."

Olivia nodded. "That's where we'll be stopping."

The slightest frown etched the doctor's forehead. "Your mother also?"

"Of course." She paused and then added, "Oh, you must be thinking of the trip overland. She'll be rested plenty by the time Father and Aaron join us. And most of the doctors she's seen have told us that once we're there—in Kansas, that is—that Mother should recover most if not all of her strength. Actually, it's the reason we're going at all. For her health."

Francis's eyes narrowed imperceptibly, and his mouth opened slightly as if he were going to say something, but instead, he lifted his glass of wine to his lips and took a long sip. There was no point telling the young woman what was on his mind: that it was doubtful her mother would live very much longer no matter where she was. She was a very, very sick woman, already in the advanced stages of consumption. And there'd been something more he'd noticed, a certain look in the woman's eyes, a look he had seen many times over his years as a physician: the look of resignation.

"It is true, isn't it?" Olivia probed. "I mean, that the Kansas territory is quite restorative for those with respiratory problems."

"For some, I'm sure it is."

"Then I think it will be just the thing for Mother. As a matter of fact, I'm rather looking forward to getting there myself. I've never seen anything but the place where I grew up, and that wasn't much."

For the next several minutes Olivia told Francis about her hometown, the farm, her schooling, which was far more than most young ladies were used to. Then she spoke of her hopes and plans for the future. Francis listened with interest, but did not comment as he would have with someone perhaps a few years older. He was already almost thirty-three years of age, and he had traveled enough during the past ten years to know the reality that faced pioneers who were moving westward

in ever-increasing numbers. They were moving away
from homes and families that were well established and
far more comfortable and prosperous than anything they
could look forward to, no matter what their romantic
notions of the West.

And there was much more to worry about on the
political front. North and South were divided on many
issues, but nothing inflamed emotions and passions like
the issue of slavery and whether or not it should be
allowed in the western states. Francis himself was ar-
dently opposed to slavery. He considered it barbaric,
and far from a mere "woman's issue," as many men
dismissed it. Indeed, much as he enjoyed a good cigar
on occasion, he could hardly bear the contentious atmosphere of the smoking car. Men's voices, raised and
punctuated by frequent shouts and curses, would grow
angrier by the hour. Morning dawned and still the debates raged.

Francis doubted that Olivia was aware of the political
issues surrounding them all, in particular the fact that
Kansas, the very place she was headed, was a hot seat
that could catapult the entire country into war. Francis
felt a certainty in his gut that outright war was not far
off.

As he watched her young face, suffused with excitement and anticipation, he remembered his own state of
mind when he had first gone into the real world after
he had finished his studies. He, too, had been naive,
had thought that nothing really bad could happen to
him, and that anything was possible. Leaving Ohio had
been relatively simple. But plenty of bad things had
happened along the way out West, most of them to other
people and not him personally, although he'd felt the
pain of such events almost as acutely. And since then,
he had discovered the humility that one learns from
realizing that, indeed, many, many things in life were
simply not possible at all.

"Anyway," Olivia was saying, her face flushed with enthusiasm, "I just can't wait to get off this train for good. I'm certain Mother will fare much better once we are in a stable environment."

"Well, it won't be too much longer. Less than thirty-six hours."

Olivia sighed and slumped back against the plush upholstery of the dining car bench-chair. She felt deflated suddenly, as if all her talking had taken the last bit of her strength. "That seems so long. I didn't think I'd feel so tired. I mean, after all, there's nothing to do on a train except sit and perhaps walk a few steps here and there."

"But you've done a great deal more than that," Francis said. "Taking care of your mother with no assistance is no small feat. I suggest that you return to the sleeper car, see to Mrs. Sands, then turn in yourself. The sleep will do you good."

Olivia stifled a yawn and said, "You are right about that."

Francis stood and then moved around the small table, placing his hand on Olivia's chair as she rose. She was touched and impressed by the gesture. Indeed, she could not recall ever having been treated so graciously or formally by a man, or anyone else for that matter. Silas had been kind to her, of course, but they'd known each other since they were four years old.

"Thank you for the wonderful dinner," she said, giving him a frank look. "I don't think I've ever eaten in such elegant surroundings."

Francis smiled, a slow, easy smile that Olivia interpreted as an indication of polish and sophistication. He was a handsome man, not in the way of her brother—indeed, she thought very few men could measure up to her brother's unique good looks—but nevertheless quite masculine and appealing. His height, somewhat over six feet, was imposing in itself, but beyond that, what

Olivia found appealing was his quiet, deliberate manner
of speaking, as if he were completely sure of what he
thought. She liked that immensely, perhaps, she mused,
because it reminded her so of her father. She liked the
way his dark gaze never left her own when he spoke,
she liked his broad shoulders and his sturdy arms, the
way the lines around his eyes fanned out when he
smiled. She liked simply being in his presence.

Francis escorted her back to the sleeper car and bid
her good evening. Inside, her mother appeared to be
sleeping again. Olivia was glad of it; she sat down on
the bench and slowly began to unbutton the top buttons
of her dress. She looked forward to seeing Francis Burton again. It was a surprising thought, and yet . . . it
did make her feel pleased. Very pleased indeed.

CHAPTER III

THE arrival into St. Joseph could not have come too soon. The last hours on the train had seemed to drag interminably, and Olivia was exhausted from lack of sleep and constant worry about her mother. Despite Francis Burton's continued ministrations, Amelia's condition had worsened. She had not gotten out of her berth once in the last twenty-four hours, and Olivia was deeply concerned about moving her mother from the train into the coach that would take them to the hotel.

Once again, Francis had come to the rescue, arranging everything, taking care of transportation and luggage, and seeing to it that their hotel, the Pattee House, provided a room that was quiet and had plenty of fresh air.

"I don't really know how to thank you," Olivia said to him as they stood in the second-floor hallway just outside their rooms.

"As I said before, there is no need to thank me," Francis replied, holding his hat in one hand. He frowned slightly and then reached up to scratch the corner of one eye.

"I will contact the best physician this city has to offer before I leave."

"When will that be?"

"As a matter of fact, this afternoon." Unconsciously Olivia's mouth parted. She swallowed, then cast her stunned gaze downward. What had she been thinking? That he would continue to accompany them and help them as he had on the train? He'd been of such great assistance to them, and she should be grateful for what he had so unselfishly offered. Still, she found it an awful thing to accept, the fact that he was leaving, in just a few hours. She would never see him again.

"I do thank you for helping us, Doctor."

"And I have enjoyed your company, Miss Sands. I'm certainly glad to have made both your and your mother's acquaintance." Francis hesitated, then added, "I trust you will not be left here long? When do you expect the arrival of your father and brother?"

"I'm not sure. When they arrive, we're to travel on to Atchison, and from there on to Salina."

Francis frowned. "You'll be traveling the Smokey Hill trail."

"Yes, that's right," replied Olivia, curious at the somber expression on his face. "And you? Which trail are you taking?"

"The same," he said slowly, as if he were thinking of something else. His eyes narrowed somewhat. "Do you and your family know much about it? The Smokey Hill?"

Olivia shrugged. "I suppose we will when we get on it."

"I'd not take on such a carefree attitude toward it, miss."

Olivia bristled slightly at his tone. "I'm not being carefree at all."

"Well, perhaps not, but you should know that it's sometimes a dangerous route. It's new-opened only this year—and the Indians don't take to travelers too much."

"What sort of Indians might we come in contact with?"

"Any of them. Cheyenne, Arapaho, Comanche, Kiowa, Pawnee. Maybe Sioux."

Olivia swallowed. "Is it possible we won't see any of them?"

"Possible. Yes. Depends on their hunting needs. Particularly buffalo. If I were you, I'd pray for buffalo."

Olivia closed her eyes and smiled, then cast him a wide-eyed look. "I'll pray for buffalo, Dr. Burton. Every single night."

Francis studied her for a moment and then said, "When are you leaving?"

"Sometime in the next two weeks. Although I'm not exactly certain when Mother will be ready to travel again."

Francis was silent for a moment, his expression somber. "Do not make any decisions for travel until you have spoken with the doctor here. Follow his advice. Don't be tempted to push your mother to hurry up."

Olivia's gaze narrowed. "What are you implying? You said you thought she would do fine in a few days."

"This is true. But I meant 'fine' under certain conditions. In other words, with the least amount of physical disturbance to her already weakened state." He paused, scratched his thumb along his jawline, then said decisively, "Look, I will speak with the doctor before I leave and make certain he understands your situation completely. Everything will be fine. Just trust him."

Olivia swallowed suddenly, forcing down a surprising lump that had arisen in the back of her throat. Her confident demeanor and her thus far secure state of mind had just been shattered. She was fighting hard to maintain the adult attitude she'd adopted during the trip with her mother.

"Yes, of course," she said, forcing a brightness to her tone.

Francis hesitated again, knowing he should be on his way, yet feeling lower than he had in a very long while. How had his emotions become so embroiled with this young woman, barely out of childhood, yet so courageous, so determined and devoted? He would not see her again, for though they were headed in the same direction, he knew too well the Great Plains. The vast grasslands could swallow up those who dared to venture across it, those who braved the dangers of the elements and the Indian tribes to stake out claims of their own upon the new land.

He'd let his emotions run away, the first time he'd been so lax with them in many a year. There had been a time when he'd been ruled by emotion. When he was twenty-five, Myra, his wife of four years, had taken ill suddenly and died within a week. Even he, a physician, had never come to a satisfactory explanation of the reason for her death. He'd been stunned by the suddenness of it, then numb, then enraged because he had been so in love with her. But he'd been even more angry with life itself. The intensity of his grief had driven him to the bottle, and almost a full two years of his life had been wasted.

He still wasn't quite certain how, but his self-flagellation had reached its peak and he'd become weary of the battle waging within him. He'd started his life anew, resumed his practice of medicine. Though every year or so he had packed up his belongings, which weren't really that much, and moved onward, ever westward, farther and farther from his native Virginia. He'd finally settled in Cincinnati—home but not home— the launching point for his excursions into the plains of Kansas and Nebraska.

In many ways, his endless running seemed to have worked. He found himself going for days now, sometimes weeks, without one single thought about Myra.

This had saddened him in the beginning, but finally he'd accepted it as a fact of life.

And now here he was, feeling the stirrings of involvement with another woman. And so it was that he found himself, standing in a corridor of the Pattee House, a gruff, stern expression on his prematurely weathered features, pulled by the necessity to leave and yet having to fight off the odd, almost foreign urge to remain where he was. With Olivia.

Habit developed over years of practice prevailed, finally, and he heard himself saying, "I'll be taking my leave then, Miss Sands."

"Good-bye, Dr. Burton," Olivia said quietly. She turned quickly and walked the short distance down the hallway to the suite she and her mother shared. As she neared the door, she heard Francis's footsteps retreating, and she paused momentarily. But she did not turn back to look at him. She had said her good-bye, and that was that. No doubt she would meet others on the journey westward, some of whom she might genuinely like but never see again in her life. A hard lesson to learn, admittedly.

Pressing the door handle downward, she inched the door open, quietly so that it would not creak too loudly, and went inside.

The following morning Olivia awoke early to the smell of coffee wafting up from the dining hall of the hotel. She'd slept only for a few hours, but those few hours had been restful, and she was more refreshed than she'd been in days. Perhaps it was because they were finally on solid ground. Or perhaps it was the down-filled mattress and pillows. She'd best not get too used to it, she thought wryly.

Patting her face dry, she peered into the mirror above the washstand. She was startled to see her mother, in the bed directly behind her, sitting up. Olivia turned around quickly.

"Good morning, Mother."

Slowly Amelia looked up at her daughter. She was absolutely gaunt and her skin was pasty, but her eyes were wide open. She appeared more alert than she had in weeks.

Olivia smiled, delighted to see her mother in such improved health. "Would you like something to eat, Mother? I was just going downstairs to get something for myself. The coffee smells delightful, doesn't it?"

Amelia tilted her head to one side. "I'm not really hungry."

Olivia rushed to her bed, bent down, and took her mother's hands into her own. "Oh, but I'm sure you really are. You haven't eaten hardly a thing in days. Please, do eat something, Mother. Please."

Amelia sighed softly. "All right, dear."

"I'll be right back."

"There's no need to rush. Take your time."

Encouraged by her mother's improved condition, Olivia hurriedly slipped into her morning dress and pulled on her leather shoes, impatiently fussing with the hook to fasten them.

"Do you have any writing paper, dear?"

"What?" Olivia, bending down to catch her hair into a topknot, spoke through the pins in her mouth.

"I'd like a pen and paper, if you wouldn't mind."

"Of course. Just a moment." Olivia crossed the pastel blue tapestry Brussels carpet to the secretary near the window. The dark blue silk and lace curtains were drawn, and she opened them slightly to let a bit more light in. She retrieved a pen and inkwell and a few sheets of vellum the hotel provided. She then picked up a hardbound copy of the Bible to place the paper on and brought it over to her mother. Carefully she arranged two pillows behind her mother's back, straightened the front of her nightgown, and then, using her own hairbrush, brushed out her mother's hair. Once dark brown and lustrous, it was now dull and limp. Olivia decided she would wash it when she helped her mother with a bath later that afternoon.

Olivia had attended her mother for so long that she was taken off guard when, as she pulled her hand away, her mother's frailer one held it firmly.

Olivia's eyes widened. "Yes? Mother?"

"My daughter," Amelia said in a whisper of a voice. Her face twitched and she winced as tears welled up in her eyes.

"Mother, what is the—"

"Shhh. Let me just look at you."

Olivia remained still, bewildered as she watched her mother's face, the peculiar expression it held. Peculiar, because she had seen none like it before. She could not understand it, could not fathom the emotion in Amelia's eyes. Then, suddenly, Olivia was gripped with fear. She forced herself to relax, then reminded herself that her mother appeared finally to be gaining strength, both physically and mentally. Olivia smiled, and her clear green eyes shone with the promise of happiness.

"I love you, you know," her mother said, sighing softly.

"I love you, too, Mother. And you are going to be well again. As soon as we are in Kansas, you will begin to feel better. You look better already. Much better."

Amelia searched her daughter's features. "You really do believe that."

Olivia pulled back slightly, a frown furrowing her brow. "Of course I do. Why wouldn't I? Everyone—all of the doctors we have spoken to—has said that's exactly what you need. A drier climate, a—"

Amelia lifted a hand. "It's all right. I didn't mean to get you upset. Why don't you go on downstairs and get a bite to eat."

"What shall I bring back for you?"

"Whatever you think best. It doesn't matter."

Once again, Olivia felt uneasy; she so hated it when her mother lapsed into apathy. It seemed Olivia had been battling such apathy single-handedly for a long time. Whenever there was a little progress, a setback followed almost immediately. But still, she could not give up.

"Coffee? Surely you would like a cup, and bread, perhaps. Toast. You'll get your strength back." Her voice was coaxing, urgent.

"That would be fine." Amelia slowly lay back against the pillows and closed her eyes, suddenly drained of the energy she'd summoned forth.

Olivia, who now had her hand on the door handle, hesitated, extremely reluctant to leave. It was alarming, how suddenly her mother had weakened, her entire being diminished in a matter of seconds. Well, the best thing for it would be to go downstairs, have a quick breakfast herself, and then hurry back up with her mother's plate.

Thrusting the door handle downward, Olivia said, "I won't be long."

But Amelia's eyes remained closed and she made no response. Evidently she had dozed off again; that seemed to be her very existence of late, Olivia thought with a renewed sense of alarm. She turned and hurried out the door and into the long, carpeted corridor.

The dining hall of the Pattee House was crowded that morning; at first glance there appeared to be no empty tables. However, within a few moments Olivia was seated and had placed her own breakfast order and one for her mother.

Cigar smoke wafted upward toward the high ceiling above the heads of men and women seated at the snow-white-linen-covered tables, the acrid odor mingling with the aromas of coffee and fresh-baked breads and pastries and fried eggs. Olivia felt her mouth water as her stomach gave a simultaneous lurch.

Her plate of eggs and ham arrived quickly, and only after she had devoured all of it, in addition to the entire contents of the small basket of sweet rolls, did she realize how ill mannered she must appear to those sitting nearby. Feeling her cheeks warm in embarrassment, she kept her gaze cast downward, reached for her cup of coffee, and brought it slowly to her lips. She lingered over it for several minutes, until the waiter returned.

"Your mother's breakfast is ready now."

"Oh, good. I'm finished with mine. If you will just follow me, I will . . ."

"Yes, of course."

Grasping her skirt, she made as graceful an exit as she could manage through the crowded room. The hotel was so enormous, so beautiful, that Olivia found it hard to believe such a place even existed, here on the edge of the territories. Only two years old, the Pattee House contained 140 rooms; it also housed various shops, offices, a saloon, even the depot where she and Amelia had first arrived in St. Joseph. It was an expensive place to stay, well beyond the standards of an ordinary farmer, but Olivia knew it was but another of her father's efforts to pamper his wife before their journey overland.

The waiter followed as Olivia made her way down the various corridors of the first floor to her room. Placing the tray containing her mother's breakfast on a small table near the door, he said, "Would you like me to bring it inside for you?"

"Yes, but if you don't mind waiting here for a moment. I must check on my mother first; she may be still asleep, and I don't want to awaken her."

"Of course." The waiter nodded again and then took a small step backward.

Suddenly the air was shattered by a scream, a long, agonized sound that sent shivering chills up the waiter's spine. It was the young lady, inside the room, he realized. He pushed open the door, which she had not shut completely, with the tip of one shoe. He saw nothing at first since the heavy damask curtains were drawn and the light was dim. The scream had stopped, and in the next instant he heard Olivia's half cry, half moan, "No. No, no, no, no, no . . ."

Galvanized, the man pushed the door open wide and rushed into the room. He saw the young woman, her back to him, crouched over one of the poster beds, her head bent over the chest of a woman cradled in her arms. The man stood stock still, chilled to the bone by the eerie, keening sound of Olivia's voice, repeating over and over the one word, "No."

He walked to the bed. The woman Olivia was holding appeared absolutely limp. Her body was so thin and wasted, he could detect the sharp edges of bones jutting against the ghastly white of her skin.

"Miss," he said, his voice cracking at first. He repeated himself in a louder voice, but Olivia made no response; indeed, it was apparent she was not even aware of his presence. He hesitated momentarily and then quickly decided to leave and summon help. He left the door open as he half sprinted down the long hallway.

Olivia half sat, half knelt against the bed, her arms wrapped around her mother, who felt as small as a ten-year-old child. It seemed as though Olivia's own heart had ceased to beat within her breast, had become as silent as her mother's.

Cold. Everything was becoming cold: her hands, which held her mother's back and arms; her cheek, which pressed against the dry flesh of her mother's forehead; the air she breathed; all cold, cold . . .

Somewhere in the recesses of her awareness came the sound of voices. Somewhere behind her. Saying her name, repeating it over and over and over. But she had no voice with which to respond.

When finally one of the voices sounded loudly in her ear, she sat still, unaware until that moment that she had been rocking back and forth, back and forth, rocking her mother's body as she hummed a tuneless melody of mourning that filled the room with haunting grief.

"Miss Sands. Miss Sands." A woman's voice, soft and kind, yet firm, spoke into her right ear, penetrating her hypnotic state.

"Let me help you, Miss Sands." Olivia felt hands touching her arm, encircling it, pulling it back from her mother's waist. Then gradually, very gently, those same unfamiliar yet gentle hands pulled her backward, allowing her mother's body to slide back onto the bed.

And then she was somehow standing, supported by hands and arms and voices that spoke quietly all around her. "So sorry, Miss Sands. So sorry. She is with the Lord now, bless her soul."

Was she? Was that where she was now? Already? Olivia's eyes, large and dry, blinked, and as she frowned, she bent slightly to peer closer at her mother, to determine if perhaps those words were correct. Wary arms, misinterpreting her motion for perhaps a faint, moved swiftly, pulling her upright again, but in that brief moment she had focused on her mother's lifeless face—had seen there, as she had seen a thousand times before, the virtues of goodness and love and self-sacrifice.

She felt herself stepping backward, though it did not seem there was floor beneath her feet. Others were obscuring her view of the bed now, and she turned her head in confusion. Her eyes met those of an older woman, kind light blue eyes, buried in a bed of crinkles in a round, rosy face.

"I'm Mrs. Clara Donovan," the woman said with a

soft brogue. "You'll be comin' with me now, all right, darlin'?"

Olivia swallowed. "Whe . . . where?"

"To my room. I'm just down the hall."

"But . . ." Olivia turned her head back to the bed.

"Now, we'll be comin' back to your dear mother. We're just going to leave the room for a few minutes so the others can help take care of her."

Olivia looked back into the blue eyes and, drawn by the magnetic appeal of their empathy, managed a nod of acquiescence.

Mrs. Donovan's room was at the opposite end of the corridor, and as they entered it, the sweet odor of a laurel sachet permeated the air within. The scent catapulted Olivia back into the past, into her mother's bedroom on the farm. She stood stock-still while Mrs. Donovan remained in the corridor, speaking in a low tone to a waiter who had followed.

Then, closing the door behind her, Mrs. Donovan hurried over to Olivia and, taking her by the arm, led her to a chintz chaise longue in one corner of the sitting room.

"Go ahead, sit down, dearie."

Olivia did as she was told. "What . . . what did you say your name was?"

"Mrs. Donovan."

"Thank you, Mrs. Donovan," Olivia whispered. "I'm not sure what to . . ." Her voice drifted off and she stared down at her hands absently.

"Darlin', don't you be thinking about a thing a'tall. Now is not a time to think. You've just lost your dear mother. I lost my own when I was about your age. Just lay your head back and close your eyes."

"What do I do now?" Olivia stared at the stranger. "I don't know what to do." Even as she uttered the words, it did not seem as though she herself were speaking.

"Dearie, you don't have to do anythin'. Just do as I say and I'll help you take care of everything."

"But why should you help me? I don't even know you."

"Please, child. You are in need of help right now, and I'm of the opinion that we are all here to help one another of God's children. I take 'Do unto others . . .' to heart. Always have, always will."

Olivia lay her head back slowly, closed her eyes, and then suddenly opened them wide. Her mother's face filled her mind's eye as vividly as if she were in the room. Olivia tried to get up, but her muscles seemed stiff, frozen. She placed the palm of one hand on her forehead, felt the pounding pain behind her eyes begin to build. "My head."

"I've ordered up a pot of tea," Mrs. Donovan said. "And I have a powder for that headache."

"What? Oh . . . No." Suddenly, as if awakening from a dream, Olivia turned her head from left to right, taking in her surroundings. She lurched forward. "I must go to my mother. What must I have been thinking? I can't just leave her. . . ."

Mrs. Donovan's reaction was swift. She had seen it coming and rushed from her own chair to the chaise; her hands on Olivia's shoulders, firm and restraining.

"Now, dearie, listen to me. There are others with your mother now, taking care of things, the way they should be taken care of. When all is ready, you'll be told, and then you'll be able to sit with her."

Olivia's eyes searched the woman's face; all she saw was sympathy and genuine compassion. Her next words leapt to her lips, and she uttered them without thinking how they might sound to a stranger.

"We shouldn't have done it. It was wrong to bring her here."

"We? Who are you talking of, love?"

Olivia blinked heavily, eyelids scraping against bone-dry eyes. "My family. My father and brother." She hesitated, swallowed, and then shuddered as the impact of what would unfold hit her fully. "They don't know. They'll be expecting her, you see. They'll think she's still . . . still . . ."

"Now, listen to me, love." Mrs. Donovan's voice was quiet, rhythmically soothing. "Tell me, where are they? Your father and brother."

Olivia looked down at the floor and then glanced back up, her frown of confusion deepening. "I don't know. They're on their way here, to meet us. We were to travel overland to some property my father bought. In Kansas." Her voice trailed off. "I just wish they were here."

"Well, I'm certain they'll arrive soon enough." Mrs. Donovan patted Olivia's hand, which grasped hers in a vise. "Why don't you lie down on the bed for a while, sweetie? I will go back to your room and see how things are progressing. As soon as they are ready, I will come and get you."

Olivia stared straight ahead; the older woman had no idea whether she'd been understood or not. Nevertheless, she grasped both Olivia's hands, tugged, and said, "Come on, dear," and Olivia rose slowly to her feet. She followed Mrs. Donovan to the small bed near one of the room's two windows and lay down on it, her head sinking deeply into the down pillow.

Her entire body suddenly went limp, as if she had been running, running long and hard for a great long distance.

CHAPTER IV

Aaron swiped at the sweat pouring down the sides of his face with the sleeve of his shirt, a garment so coated with the grime of dust that it was as stiff as the calfskin boots on his feet. His voice croaked as it had when it was changing two years ago, as he called out, "Hyaaa! You danged mule! Hyaaa!"

The prairie schooner lurched forward as the horses heeded the sound of Aaron's voice and the crack of the whip, pulling the rear wheels out of yet another muddy rut on the road, which in a few miles would join up with the main one into St. Joseph. He'd passed at least a dozen other similar vehicles during the past ten miles or so, and though everyone called out some form of greeting, he merely managed a nod of his head in return. He could not have called out a decent hello if his life depended on it.

His voice was shot. His throat felt as raw and swollen as his eyes, which he kept hidden beneath the brim of his hat, not wanting others to see how he must look. How he must feel. Which was like a child. No . . . worse. Like a baby. His throat constricted again in that awful pain, and his eyes brimmed with tears that mixed with the dust on his eyelashes, burning and stinging like acid. He couldn't stop crying, just as he couldn't stop the one thought going round and round in his head. What was he going to tell them? How could he explain to his sister and mother what had happened? God Almighty, what in the world was he going to say to them?

Once again his eyes filled and he fought off the urge to pull the wagon off the road, climb inside, and just let himself go. But he couldn't do that. He had to get to them, to tell them, to explain things. "They'll need you, son," he kept hearing his father's last words. And he kept trying to believe it, to make himself feel capable of carrying out his duty.

But deep inside he felt that his father's words were the exact opposite of what was really true. For he needed *them*. More than he'd ever needed anyone in his life.

Aaron reached St. Joseph by nightfall. The moon was full, so there was good enough light to make his way easily, and after asking a stranger for advice, he was able to locate the Pattee House, where his mother and sister were staying. He made arrangements for stabling nearby, then set off toward the hotel. He hesitated as he approached the imposing entrance of the enormous hotel, the likes of which he'd never seen in his life. He considered for a moment returning to the stable and jumping into a water trough; not for the first time aware of his own filth.

But observing some of the other men he passed entering the front doors of the building, many of whom looked as weary and rough as he did, decided him in favor of just going on ahead, filthy or not. The sooner he met with his mother and sister, he figured, the better.

Determinedly he strode into the center of the high-ceilinged lobby, hesitated, and then stopped, his gaze arrested by his surroundings. The marble floor and richly paneled walls, the pots of fresh flowers and plants, set him back for a moment. He was as much out of his element as an elephant in a tree. For just a moment he wondered if indeed he was in the right place, for never, ever had the Sands family seen such luxurious surroundings.

Swallowing, he ducked his head as a man and woman dressed in splendid finery passed by him. He felt his hat slip down onto his forehead and then hurriedly reached up and pulled it off, hoping most of the dirt in the brim stayed put. A man in a dark woolen suit approached him, gave a slight bow, and, with an officious tone, said, "May I help you?"

Aaron scratched his jaw, which was covered with a short, coarse beard, and cleared his throat. He swallowed, not trusting how his voice might come out. "Ah, yes," he said in an almost whisper. "I'd like to find out exactly where my mother and sister are staying. I mean . . . um, they're staying here, in this hotel, but I want . . ."

"You'd like their room number?"

"Yes, sir."

"Come with me please."

The man led him to the registration desk and turned to Aaron, saying, "You may inquire here."

"Thank you."

The man behind the long, glossy oak counter had his back to Aaron, but after a few moments he turned round and lifted one eyebrow as he examined Aaron's trail-worn appearance. His tone, when he spoke, was icily polite.

"Yes?"

"Um, yes, sir, I'd like to find out the room my mother and sister are staying in."

The clerk's eyebrows rose even farther upward. "Name, please?"

"Ah, my mother's name is Mrs. Claude Sands—Amelia Sands. My sister is Olivia Sands."

The clerk appeared confused for a moment, and then his entire demeanor changed, and a frown drew his brows together as he pursed his lips. "Ah . . . yes. Just a moment please."

Aaron waited, more uncomfortable with each passing minute. It seemed forever until the clerk returned. With him was another man, a portly, nattily dressed man with slicked-back hair. The two men stopped some twenty feet from where Aaron stood, and it was several moments before they stopped speaking with each other and turned to him. Both men proceeded cautiously toward Aaron, and as his gaze flicked back and forth from one man to the other, something gave a little twist in his gut. He swallowed, squinted as though bright sunshine were streaming into his eyes, and then swallowed again.

"Mr. Sands," said the portly man, extending his hand, which Aaron took and shook, hardly aware, as he would have been a few moments before, of the impropriety of shaking hands with such a polished gentleman.

"Yes, sir." Aaron nodded.

"I am Sinclair Davis, proprietor of the hotel. The clerk tells me you are here looking for your sister."

"Yes, sir, that's right. And my mother. Amelia Sands is my mother, and my sister's name is Olivia."

The proprietor cleared his throat and indicated with a slight movement of his head a leather-covered bench alongside a nearby wall. "Would you care to sit down for a moment, Mr. Sands?"

Aaron looked over at the bench and back at the man, confusion in his expression. "I thank you, sir, but no, I don't really want—"

With a hand on the young man's shoulder, the proprietor firmly guided him in the direction of the bench;

the clerk followed along behind. Aaron looked at both men in amazement, his confusion rapidly escalating into annoyance. Incredibly, he found himself seated, indeed cornered, with one of the men standing before him, the other next to him, as though to prevent him from bolting, which was exactly what he felt like doing at that moment.

"Look here," he sputtered, not caring a whit at this point how he looked or how he must sound. "You can't—"

"Mr. Sands, please," the proprietor interrupted. "You must listen to what we have to say."

Olivia was seated on a small wooden bench near a freshly turned mound of soil, the grave lacking even the simplest of crosses. She was dressed completely in black, head to foot, and Aaron swallowed back the painful lump in his throat, his eyes filling with tears until her image became swallowed up in the watery blur. He blinked, and Olivia came back into focus; she was looking up at him now, not surprised at his presence, but as though she expected him.

Her features were devoid of emotion, or so it seemed, as he approached her. But perhaps that was the way it should be; one of them should be strong, capable. He felt as if all the world had gone gray . . . lead, dirty gray. He felt none of his six feet two inches of height.

His voice croaked out, "Sis, I . . ."

When she spoke, her voice was surprisingly, almost jarringly, clear and precise. "You're here. Who told you I was here?"

"The, um . . . the proprietor of the hotel."

"I see. What else did he tell you?"

Aaron frowned. "About Mother, of course."

"Of course." Olivia glanced at the grave and stared at it for a long while. Suddenly she looked up at her brother, then beyond where he stood. Aaron looked back over his shoulder; no one was there. Still his sister stared, for all the world as if she saw someone there.

"Where is he?" Olivia asked, finally looking back at her brother.

"Mr. Davis? I'm sure he went back to the hotel. He only took me as far as—"

"Not him," Olivia cut in. "Father."

Aaron swallowed deeply, and visibly paled. He shifted his weight and lowered his head.

Olivia could not see his expression. "Aaron?" Suddenly the leaden weight inside her gut shifted, allowing the emotions that had been forced down to race to the surface again; inexplicably she was overcome with dread and fear. "Aaron!"

But her brother remained rooted to the spot, his only movement the twitching motion of his broad shoulders. He was crying. Olivia got up and went to him. Even though she was shorter by several inches, her hands clutched his arms in a strong grasp, and he was suddenly slumped over her, his body bent in a half crouch as his chin rested on the top of her head. His whole body shuddered in great, half-strangled gasps of grief.

When he managed to speak, finally, he sounded like the little boy Olivia remembered so well, his voice high and plaintive, his lower lip quivering uncontrollably.

"He's . . . he's . . . Oh, Olivia, our father is dead, too. It was an accident on the trail, a pure accident." Again he shuddered from head to foot, his entire weight almost collapsing against her own.

So stunned was Olivia, however, that she became rigid, supporting her brother completely. Unlike him, she remained dry-eyed, though she was certain her heart was barely beating now. She struggled to comprehend what he had just said.

Their father was dead. It couldn't be so; and yet she knew it was, recognized that she somehow had already known, perhaps even before her brother had arrived.

For in the overpowering grief she'd felt during the two weeks since her mother's death, she had not once been able to summon to mind, even to comfort herself, the day she would confront her brother and father.

Now she knew why.

She and her brother stood, clinging to each other, for a long while. The moon shone brightly in the evening sky, lighting the path clearly as they made their way slowly back to the hotel.

CHAPTER V

THE Conestoga swayed precariously as they crossed the span of wooden bridge over the Missouri. Aaron walked ahead of the two horses, a roan and a dappled gray their father had decided would be the most likely of their stock to stand the journey westward. And indeed, Aaron had informed Olivia, neither of the two geldings had even thrown a shoe since they'd left the farm.

But Olivia's face furrowed slightly as she watched the gait of the gray from her perch on the driver's bench; something was amiss, though she wasn't quite sure what. Ah, well, she thought with a sigh, they would handle that problem when the time came. Nothing seemed like a serious problem anyway, compared with the tragedy of their parents' deaths. She thought she could handle just about anything after that.

Her brother, she wasn't so sure about. As he walked ahead, one hand on the leather shank with which he was guiding the roan, there was a slump to his posture she'd never noticed before. He'd been sullen since the day before yesterday, the day they'd finally been able to face each other and discuss their plans. Neither could fully express the confusion and doubts that were almost overwhelming, but Olivia could see her brother was also possessed by a fear the likes of which he had never known in his sixteen years. It was she who had finally taken over and suggested that they go on with their father's plan.

Aaron, sitting on the sofa in the hotel room, had looked at her, blinked hard, and asked, "You think we should?"

Olivia, standing near the window, pulled back one curtain panel and gazed outside. Down below, the streets were jammed with traffic: horses, mules, and all manner of vehicles. Wooden walkways were crammed with men and women taking advantage of the cool, sunny weather to go about the business of their lives.

Lives. Olivia mulled over the word for a moment. What had happened to their lives, hers and Aaron's, in such a short time was almost too hard to conceive. But it had, and time was moving forward, pulling them along into the future.

"Olivia?"

"Yes?"

"Did you really mean that? About not turning back?"

"Yes, I did, Aaron," she said, turning to face him. "Would you really want to go back?"

Aaron mulled this over for a moment. "Not really. There's not much we can go back to. Everything Papa had, he sold. Only thing he had left is the land in Kansas."

"Exactly."

"But what about you? What about Silas?"

"What about him?"

Aaron looked embarrassed. "He . . . well, he would want you to come back. He . . . uh . . . well, he told me once how much he thought of you."

"Yes," Olivia said, glancing back out the window. It seemed so long ago that she had known Silas, had considered marrying him and settling down in the same part of the country as their parents. She had always, since a very young age, wanted to leave, wanted to see more of the world. But never could she have imagined how far away a person could feel. How alone.

She could never go back; she knew this fact as surely as if it were carved in granite. Even, she thought, with a deep, agonizing pang, even though it meant that she would never again see the house and land on which her parents had raised her. That was the past now . . . and forever.

Olivia looked her brother squarely in the eye. "I will never go back. Never."

Aaron frowned. "But what about . . ."

"Silas? I liked him well enough, but even if I loved him, I wouldn't go." Her jaw clenched, she swallowed tightly and then said, "And you? Do you want to go back? Really?"

Aaron's face rippled with emotion; confusion, anger, fear, anguish, as he considered his sister's question. Finally he shook his head, then let his chin drop downward.

"No," he whispered.

Olivia drew in a breath and let it out. "Then I suppose it's settled. We'll just go on."

"Where?"

"To the land Father bought. Where else?"

"But we know nothing about it. We're not even sure where it is."

"We have the deed, and the map. . . . We have everything Father had. I don't see what else we will need."

Aaron sat down on a nearby chair. "But how do we know if we'll like it?"

"We were going there anyway," Olivia said. "I don't see why you should be mentioning such a thing now."

"Yes . . . well. That was because our parents were going with us." Suddenly his voice broke off, choking.

Olivia crossed the space between them and put her arm around her brother's wide shoulders. "Don't cry, Aaron. Please don't cry. Not now. We have so much to do. I know how you are feeling right now, but I've been thinking a lot. I really do believe Mother and Father would have wanted us to go on. To carry out their dreams."

Aaron sniffed, wiped his face with the shirt-sleeve on his forearm, and said, "It was only Father's dream. Not Mother's."

"That's true. But it was also mine. And, I thought, yours, too."

"I was just doing it for them."

Olivia dropped to her knees in front of her brother and looked directly into his eyes. "Aaron, we own the land in Kansas. It's all we have. I know it will be hard without Mother and Father, but if we don't go there and claim it, what do we have? If we hate it there, we can at least try to sell it."

Aaron nodded slowly. "I know. You're right. It's just . . ."

"I know, Aaron, I know." Her voice lowered to a whisper. "But we'll make it, Aaron. We will. Together."

He hadn't answered, but now, here they were crossing the Missouri into Kansas, on their way to Atchison, where they would join up with a party of travelers headed west. They'd spent several days in St. Joseph outfitting the prairie schooner with extra sacks of meal and grains, salted beef and pork, tins of teas and coffee, crackers, and as many "special" items, such as jars of jam and preserves, as they could locate. Most of the supplies were readily obtained, but the wait at the smithy to repair a rear wheel had taken an extra day and a half.

There were other vehicles waiting to cross the bridge, and after a while Olivia got used to giving a friendly nod to other travelers, saying a word here and there in response to inquiries about their destination. Many were men, headed toward the Rockies to mine for gold. But wagons of entire families, carrying every last possession they owned, were not uncommon.

One party consisted of a man, his wife, and two small children, who were seated inside the covered wagon, their towheads popping up behind their mother as they listened to her chatter. The husband was walking ahead leading the team, as Aaron had elected to continue doing.

"How far are you headed?" the woman called out to Olivia. Her face, which was only partially visible beneath the tattered calico bonnet she wore, was reddish brown, and lined heavily, the effects, no doubt, of hard work, and heavy exposure to the sun.

"Kansas," Olivia replied, her fingers unconsciously gripping the leather traces a little tighter. She so hoped the woman would ask her few questions and be done with it. She was tired of conversing with strangers, tired of answering the same inevitable questions.

"Whereabouts?"

"I'm not exactly certain." She glanced over at the woman. "Where are you headed?"

"Past Kansas, that's for certain. They don't call it 'bleedin' for nothin', you know. Can't figure why a person would want to set down roots here. No, we're headed toward the Rockies, to let my man decide whether or not there's anything to all the claims of gold. If nothin' comes of it, we'll head on up toward Oregon."

The term "bleeding Kansas" was one Olivia had never heard until just the past few days. She was curious about the phrase, but she wasn't about to ask this woman.

"That your husband up there, a-walkin' the horses?" The woman gave a quick backward toss of her head. "Any kids back in there?"

Olivia's jaw tightened. "That's my brother. And no, there are no children in the wagon." She kept from retorting, "Is there anything else you would like to know?"

Still the woman would not desist. "Brother? That's all in your party? He does look on the youthful side, though he's built like a man. And I'd be hard-pressed to believe you were outside of nineteen yourself."

Something inside Olivia snapped. The anger bottled up inside since burying her mother and then finding out about her father had not dissipated; indeed, it had been bubbling dangerously close to the surface of her all-too-strained emotional state.

"Our parents are both dead. We are alone. We are settling in Kansas. Anything else you would like to know?"

The other woman was silent for a few moments. When she spoke, her voice was soft and kind, filling Olivia with instant regret at her own rudeness. "I'm so sorry for you, miss. Simon is forever reminding me of my mouth. I cain't ever seem to keep it closed. I'll leave you in peace." She paused and then added, "My name is Leona McGill. I wish you good fortune in Kansas."

Olivia said nothing in return, merely kept her gaze straight ahead. Her heart was breaking inside her chest. The woman's last words had been so kind and sweet, the very thing she longed to hear. Now that the woman was finally leaving her alone, Olivia found herself wanting nothing more than to apologize, to continue the conversation in a friendlier tone. But she dared not at this point. She'd have to hold back her emotions and unshed tears. To break down now would do no good whatsoever. One look at Aaron, trudging ahead, told her that. She was the one with strength, or so Aaron believed, and to let him down would change everything. And now that they had made up their minds to carry on with their father's original plans, she felt committed to it. She couldn't turn back, just couldn't. It was the only possibility for their future.

The horses plodded along on the dry, dusty road. The mule had balked a bit at crossing the bridge, but after being prodded and poked, he'd resumed following behind the wagon.

As he walked, Aaron kept his left hand on the gray's shoulder, out of habit more than anything. Also, though he did not recognize it, he found it soothing to be holding on to something. From time to time his eyes would fill, and he would be so lost in thought that he didn't know it until he tasted the hot, salty tears seeping inside the corners of his mouth. Then he would swipe the back of his shirt-sleeve across his face, smearing the dirt even more. Occasionally he'd reach up and take off his hat, the blue felt one his dad used to wear, knock off the layer of dust that coated it, and then set it back atop his shock of dark brown hair.

He was so confused, felt so strange. Unconsciously he wore a perpetual frown on his face. He didn't understand anything right now. Where were they going? How long would it take? Why were they making all this effort? He didn't understand his sister, who was so bent on carrying out their father's plan. Of course, she was right about there being no reason for them to go back home, since the farm was no longer theirs. When he pictured being back in Ohio, he could not even conjure up a vision of it anymore. What it looked like, how it smelled . . . nothing. It was as though the memory of it had been erased from his mind.

But neither could he envision what lay ahead. Claude Sands had said precious few words about the section of land he had purchased. Hadn't described it in any way other than to say it was prime land, much larger than the farm in Ohio. Mostly, though, it was to have been a place that would cure Amelia. That had been really all that counted for him.

Now both he and Amelia were dead. So, to Aaron's way of thinking, what was the point in their going? They could just have easily settled in St. Joseph. Neither he nor his sister had need, as their mother had, of moving to a dry, arid climate. And just picking up bits and pieces here and there along the way, Aaron had figured there was probably plenty reason *not* to live in Kansas. He'd heard more than his share of arguments on the slavery issue, seen more than a few polite conversations escalate rapidly into fisticuffs between an irate Missourian and an enraged Kansan. Slavery was wrong, he knew that; but he also knew enough by now to keep his mouth shut about his own opinion.

The subject that did interest him greatly was that of the Indians. On one hand he was fascinated by tales of their way of life, their savagery, their sheer strangeness. On the other hand—and he would have told no one of this—he was terrified of encountering them. He expected it was inevitable, but still, he couldn't rid himself of the irrational fear that penetrated his dreams every night. He felt the fool. He was a strong man, taller than his own father had been by almost three inches, and towering over most other men. Yet physical appearance and strength did nothing to banish such feelings.

In the end, though, he was swayed by the high regard he'd always had for his sister. She was smart, much smarter than he could ever hope to be. He respected that about her, envied her a little at times. But mostly, he trusted her. And since he was so confused himself right now, he reasoned that perhaps it was best to simply trust in what she thought was best and go along. Besides, where else could he go?

Maybe after a time he would lose the fear that lurked

inside him, maybe even prove to himself that he was really a man.

They reached the outskirts of Atchison late in the evening on the last Sunday of the month of June. The weather, warm during the day, turned at least ten degrees cooler as soon as the sun went down. There were other trails than the one Olivia and Aaron had arrived from, and at the terminus of each trail, a mile or so from the outskirts of Atchison, were groupings of all manner of vehicles. Covered wagons were lined up one behind the other, people milling about them, setting up or breaking camp, tending to the assortment of animals, who were either staked out or gathered in makeshift corrals. A few children were running about, their shouts and laughter ringing out in the clear night air. Women were bustling about campfires and wagons, preparing evening meals or cleaning up. A man strummed a banjo and began singing in a not so bad voice.

It was a homey atmosphere, and it filled Olivia with a sudden urge to cry. Mother and Father should have been here tonight, she thought. Especially Mother. She would have loved seeing so many people together, would have been cheered by the music. Swallowing, she pushed back the thought. No use even thinking that way, she thought. It only made her feel worse.

After selecting a spot, she and Aaron went about immediately setting up camp. Aaron watered and fed the horses, then staked them out on a grassy knoll a few yards from the wagon. Olivia built a fire in the iron stove they'd brought along in the back of the wagon and set about preparing the evening meal. It wasn't much—biscuits and gravy and a bit of ham were all they would eat that evening—but the aroma coming from the cast-iron skillet roused ravenous appetites in both of them. Aaron came back in short order, and both of them sat down on the wagon's tailgate and began to eat, mostly in silence.

Olivia made an effort to draw her brother out for a moment. "It's strange that they're not here, isn't it? I keep expecting to see Father coming round the side of the wagon and telling us what to do."

But Aaron merely gave a brusque nod of his head and looked down, picking up the last of his biscuit. He popped it in his mouth and turned his head away from her, but not before she saw the telltale glistening in his eyes.

She said nothing further, deciding not to press him. Everything was still much too raw for him. Best to leave him to his private thoughts for now.

After cleaning up, Olivia wanted nothing more than to shuck off her clothes, slip into a deep bathtub like the one at the hotel in St. Joseph, and sluice off the layers of grime from her body. If only she weren't so tired, she would make her way down to the stream where Aaron had gathered water for the horses and indulge in a sponge bath. But she was simply too weary to do more than think about it. Aaron checked on the horses one final time before climbing inside the wagon and rolling up inside his bedroll. When Olivia finally lay her head back on the small pillow on her pallet, she could not imagine getting up again.

Morning light filtered through the heavy canvas of the wagon. Olivia opened one eye, calculated that it was probably not too long after daybreak, and turned over onto her other side, her body and mind both reluctant to face the dawn of a new day. But there were noises about outside, man and beast astir, and as the minutes passed, they became more intrusive. At last Olivia opened both eyes, rubbed them vigorously, and gave herself a long, invigorating stretch.

Rolling off the pallet, she noticed that Aaron had already gone. She removed her muslin gown, pulled over her head one of five calico dresses she and Amelia had made, laced up her shoes, then stepped out the back of the wagon. She stood in one place for a moment, looking all about. The sky was a deep robin's-egg blue, and there was a brisk breeze which countered the warm rays of the summer sun. It would be a nice day, she thought, walking over to the campfire and tossing a few branches onto last night's ashes. She coaxed a fire quickly, then stood up and dusted off her hands. It was the perfect day to make the trip into Atchison, to the land office, where she hoped to clear up a few details about the papers her father had left them.

But first things first, she decided, remembering the small cloth bag that contained two soiled calico dresses and a few undergarments. She retrieved it from the back of the wagon and hastened toward a well-beaten path that led to the creek. She found a convenient spot on the grassy bank and set about washing her precious garments. Other women were already doing the same. All of them seemed intent on the task at hand. After a few minutes, one of them lifted an arm and waved to Olivia. Olivia squinted against the sunlight and then recognized the woman as the one who had spoken so forthrightly with her on the road yesterday.

The woman approached, a large straw basket propped on one hip. "Hello there." She grinned broadly, and Olivia could see that despite the lines on her face, she was probably no more than thirty years old.

"Hello," Olivia returned the greeting.

"You look a sight better than you did yesterday," the woman said. "You probably don't remember my name. Excuse my manners. Don't much have any to start with, Simon's always sayin'." She nodded. "Leona McGill."

Olivia, twisting the water out of a chemise, smiled

back at the woman. "Olivia Sands," she introduced herself. "Glad to meet you. Again."

"Well, I'm happy to see you lookin' a lot more spry. Where's your brother?"

"Actually," Olivia said, spreading the damp garment across a low bush nearby, "I'm not too sure. He was tending the horses when I left the wagon. He usually wakes earlier than I do."

Leona shifted the basket onto her other hip. "So have you joined up with a party yet?"

Olivia frowned. "No. I'm not sure what we'll be doing."

Leona raised her eyebrows. "Well now, you should already be aware that gettin' in a good company of wagons is real important. Most people you see hereabouts are already signed on to one."

"That so? Well . . . I suppose I might find out some information today in town at the land office."

"Which trail are you headed down?"

"The Smokey Hill trail is the one our father intended to use. Have you heard of it?"

Leona nodded. "I sure have. Matter of fact, it's the one we'll be taking. But that's because Simon's so all-fired determined to get to Colorado the fastest route possible. It's new, you know. Not much favored by most."

Olivia wasn't bothered by the warning note in the woman's voice. "I'm certain our father had good reason for wanting to use it."

"Where you headed?"

"Near a town called Salina."

Leona nodded briefly. She arched her back and took in a deep breath of the clean, dry air. "Well, I've got to go on back to camp. I've lingered too long. The youngsters'll be scroungin' round for their breakfast." She smiled. "But it was sure nice to see you again. If you decide to leave in the next few days, I'd advise you to join up with our party. It's a good one. As safe a one as you'll find."

"Thank you. We'll consider it," Olivia said, turning back toward the creek. She finished her wash with haste, for she needed to get back to camp herself. Her stomach was growling and gurgling as hunger started to build.

Aaron was stirring up the coals and had already set the coffee to boiling when she got back to the wagon.

"Morning," Olivia greeted him. "That smells wonderful. Let me put this away and I'll fry up some bread and ham."

"All right," Aaron answered. His hair was wet and his face seemed reasonably clean. Olivia surmised that he'd made his own trip down to the creek. He looked in better spirits, too, which was good, because from now on, both of them would have to set their minds to the upcoming journey overland.

As they sat on the ground atop a straw mat, sipping coffee and eating thick slices of the sourdough bread Olivia had fried, they discussed venturing into Atchison that day.

"We've got the plans already," Aaron said, taking a loud slurp of his coffee. "I don't see why we need to talk to anyone at the land office."

"I just think it would be wise, is all," Olivia answered. "We need to verify the map and the deed at the very least. I reread everything yesterday, but it still seems confusing."

"Well, if you're confused, then I sure can't help." Indeed, Aaron had never applied himself to learning the way his sister had, choosing instead to help his father on the farm. Oh, he could read a little and do his sums, but legal documents were beyond him.

By ten o'clock they had redded up the campsite, took stock of what supplies they needed to replenish, and then saddled up the two horses. A good many of the

wagons they saw—and there were all manner of them—
were using mules or oxen for pulling, but already the
advantage of having two sturdy horses was apparent. It
sure did make for a better form of transportation than
walking or kicking the sides of their stubborn mule.

They rode side by side on the dirt road into the city,
keeping the horses at a walking pace.

"I think old Sampson and Whiskers are enjoying
having somebody on top instead of behind," Olivia
commented, grinning as she observed the long necks
of the two animals, completely stretched out and relaxed.

"That's for sure," said Aaron, and his face, too, lit
up with a smile.

Olivia noticed it and suddenly felt a lurch in her mid-
section. How long had it been since she had seen a
smile on her brother's face? How long had it been since
she herself had been capable of smiling? She looked
away, consumed with guilt suddenly. Aaron must have
felt the same, for he looked embarrassed now, almost
ashamed.

It didn't seem right, Olivia thought, didn't seem right
that they could be smiling now. So soon, so very soon
after their parents' deaths. And yet both of them *had*
smiled, and here they were riding together into town,
just as if this were the way it had always been intended.
And who knew, really? Who knew that this wasn't the
way it was supposed to have been all along? Who knew
this wasn't God's plan, after all?

Just the two of them together, facing the future alone.

CHAPTER VI

THE land office was located on Main Street, and even though it should have been an easy place to find, it seemed at first as if they never would. There were so many people crowded around the building that its sign was almost completely obscured. They'd found a stable right away, had seen to the horses' care, and then set out on foot along the wide, dusty street.

Olivia felt out of place in the throng that spilled out the door of the government land office. It appeared she was the only woman present, which made her feel distinctly uneasy, especially after enduring a few rather impolite stares from some of the men, many of whom were loud and boorish and obviously fond of imbibing spirits with breakfast. She stayed as close as possible to her brother, at one point deciding to tuck her arm inside his elbow for extra security. After that she simply kept her eyes fixed on the ground and tried to block out the rude, indecent talk and raucous laughter.

Aaron stood with his sister on his arm, red-faced and totally unsure of himself. Embarrassed, too! He'd never been around such wild talk before. And to have his sister right there beside him, hearing all of it. He thought for a moment about suggesting to Olivia that perhaps they should leave and come back another time when the place was less crowded, but her look was stern; she would, he knew, want to stay.

The sun directly overhead was intense, and because the breeze had died down, the heat was rapidly growing unbearable. Flies swarmed aggressively, and Olivia was kept busy fanning them away from her face. She remembered her handkerchief in the small reticule on her wrist and placed it across her nose and mouth, which also helped to keep out some of the dust being kicked up by the throng of restless men.

"Miss Sands? Is that you?"

The deep, resonant voice made Olivia whip around. Behind her stood Francis Burton, his handsome features darker than she remembered, his eyes a deeper brown. His clothes, everyday wear instead of the formal attire he'd worn on the train, were coated with dust.

"Dr. Burton." Olivia felt herself blush, and was irritated to display such emotion.

"What are you doing here?" she asked, almost at the same time he did.

Francis smiled and nodded toward the land office. "I'm here for the same reason everyone else is, I suppose. To see what the government's selling today. You never know. Might be worth the price, might not be."

Olivia nodded and, for several moments, was tongue-tied. She felt a nudge against her arm and turned to see Aaron looking down at her quizzically.

"Oh! I forgot my manners. Dr. Burton, this is my brother, Aaron. Aaron, this is Dr. Francis Burton."

Francis extended his hand toward Olivia's brother and explained, "We met on the train into St. Joseph. I cared for your mother while she was ill." His eyes narrowed and he turned his gaze to Olivia, who had dropped her own. "Is she all right?"

Slowly Olivia shook her head. "No. She didn't . . . she didn't make it."

Francis's expression was somber and he was quiet for a long while. "I'm truly sorry to hear that. She was a true lady. I'm very sorry for both of you."

Neither Olivia nor Aaron seemed capable of speaking, so Francis searched for something else to say. "And your father? Is he here with you, then?"

Aaron spoke for the first time. "He's dead, too."

Francis appeared stunned. "What happened?"

"He was killed on the journey over. It was a freak accident."

Francis lowered his head, then looked up several seconds later. There were no words, really, that were appropriate. He'd been exposed to much tragedy before, that was certain; it never got any easier to deal with.

"I'm so very sorry." He paused, fiddled with his hat, and added, "Would you both like to go with me for a bite to eat? Doesn't look like this crowd is going to thin out any time soon." He frowned. "Are you here to buy land?"

"No," Olivia answered, "we just wanted to check on a few matters concerning the land we already own before setting out."

"Whereabouts is it located?"

Olivia frowned. "That's what we're here for, actually. We're not exactly certain. Somewhere along the Smokey Hill River. Near a place called Salina. West of it, I believe."

Francis suddenly thrust out his chin. "Salina? Why, that's not far from the Smokey Hills."

"Yes," Olivia said, "I know."

Francis scratched his jaw and considered the young woman and boy before him. As travelers, they were mere greenhorns. They weren't sure of what they were doing now—or what they were about to do. The route they would have to travel to reach their destination was one of the newest and most dangerous trails heading into the territories. First they'd have to travel the trail that was used by the Leavenworth and Pikes Peak Express stage route till they reached Junction City, and then switch to the Smokey Hill trail. He intended to use it himself to reach Colorado.

"Look," he said in a louder voice, for suddenly a group of men nearby had burst out in raucous laughter. "It's really hot, and the flies are awful." He glanced off into the distance, wincing. "Why don't we get some shade under that oak?"

Olivia glanced back toward the front of the land office building and then back at her brother, who was growing increasingly uneasy. "Well, I'm not so sure we should lose our place in line."

"Most likely you won't get to the head of it today. Besides, I think I could help you more than the men inside."

"How so?"

"Do you have the property papers with you?"

"Yes."

Francis jerked his head sideways. "Then come along."

Aaron took an immediate step forward. This gentleman was being so polite to them, and he'd had enough of the rowdy, crude crowd.

Olivia considered staying for only a moment; she hated to lose her place in line. But she quickly followed Francis Burton, her brother close behind. When they finally stopped beneath the oak, Olivia let out a sigh of relief. The temperature beneath the umbrella of its spreading branches was a good ten degrees cooler; a light, steady breeze soughed through the leaves, caressing her nape, her perspiring brow.

Pushing off her sunbonnet, Olivia leaned her head back, letting her head rest against the trunk.

"Over here, sis," Aaron said, indicating a smooth-surfaced log nearby.

"Perfect," she said as she sat down.

"Sure is," Aaron said, straddling the log and taking off his own hat. He fanned it against his face and closed his eyes as he spoke. "Sure is nice to be away from that bunch."

Francis chuckled. "I'll agree with you on that." He sat down a few feet away from Olivia, took his own hat off, and placed it a few inches away. "Now. Let's see what sort of papers you have with you."

Olivia untied the strings of her reticule and removed a carefully folded brown envelope. She opened it and began to withdraw the contents, but hesitated before handing them over to Francis. "It's awfully nice of you to help us like this."

"I'm rather curious, to tell you the truth. I've not heard of too many people purchasing land where you say your father did."

She handed him the papers and waited as he looked over each and every one of them. "It's all here. Your father did acquire a section near Salina. It's all legal. Don't see anything you're missing, and according to the description here, it shouldn't be too hard to find."

Francis shook his head, the furrow beneath his brows deepening. "I don't know. I just don't know."

"You sound disapproving," Olivia said.

"Well, it's a very sparsely populated area. I know some about it because I've traveled the route once before. Salina was just a settlement back in fifty-six. Then there was the battle at Indian Rock nearby. Conflict between the reservation Indians and the Cheyenne, Sioux, and Arapaho tribes. Pretty bloody, from what I heard. Of course, by now there's been some sort of peace made." He raised his shoulders. "Salina is scattered farms—a township. Not exactly a hub of social life."

Olivia suddenly sat up straighter. "Social life is not what I'm looking for, Dr. Burton."

Francis glanced at Aaron; the young man was frowning.

"What are you looking for?"

Olivia pondered how exactly she should answer Mr. Burton's question. As she spoke, she realized she was answering not only him, but herself.

"I'm looking for a home," she said, softly and slowly. "The home our parents would have wanted. A home like the one we left and the one we were going to build."

Francis noticed the way Aaron watched his sister; he appeared completely reliant on her, no matter his own thoughts.

"I see," Francis said.

"And I don't care how far away this place is that my father bought. It belongs to us now, and I intend to carry out his plans. I intend to see to it that he did not set out on the journey for nothing."

Francis twisted the leather rim of his hatband back and forth. "Well, that's certainly an honorable goal. And I wish you luck." He took in a breath and let it out in a sigh. "I think you'll need it."

"One needs luck in everything," Olivia answered, firm now in her resolve to do what she believed was right. "And a lot of hard work."

"That's certain."

"I've never been one to be afraid of hard work," she said firmly. "And neither has Aaron." She paused as she looked at her brother, and a slow smile spread across her face. "Well, usually he's not afraid of it. Right, Aaron?"

Aaron gave a lopsided smile back and then nodded. "I do what it takes."

Francis stood and brushed the tops of his trousers with his palms. "It's a good thing, then, that you both agree."

Olivia looked up at the tall, handsome man and

cocked her head to one side. "What were you doing in Salina before?"

"Well . . . I was on my way to Colorado."

"Didn't you say that's where you're headed now?"

"Yes. I did. I've joined a party traveling the Smokey Hill trail. Which is the same one you'll have to take."

"Is your party still open to others?" Olivia asked.

"I think so. We don't have too many yet. If you're certain you still want to go on . . ."

Olivia bristled with irritation. "I'm absolutely certain."

Francis gave her an assessing look. "All right, then. I just think you should understand what lies ahead. . . ."

"I've heard your warnings."

"Fine. Fine. But there are other options open to you. You'd do well to consider them."

"What options?" Aaron asked.

"There are plenty of places where you could wait and think things through before heading out into such desolate territory."

"That won't be—" Olivia said testily, but was interrupted by Aaron, who asked, "Such as?"

"Such as Topeka. Or Kansas City. Or St.—"

"We are going to settle on our land, Dr. Burton. And that's final."

Aaron looked at his sister, frowned, but then quickly looked away.

"Well then," Francis said, "I'll tell you what. I'll talk to the wagon master and get you a place in the lineup. We'll be leaving day after tomorrow."

Olivia's heartbeat quickened. "So soon?"

"Yes. Most of our party is already well equipped, and we're only waiting on a few repairs to be done with."

Olivia turned to Aaron. "Well, Aaron. Sounds like we'd better get to our shopping."

"I'll be seeing you then, soon, I suppose. Why don't you drive your rig up to our group—up near the bluff at the end of that road. Look for me, and I will introduce you to Mr. Turley, the wagon master."

"Thank you," Olivia said, feeling more excited with each passing second. "We'll be there this evening."

Francis placed his hat back on his head and gave a curt nod. "That's settled then. Have a good afternoon."

Olivia's eyes stayed on his retreating figure as he walked away from them, back in the direction of the land office. He carried himself very well, she mused, for a tall man. Unexpectedly she remembered his kneeling figure next to her mother's bedside and felt a powerful pull toward this man who had entered her life for the second time. Both times had been moments of crisis, or, at the very least, profound change.

Unbidden, the image of Silas came to her, and she found herself comparing the two men. Next to Francis Burton, Silas seemed callow, inexperienced. One had been a boy still; the other was a man.

"Sis? Are you listening or has the heat got the better of you?"

Olivia looked at her brother and shook her head slightly. "I'm sorry. I didn't hear a word you said."

"That's certain. I asked if you're ready to go on into town yet."

"Yes, of course. Perhaps we could stop for something to eat first, though, before we do our shopping. I'm starved."

"Suits me. I'm always starved."

Olivia placed a hand on her brother's forearm and gave it a playful shake. "You've been hungry since you were born. I don't think Mother ever could fill up that stomach of yours."

Aaron looked startled for a second. It was the first time either of them had made an offhand remark about one of their parents. It marked a turning point . . . a letting go.

Neither of them acknowledged this aloud, but as they walked onward, both were very much in tune with the other's thoughts and emotions. The bond that they'd always shared had grown stronger.

The town of Atchison was busy as St. Joseph, Olivia decided, its population mostly transient, since it was one of the jumping-off points for the trails westward.

She and Aaron had a satisfying meal in a hotel restaurant, and then separated for a while to shop. Aaron set off first to locate a smithy, in search of a few extra tools. Olivia, having already seen a large general store, went in that direction.

She spent over an hour inside the large, well-stocked emporium, debating for a long while over how much she should purchase. Money was not an issue, for Claude Sands had left his family enough to stock the farm, but supplies might be unobtainable in Salina.

At last she set her mind to obtaining each and every article she thought they might possibly need for the next year. She splurged on a few yards of calico muslin and various needles, spools of thread, buttons, and button hooks. She added two pairs of shoes, one pair practical, made of sturdy leather, the other a more delicate fashionable pair, which she imagined wearing to church on Sunday. The thought flashed through her mind that she wasn't even certain if there would be a church near their new home. She grimaced at the thought, for it brought to mind a host of other unanswered questions. The truth was that she had little idea what living in Kansas would be like. However, one way or another, she would find out, and that would be that.

She made her way to the grocery section, where she purchased extra rations of staples already stored inside the Conestoga; bacon, dried apples, coffee, sugar, flour, cream of tartar, and baking soda. Then, on a whim, she added a few other items she was certain they'd be hard-pressed to find in the future: jars of pickles, mustard, and tins of dried herring. At the apothecary, across the street, she selected liniments, tinctures, an assortment of differing lengths of cotton cloth, and boxes of clean cotton. On final consideration, she added bottles of tincture of turpentine, calamine, and tins of sassafras and buttercup tea. Packages in hand, she left the store and then retraced her steps inside. She purchased two precious vials of laudanum, hoping there'd never be need of them.

Finally done, she met her brother, as they had agreed upon earlier, at the feed store, where she found him paying for sacks of grain and bales of hay.

Aaron's eyes widened as he saw his sister; she was barely visible behind the bulky packages she had awkwardly arranged and managed to carry.

"Here, give me those," he said with a chiding tone. He poked his nose inside one box and said, "What in heck did you buy?"

"A little of everything." Olivia wiped her dampened brow with a small handkerchief. She gave her brother an appraising glance. "You could do with a bit of extra clothing, you know. A new pair of shoes wouldn't hurt, and a couple of new pairs of jeans and—"

"I've got Pa's things," Aaron said quietly, looking off into the distance. He swallowed deeply and cleared his throat, and Olivia knew in that moment the pain he still felt. Would always feel.

"Yes, that's true. You do have Pa's things. It . . . it would be a shame not to use them."

Aaron looked back at his sister and said, "Well, are we ready?"

"I am. Are you?"

"Yep. The man here said he'll deliver all my purchases in his supply wagon this evening."

"Good."

"I'll go round back to the stable and bring the horses. You wait here." Aaron placed the boxes and bags on the wood plank floor, walked down the steps, and then headed to the rear of the feed store toward the stable and carriage house.

It was as he walked away that Olivia recognized he was wearing their father's old blue chambray shirt and his wide leather belt. How could she not have noticed until now? Her father had worn that shirt and belt for years. She struggled with a pang of guilt for a few uncomfortable moments; how much else would she forget, not only about her father but her mother, too? No, she wouldn't allow that to happen. Never! She would remember everything about them.

But as her brother rode up a minute later, leading her mount by the reins, she realized that she had already forgotten something, and it was frightening how soon it had happened.

Locating the party Francis Burton was in was not difficult, for it was only a mile east of where Olivia and Aaron had spent their first night on the outskirts of Atchison. It was also the smallest group of wagons she had seen; there were only ten, most occupied by men headed for the Rockies to mine for gold. The only other woman, Olivia soon discovered, was Leona McGill.

Leona spotted Olivia as soon as she and Aaron had parked their rig near the crescent of vehicles.

"Welcome," she said, her hands on her hips as she waited for Olivia to climb down from the driver's seat.

"Hello there," Olivia said, pleased to see her friend. She pushed her bonnet off her head and smoothed the braided coil of her hair.

"Had a hard day, it looks," commented Leona.

"No. Not really. Just did a lot of shopping in town, and I suppose the heat got to me a little."

"Well, make sure you make the most of tonight and tomorrow and get plenty of rest. There's no tellin' what's awaitin' us on that trail."

Olivia shrugged. "I wouldn't think it would be much worse than anyone else has to face. Besides, so far I've found travel to be fairly boring."

"You'll find out the difference soon enough," Leona retorted confidently. "Well, I better get back to my two little ones. They've been napping in the wagon, but they'll be screamin' their lungs out for their supper soon enough."

"I should set about preparing ours, too, now that you mention it."

"I'll see you later."

Fifteen minutes later, as Olivia tended thick slices of ham sizzling in the heavy cast-iron skillet, she thought how curious it was that food should taste more flavorful out in the open than it had at home, where it was prepared in the comfort of a fully stocked kitchen. Certainly she was doing nothing different; if anything, she was using even less in the way of spices.

She heard footsteps behind her and turned, thinking it was Aaron, back from his chores taking care of the horses. But it was Francis Burton.

"Did you get everything you wanted in town?" he asked.

Olivia placed the lid on the skillet and stood, wiping her hands on her apron. "Yes, I think so. I just hope I don't discover something later that I forgot to buy."

Francis nodded. "I saw you talking to Mrs. McGill. She's a friendly, helpful woman. I'm sure if you're in need of anything, she'll help you out."

"Yes," Olivia said, giving a half smile. "She is friendly."

"Come around to my wagon after supper and I'll introduce you and Aaron to Mr. Turley."

"Thank you. I'd appreciate it."

Francis's dark eyes were disconcerting, she realized suddenly: so intense, penetrating, and direct. Of all his features, his eyes were by far the most arresting. Almost captivating.

Thrusting the thought aside, she turned and walked toward the back of the wagon. Opening the supply box, she busied herself arranging the new purchases, and when she glanced up, Francis was gone.

The sun was setting on the western horizon, and the light breeze that had picked up late in the afternoon was rapidly developing into a stiff wind. The canvas tarp billowed out, pulled taut against the span of hoops connected to the sides of the wagon. Like a sail on a ship, Olivia thought. She closed her eyes and listened, not to the sounds of the people and animals and various other noises, but to the sound of the wind as it snapped and flapped the tarp. It was like the sound of a ship, sailing onward through sometimes silent, sometimes turbulent, waterless seas.

She opened her eyes and stepped onto the rear stoop of the wagon. She paused, gazed at the darkening horizon again, and then turned, entering the ship that would take her into her future.

CHAPTER VII

THE caravan of wagons, some twelve altogether in the final count, departed the outskirts of Atchison toward the south-southwest on the first Monday of July. Olivia had been awake all night, or at least had no recollection of sleeping, for she had been too excited to do anything other than anticipate the morning.

She had arisen long before daylight and, by light of the kerosene lamp, stoked up the fire. Breakfast was ham and fried bread, over which was poured a generous measure of molasses. And, of course, coffee. Rich, aromatic, and strong coffee, made exactly the way her mother had made it. Half an ounce of ground beans and a pinch of salt boiled in water and allowed to settle for a few minutes.

By midmorning the wagons had gone about six miles; and by then, Olivia had grown used to the sounds of grinding wheels and jangling bells intermingling with the noise of the mules, oxen, and draft horses that pulled the various wagons. And of course, there was also the friendly chatter of the people who were traveling together, headed toward the Smokey Hill trail.

Most of the conveyances were light wagons, similar to the Conestoga she and Aaron were in, but as far as

Olivia was concerned, none of them were as sharp-looking. Theirs was painted in the original bright colors of deep blue on the underbody, crimson along the upper body, with a canvas as close to white as any could get. She felt confident in their sturdy horses and two mules, and looked with pride upon her brother, who was riding comfortably on the left-hand wheel horse.

By noon the sun was bright and hot, and the wagon master sent word along the line that the party would stop near a small creek a few hundred yards away.

Francis Burton rode up on his own horse, a dark dappled bay thoroughbred, seventeen hands high, just as Aaron was dismounting and setting about releasing the harness yokes.

"Looks like you two are getting along just fine," Francis said, a wide smile on his face.

Olivia jumped down from her perch on the bench seat, a maneuver she had perfected by now, and put her hands on both hips. "Well, did you expect we wouldn't?" There was a teasing glint in her eyes.

"No. I think you two have what it takes."

"For what?"

"For just about anything." He tipped his hat and turned his attention to Aaron. "Need any help, son?"

Aaron glanced up quickly, a rather startled look on his face. He had not been addressed as "son" in many a week. It stirred some warm emotion in him, one he wasn't quite sure what to do with.

"No. But thanks anyway."

Francis tipped his hat and pulled gently on the reins, pressing into his horse's sides with his legs. The horse began to back.

"Would you care to join us for dinner, Dr. Burton?" The words were out of Olivia's mouth before she had time to think.

"That's very kind of you, but I must make my visits to everyone here. I've agreed with Mr. Turley to try and keep this company as healthy as possible. If you care to extend that invitation to tonight, I'd be glad to accept.''

"All right. Tonight, then," Olivia said, and then turned to walk round to the opposite side of the wagon where the kitchen supply box was nailed. As she rummaged inside the box, she thought how comfortable she was feeling with Francis Burton.

She and Aaron sat on the tailgate and ate their lunch, which tasted even better than breakfast had. She had reheated the leftover coffee, and even that tasted good.

"How are the horses?" she asked her brother.

"Doin' fine. Sure did like that fresh, cold water down in the creek.''

Olivia sipped some more of her coffee. "I hope you didn't mind that I asked Dr. Burton to join us for supper.''

"Why would I?"

Olivia shrugged. "I don't know. I . . . didn't know if you liked him or not. You do, don't you?''

"Sure I do." Aaron paused, finished chewing on the last bite of his biscuit, and then added, "He's a good enough man.''

Olivia said nothing, but inwardly she was reassured. She, too, felt he was a "good enough man." It was silly, really, but her brother's opinion did make her feel more confident in her own judgment.

Leona McGill found her way over to the Sandses' wagon as Olivia was cleaning up. The two-year-old on her hip was sucking on his milk flask, his clear blue eyes staring intently at Olivia.

"Hello," she said in response to Leona's greeting.

"You about redded up yet?"

"I think so," Olivia said, placing her hands on the small of her back and arching backward.

Leona shifted the child to her other hip and said,

"Too soon to be getting all sore. We've a ways to go, you know."

"That's for certain. I've been told it's over a hundred and fifty miles to Salina. Wonder just how long we'll be in getting there."

"Well, I'm not the one to ask. Guess it depends on the weather and this here new route we're taking. To tell the truth, I don't like to think about it at all. Makes me plain tired. Course, you're lucky, not going as far as we are."

"I guess so."

"Why don't you ask Turley about the distance?"

"Well, I did, actually. And he said two, maybe three weeks."

"Well, then, there's your answer."

Olivia sighed. "I suppose so. I just wish . . ." Her voice trailed off.

"Girl, let me tell you somethin'. There's no good in wishin'. Won't get you something back that you lost, and can't guarantee you the future. Best thing to do is move on one day at a time."

As the days rolled by, the caravan traveling on the open plain toward an ever-disappearing horizon, each seemed different and yet somehow the same. Like hundreds before them, the wagon train party Olivia and Aaron had joined followed a well-established routine, one that kept both the humans and livestock as safe and sound as possible. Olivia, like most everyone else, was fearful of an Indian attack. But each day ended peacefully.

The sky remained clear and high, spilling no rain to wash out the trail or turn the dusty land into a mud trap for the animals' hooves or wagon wheels. Nights were still cool and pleasant, allowing for restful sleeping, but by the nooning stop, the sun blazed overhead, its rays bearing down on the vast land below with sizzling intensity. Many were the moments that Olivia fought the urge to climb into the wagon, strip down to her undergarments, and lie down, away from the dust, intense heat, and flies. But, of course, that was impossible, and so she, like everyone else, forced herself to endure those unbearable hours of the day, her every thought focused on the evening and its cool respite.

Everyone in the party was assigned a daily chore. To Olivia had fallen the duty of supervising the cooking for the evening meal, which took several hours from start to finish. But she found she didn't mind at all, because she was left to enjoy a few more precious minutes of predawn slumber and could retire immediately to the wagon bed after lunch for a much-needed nap. The first night Francis joined the Sandses for supper was the first of many to come. Indeed, for the entire journey, he spent all but one evening on the stoop of their wagon, where he enjoyed an extralarge portion of whatever was being served that night, and, of course, the company of the young woman.

Francis was perplexed by his state of mind; all day long, when he was busy riding scout with Herb Stanley, or tending to those who had taken ill, she was there, just beyond his thoughts. He checked on her frequently when the wagon train was moving, although most of his conversations were with Aaron. He really liked the boy. Though he was still young, he had a disarming frankness. Got straight to the point, a characteristic Francis much appreciated. And it was obvious that he had a great love for his older sister. Francis found himself sharing stories about his past, relating details he'd thought long forgotten, stories that revealed how he had handled certain situations, certain decisions. Practical, useful information that Francis had gotten from his own father. He saw what he was doing: trying to fill in somehow for the boy's dead father. As far as he could tell, Aaron was receptive, as was his sister. Though she had said nothing, he noted the expression of approval on her face whenever she saw them together, deep in conversation.

The trail they followed now was closer to the Kansas River, and frequently the wagons were in the shadow of the tall cottonwoods that grew in abundance. The shade made it possible for the wagon train to travel a little more distance every day.

One evening, as Francis joined Aaron and Olivia on the back stoop of the Conestoga to share supper, he said, "We'll be reaching your land soon."

"How long?" Aaron asked, taking a bite of a soda biscuit.

"Five, maybe six days."

Olivia sat up straighter. "Do you really think so?"

Francis nodded. "Looks that way. We've had a remarkable journey so far. The scouts haven't reported sighting any Indians. There hasn't been much illness among the stock, and the trail's been so smooth, most of the wagons have been holding up fine. I don't think there've been but two wheels needed repair so far."

"We have had wonderfully good luck, haven't we?" Olivia said. The entire trip had turned out to be so routine, so predictable, that it seemed almost impossible to believe that some wagon companies met disaster. Suddenly she realized that in less than a week Francis Burton would be on his way, without them. The thought was unexpectedly painful. Unconsciously she set her fork on the tin plate in her lap and turned to stare off into the distance.

Aaron was talking with Francis, but she heard none of what either was saying.

"Sis?" Aaron spoke up loudly.

Frowning stiffly, she turned to him. "Yes?"

"I was just sayin', I think I'll hay the horses again. Make sure they're all right. I'll be back in a few minutes."

"Of course," Olivia said, then watched as Aaron walked off around the side of the wagon.

"Your plate."

She looked up questioningly.

Francis nodded toward her lap. "You're about to lose it."

"Oh," she said, righting the plate, which had been about to slip off her lap onto the ground. On it was still half of her venison stew, now cold.

"You didn't eat much."

"I know." She felt bad about it, for it was wrong to be wasteful, wrong to take more than one could eat. Yet looking at the congealed food, she had neither the heart nor the stomach to finish it.

"Here, give it to me," Francis said. "Turley's hound will love it."

"It's more than scraps," she said.

"Doesn't matter." And then he reached over and took the plate off her lap, the outside of his palm brushing her calico skirt lightly.

An involuntary shudder ran up the length of her spine and she froze. Francis set the plate down on the tailgate. His eyes looked into hers, and yet she could not read them, had no idea what he was thinking. She swallowed, strangely unable to think of a word to say herself.

"It will be hard, you know," he said, quietly.

"What will be hard?"

"The new life you have planned for yourself."

She gave an upward lift of her chin. "Yes. I'm sure it will."

"I was married a few years ago," he said. He looked away for a moment and then back at her. "She died."

Olivia looked down. Why was he telling her this?

"She had a mother and father, lots of brothers and sisters. Me. She would have never even thought to attempt what you are doing. She liked her life as it was.

Easy. Safe. But you . . ." He shook his head. "Well, I don't think I've ever come across a woman like you. So . . . determined."

"So unwise?"

"Well, maybe that, too. I just hope you do all right."

"Thank you," she said somewhat tersely. She stood up suddenly, began cleaning up.

As she reached for her brother's empty plate and cup, she felt Francis grasp her upper arm. She stared at his hand and then looked up at him.

"I want you to know . . ." he began, then paused for a few seconds. "I want you to know that I think you are a very beautiful woman. I've enjoyed your company—and your brother's—immensely, on this trip. Perhaps we'll see one another again."

"I doubt that very much," she answered, surprised to hear an edge of bitterness in her voice. How had it come to be that she cared so much about this man? She didn't have the answer for that; only felt a strong urge to move away from him now.

She took a step, but his grasp was firm.

"One more thing," he said. "I . . ." He cleared his throat. "If I ever thought about marriage again, it would be with a person like you."

Olivia just stared at him. What sort of statement was that? If he ever "thought about" it again? And what was she supposed to say, how flattered she was? Suddenly white-hot anger flared up inside her, and she jerked out of his grasp. She gathered up all the dishes, except her own, and managed a tight-lipped "Excuse me."

Francis stood where he was, watching Olivia as she marched toward the women who were in charge of the cleanup crew. Thinking over what he had just said to her, he winced. He'd meant what he'd said, but he'd said what was on the top of his head, hadn't considered that it might be ill-sounding to her ears. Confusion engulfed him; he had meant to compliment her, let her know how much he . . . how much he what? It hit him then, the realization that he cared for her deeply, more deeply than he'd ever imagined possible.

He felt a stab of anger within; anger at his uncharacteristic ineptness. He waited around for a couple of minutes, but when she didn't return, he left for his own wagon.

He slept that night, as many of the men did when the weather was cool and dry, beneath his light wagon, on a comfortable heap of blankets. But it was a restless, unrefreshing sleep.

The wagon train was traveling through a cool, wooded stretch of terrain two days later, within earshot of the gurgling waters of the Kansas River. Olivia, tired of walking alongside the wagon, had gotten up on the seat; the normal jostling and bumping wasn't so bad today. In fact, she had long grown used to it, her body having learned to give and sway with the rocking, often jolting, motion. It was truly amazing, she had thought many times, how fortunate were the circumstances of their journey. The days had remained dry, and the ground was firm and accommodating to the wagons and animals. They had never been approached by any Indians, though the scouts had reported evidence of several newly abandoned campsites. Probably Pawnee, sometimes referred to as Noisy Pawnee, the travelers were told. Small, dark shadows on the horizon had been recently spotted—herds of buffalo—and so it was assumed this was the diversion that kept them safe from confrontations with the tribes.

Many of the men discussed, in the evening, the possibility of going on a hunt; after all, they declared, everyone would benefit from any kill they made. But Mr. Turley always made it quite clear, in a firm though friendly tone, that there would be no hunting whatsoever. If buffalo were keeping the Indians at a distance from the wagon train, then it would be absolute folly to invade their hunting grounds.

The men understood the reasoning, though it was evident in their expressions the disappointment they felt. Most were becoming bored by now, since the journey had gone so smoothly.

They had come within a few miles of Topeka a few days before, and some of the men had wanted to ride into town, which would have meant an extra night on the trail. Turley had said no, and so the party had set off as usual the next morning.

When the wagons stopped for the night, on the western outskirts of Abilene, however, there was nothing Turley could do to dissuade the men from riding into the town. According to the papers and maps in their possession, Olivia and Aaron's land was located south-southwest of Abilene, near the infant township of Salina. It was less than a day's journey away, and Olivia was feeling excitement about finally reaching their destination. But Abilene would be the last city that could furnish the men with supplies and entertainment before they set out on the long, desolate trek westward toward the Rockies.

Francis decided that he, too, would join the men, and he asked Aaron along. Aaron looked toward Olivia, his expression revealing a strong desire for her approval, and so she said, "Go on, Aaron. Enjoy yourself. You deserve it."

And so the men set off into town, some of them impatient and spurring their horses a bit more than necessary as they galloped toward the south. Since they left before the evening meal, Olivia and Leona were happy to have only themselves, the children, and the few men who had remained behind to prepare supper for. They fixed a light meal of leftover rabbit stew and cornmeal mush, or hasty pudding, as it was often called.

Leona asked Olivia to sit with her and the children at the rear of their wagon.

"Are you gettin' excited about reaching your land, Olivia?" Leona handed a plate to one of her youngsters and then sat down next to Olivia.

"Actually, yes." Olivia narrowed her eyes and ruminated for a moment before going on. "But you know, I think I've gotten used to traveling. The trip wasn't too bad at all. I had all sorts of horrible imaginings before we left."

Leona scooped a lock of hair back behind one ear, shifted the toddler propped up on her lap, and said, "Well, I don't know. I think we've all just been lucky so far. Good weather, no Indian problems. But there's a lot of miles between here and where we're headed. And," she added, "I don't think the land will be as hospitable as it's been so far."

"What do you mean?"

"Well, Simon has talked to some of the men who've been out the Smokey Hill before, and they seemed of one mind that the next part's a no-man's-land."

Olivia felt concern for the woman she had grown to think of as a friend, but more than a little relief that she and Aaron were within hours of what was to be their new home.

"How you been gettin' along with the good doctor?" Leona asked, pulling off a hunk of bread and popping it in her mouth. "Haven't seen you and your brother spending as much time with him lately."

Olivia pretended to shrug off the question. "We haven't had any need to see him."

Leona raised one eyebrow. "I could have sworn Dr. Burton was taken with you."

Olivia stared at the woman for a moment. They *had* spent a good deal of time together over the last three weeks; it must have been obvious to everyone, given appearances of a relationship that was simply nonexistent. "No, I think you are mistaken about that. He formed a friendship with both Aaron and myself. That is all."

"I see," said Leona, though her tone was dubious. "Well, it's none of my business. Sarah, don't put that in your mouth after you dropped it in the dirt." She leaned over and fussed with her young daughter for a moment, giving time for Olivia to think. It was hard to believe that tomorrow she would be seeing Francis for the last time. Suddenly, inexplicably, she was seized with a searing sense of loss. Images of her mother and father, and now Francis . . .

"Excuse me," she muttered, putting her plate down and standing up. "I really would like to . . . um, take a walk down by the river."

"You didn't eat much," Leona observed.

"I know. I'm not that hungry. Give it to Sarah or little Jimmy."

Leona nodded her head briefly and reached for the leftover food on Olivia's plate. "If you insist . . ."

"I'll be back in a few minutes," Olivia said, scooping up the hem of her skirt as she started off into the knee-high grass just beyond the wagon.

Leona was too busy dealing with her youngsters to answer, but Olivia was already descending the rather steep embankment that bordered the Kansas.

The water was clear and flowed quietly, peacefully, over the shimmering layers of pebbles and larger rocks that formed its bed. Olivia stood staring down into it, seeing not a reflection of herself, but of her past, all that had gone before her and which now would be coming to an end. For tomorrow there would be no more journey, no more sense of moving forward in time toward the future. The future was now, within the span of a few hours.

And suddenly all the doubts she had shoved to the back of her consciousness, all the possibilities for some other life that she and Aaron could have had, loomed up in her mind so hugely that she found there was no more escape from them. What if she *had* made the wrong decision? What did they know about this country, this land to which there had originally been no reason to move, other than to find a new home for Amelia Sands?

Olivia knew some about farming, and a lot of how to run a household; indeed, it had been she and not her mother who had been the real mistress of the household for the last few years. There was hardly any sort of work she would not, or could not, do. But could she have been wrong in insisting they carry on with their father's plans? Was doing so in Aaron's best interest? As mature as Aaron looked to others, Olivia realized his still very immature nature. He had suffered the same devastating loss as she had and was dependent on her.

A small fish wiggled its way from beneath an outcropping, its sudden movement producing concentric circles across the glassy surface of the water. Olivia stared at the hypnotic rings for a long while, her thoughts mimicking the motion of the water. Round and round and round they went, and still there was no answer to the questions in her heart and in her mind.

CHAPTER VIII

Francis Burton rode his dark bay thoroughbred back to camp at a faster pace than he had left. After starting at a brisk trot, Francis had legged the gelding into a canter and then into a full gallop.

None of the other men who had gone into Abilene could understand why he was already heading back to camp. The day had hardly begun for them. There was more than enough room at the saloon, and plenty of ladies of the evening to go around. Their hard-earned money would be well spent. Aaron had seemed surprised, too, when he said he was heading back, but he shook his head when Francis asked if he wanted to go back also. As Francis left him, the boy was walking along the dusty plank sidewalks, trying to work up the nerve to step inside the noisy saloon just across the street.

Burton had other things in mind than an afternoon of corn whiskey and willing women. He had felt the fool since his comment to Olivia Sands a few days earlier. Since she'd walked off, obviously offended, she'd taken care to keep her distance from him. Aaron apparently hadn't noticed what had happened, or learned of it from her, for he was as friendly as ever.

Fool or not, however, he'd been faced with having to think over his own words. He'd meant what he'd said, but the more he thought about it, the more it ate away at him, and he realized just how much he was holding back from himself. He cared deeply for Olivia Sands. The closer they got to the point at which she would be leaving the wagon train, the closer he came to recognizing what was right there in his own heart. Now he was on top of it, and he realized his caring was more than simply that. He was in love with Olivia and he wanted to marry her.

He saw Leona McGill leaning over one of her children near the back of her wagon; pulling a fresh muslin shirt over his blond head. She turned when she heard his horse's footsteps. "Doc Burton! What are you doing back here? I'd a thought you men wouldn't be back before sundown." She frowned. "Anything wrong?"

Francis reined up a few feet away from her. "Something I need to take care of."

Leona straightened her back and looked him squarely in the eyes; she watched his gaze perusing the campsite as he spoke, noted the alarm in it.

"She's down by the creek," Leona said, a little smile lifting one corner of her mouth.

Francis reacted immediately, pulling the inside rein against the horse's neck, turning him in the direction of the grassy knoll that sloped down to the creek. His gaze locked with Leona's for a few seconds, hers communicating all she understood, which was everything. Yes, his eyes told her, yes, you are right.

He let the reins slacken, allowing the horse to pick his own way down to the creek. The brush was thick, and he had to lower his head all the way down to the horse's withers to escape low-hanging branches. When they came into the clearing, he lifted his head, looked to the left, and saw her at once.

She was half squatting beside the water, her skirt

pulled up and twisted around her thighs, revealing a good portion of her bare legs. He cleared his throat loudly.

Olivia turned and looked behind her, and her eyes widened in disbelief. She could hardly believe it was him. It was as if her thoughts had produced him.

"Hello," he said.

She swallowed and, quickly realizing the state of disarray she was in, stood up, her skirt, now wet, dropping slowly to her ankles.

"I thought you were in Abilene today."

"I was," Francis replied, swinging down off his horse. He tied the reins around the horn of the saddle and slapped the horse on the rump, encouraging him toward the creek, where he could drink his fill. Tentatively he walked toward Olivia. "I got tired of the dust and the noise and . . ." His voice trailed off; he reached up and removed his hat, and ran one hand through his hair. His face, he knew, was covered with grime from the incessant dust, and his hair could use more than one or two good dunkings. The thoughts about his personal appearance brought him up short; he hardly ever gave so much weight to how he looked to others. But this was different; one hell of a lot different.

Olivia watched him, nonplussed by his uncharacteristic behavior.

"That's not the reason I came back," he said in a brusque voice. "I came because I wanted to be alone with you. I wanted to ask you something."

Olivia answered tentatively. "All right."

"When I said . . . those things the other night . . . the things that made you upset and all . . ."

"I wasn't upset," she inserted.

"You weren't?" He frowned. "You've avoided me ever since."

"Yes, well . . . I knew you were busy."

"No more than before."

Olivia looked off to the side, saying nothing.

"So anyway, as I was saying . . ." He cleared his throat. "These things I said, well . . . they were true. About wanting someone like you if I ever get married again."

Suddenly Olivia's head snapped back toward him, her eyes flashing. "That's all well and good, Dr. Burton, and I hope you will find someone who you actually can marry one day."

"I have." He spoke the words so quietly that at first she just stared blankly at him.

Unknowingly she blanched, her mouth tightened, and then she said crisply, "Well, that's wonderful. I hope you will be happy with her."

Francis took a step forward, shaking his head. "I mean you."

Olivia stared at his mouth. Then his chin. Then back into his eyes.

Francis repeated himself. "I meant it. I would like to . . . well, I would consider it an honor to have you as my wife."

Olivia swallowed, still staring. But strangely, no words came to her tongue.

He moved a step closer but remained quiet, allowing her to think it over. She seemed so much in shock that he didn't know what to make of the situation. Slowly she turned and looked toward the river, and then suddenly, right there in front of him, simply sat down on the grass, her feet brought in close with knees near her chin, her arms hugging her skirt tight around her calves. It was such an unusual, completely unexpected movement that Francis was dumbfounded.

"Olivia?" he asked, softly. "Are you . . . are you all right?"

"Yes. I'm fine." Her tone was strangely flat, and his heart sunk. What an idiot he must seem. He should have known better, should have realized he couldn't just make an instant decision, then ride up on her and expect her unquestioning compliance.

"I'd like to ask you something," she said, very softly, very quietly.

"Yes?"

She was still looking at the water, speaking to him over her shoulder. "Exactly why do you want to marry me?"

"Why?"

"Yes. Why."

He took in a deep breath and let it out slowly. "Well . . . I . . ." He scratched a nonexistent itch at the corner of his right eye.

"Go ahead."

"I . . ." He cleared his throat. "I suppose it's because . . ." Damn, but he was as tongue-tied as any fool he'd ever come across, and he'd come across plenty in his life. "For one thing, I like you. I like you a lot. And . . . well, I think we could do well together."

"Where?"

"Where?"

"Yes. Where?"

He hadn't talked to a woman in this fashion since he was a young boy engaged in conversation with his mother. Most of the time, with both men and women, it was he who issued the questions, they who gave the answers. "Why, here. In Kansas. I mean . . . I thought you wanted to stay here."

She had turned to look at him finally, and her clear green eyes were penetrating. He was shocked. He'd never had a woman look at him so . . . so scrutinizingly. He'd never thought about it before, but most women held a man's gaze for a few seconds or more and then averted their own, sometimes even dropping or lowering the chin. But Olivia did nothing of the sort. Her gaze was so different, so riveting, it almost unnerved him. Once again he scratched his eye, more vigorously this time. "You do, don't you?"

"Absolutely."

"All . . . right," Francis said slowly, still utterly confused by her manner.

"The question is," she said abruptly, "what is it that you want?"

"Well, I said what I want. I want you. And . . ."

"And? Yes?"

"Well, to stay on here with you, to help you and . . ." Damn, he hadn't counted on it being this hard.

"I appreciate what you are saying, Francis, but your original plan had been to travel toward Colorado. The gold mines. Most of the men on this wagon train are obsessed by it. I suppose I find it difficult to believe you could just give up that dream to settle down here—in the middle of Kansas."

"Well, it was my intention. But it's not now."

"We could certainly use the help, I'm not denying that . . ." Her voice trailed off and she sighed, her shoulders slumping as she bent forward to break off a blade of grass near her skirts. She rolled the long blade between her fingers slowly and then looked back up at Francis. "My mother and father married for a completely different reason."

"They did?"

"Yes. They married for love. They wouldn't have thought of getting married only because they could do well together, or however you put it."

"But . . . I didn't mean it . . . Well, I didn't mean it to sound so . . ."

"So what?"

Suddenly he crossed the remaining space between them and squatted down beside her. She was surprised when his hand grasped her own, the one that still twisted the blade of grass between thumb and forefinger. She stared at their hands, touching for the first time ever.

"Look, Olivia, I would like to tell you I love you. I think I do. I mean, I surely haven't felt this way in a long time about any woman at all. I guess I'm just, well, I'm a little afraid I might . . ."

"Yes?" Olivia asked softly.

His words came out rapidly. "I don't want to jinx anything . . ."

Olivia looked up and saw the sincerity in his expression, and she quite suddenly felt a mirthful chortle surface to her lips.

Francis frowned, lifted his chin, and released her hand abruptly. Just as abruptly she reached out and grasped it again within her own. "That's just about the silliest thing I ever heard," she said, smiling gently. "And the most believable."

He was looking at her hand, encased in his. It was smooth and slender, and tanned a rich golden brown. Her next words brought his gaze up to meet hers.

"I suppose," she said, still smiling, "I suppose that if we don't know one another well enough at this point, we'll have plenty of opportunity to do so in the future. I accept your offer of marriage, Doctor."

He was dumbfounded. He had thought . . . he had been so sure that he'd been such a fool . . . and now, now, here she was holding his hand, accepting his proposal!

"There are only two questions I'd like to ask," she added.

"Yes?"

"Where and when? I mean, we are arriving in Salina tomorrow, and we have no idea if anyone there will be able to marry us."

"That won't be a problem. In fact, I'd already given it some thought."

"You had?"

"Of course. Turley was a Lutheran minister back in Indiana before he took on this job. We'll have him perform the service before we break camp in the morning.''

Olivia frowned. ''But . . . well, that doesn't give me much time to . . .''

''To what? There's not that much to a wedding ceremony.''

Olivia's eyes narrowed. ''I intend to get married once, Dr. Burton. And if I can't have a church, then I'll at least have the proper dress.''

''Dress? You think there'd be time to ride into Abilene and purchase . . . ?''

She waved a hand dismissingly. ''I have my wedding dress already. It was my mother's.'' She paused, thinking for a moment. ''Of course, it's not the proper size, but I can work on it tonight and part of tomorrow, and by the time we reach Salina, why, it'll be ready.''

He swallowed, and gave a shake of his head. Then he gave a self-deprecating laugh. ''I sure never thought it would turn out like this.''

''You're not changing your mind, are you?'' Olivia asked, her tone teasing yet gentle.

Francis glanced up at her, and slowly the smile on his lips spread to his eyes, encompassed his entire face until he no longer appeared his nearly thirty-three years of age, but more like the innocent teenager he had once been. He felt wonderful! Joyous, exhilarated! All the things a man was supposed to feel when he was in love . . .

His thoughts brought him up short. So there, he'd finally admitted it to himself. And . . . well, it didn't feel bad. Not bad at all. He was in love for the second time in his life, and for all he could tell so far, it was much better this go-round.

Taking her hand, he stood up and then helped her rise to her feet. There was no one around, at least not to his knowledge, and so he slowly moved his face toward hers. She looked at him with those clear green eyes—ever so intense and penetrating!—but he saw his image mirrored in them, and if there had been any vestige of doubt in his mind, at that moment it vanished forever. He pressed his lips against hers, very briefly, barely brushing his flesh against hers. But to him that first kiss meant everything. It was a seal, a seal of their promise of betrothal and a seal guaranteeing the future that was now theirs.

The township of Salina was so tiny, it was hard even to think of it as such, let alone to call it one. A Mr. W. A. Phillips had been successful the year before, in 1858, in organizing a Town Company, appointing himself president and four others to complete the company board. The company was granted a town charter on March 30, 1859, but hadn't yet completed the platting survey.

Olivia was disheartened that it was so sparsely populated; nevertheless, it gained her instant admiration by virtue of its truly beautiful location. Sitting in the lap of a lush and fertile valley, it was near the banks of the Smokey Hill River, whose waters, just coming up from the south, took a sharp bend to the east. The few settlements so far were positioned on either side of the river. What little business portion there was, was located on the western side. This included a large log house, obviously a residence, and three general stores, all of which were also made of logs. Across the front, sides, and back of one were strung all manner of robes and skins, which, Olivia later learned, would be loaded onto wagons by traders and sent back to Leavenworth or Kansas City. The Indians who brought in the skins exchanged them for provisions, ammunition, and whiskey, when it became available. As far as Olivia could see, there could hardly be more than a dozen families who'd settled here thus far. It was a strange feeling, knowing that she was going to be putting down roots here herself, and yet . . . yet somehow, she felt a sense of elation, of pride . . . and a feeling of something else, something indefinable for the moment.

But as she stood inside the wagon late that afternoon, the day she was to marry Francis Burton, slowly pulling on each article of her wedding attire, it struck her that she felt—finally—after all this time, a sense of belonging. Sad as she was that her mother and father were not here with her on such a momentous day in her life, she felt that somehow they really were. They were beside her in spirit, urging her on with their support, assuring her that this was what they would have wanted for her.

And so it was that on the fifteenth day of August, Olivia Sands took Francis Burton's name as her own. They stood with Mr. Turley beneath the wide canopy of a maple grove on the northern bank of the Smokey Hill River. Every member of the wagon train party was there, standing quietly several feet away. As Olivia's gaze took them all in, she suppressed a smile. Except for Leona and her young daughter, they were all men. Had she been married back in Ohio, it would have been so completely different; the women would have taken over the entire event and constituted at least half of the wedding guests.

But this was a long way from Ohio, and her life itself had changed more radically than she could have imagined when she left. Now it seemed perfectly fitting to have such a wedding as this.

Aaron stood to Francis's right and Leona to her left, as their witnesses to the wedding ceremony. Mr. Turley, dressed in worn yet clean shirt and trousers of woolsey linen, stood before them, cleared his throat, and then began to read in a somber tone from a worn copy of the Bible. Within moments, it seemed, Olivia was reciting her vows and turning to her new husband.

". . . man and wife."

She heard the words and stared down at the thin band of gold Francis had just slid onto her finger. He'd made another trip into Abilene and luckily had been able to secure the piece at a fairly decent price. From somewhere in the crowd came the jubilant shout, "Well, whatcha waitin' for? Give 'er a kiss!"

And then Francis was turning her by the shoulders toward him, and staring downward into her eyes, the smile on his face pouring into her own gaze, flooding her with a happiness and contentment she had not thought again possible. He bent his head gently down and pressed his lips to hers. Impulsively she rose up on tiptoe and flung her right hand, holding a bouquet of freshly picked wild flowers, around his neck.

A cheer went up from the men when Francis pulled back. Olivia looked over toward them with an expression of astonishment. These men were genuinely happy for the two of them; she was certain of it, and the joy and excitement in their voices was infectious and uplifting.

She felt Leona's hand on her shoulder and turned to face the woman, whose tanned, prematurely lined face was wreathed in smiles. "I'm real happy for you, young woman." Leona turned to Francis. "And you better be a good husband to this here lady. If word gets to me otherwise, I'll be back in no time to straighten things out."

Francis, the smile on his face widening, gave a nod. "There's no need for worry about that."

"Well, good. Better not be."

The men had gathered round and were congratulating Francis and Olivia. Here and there she could see a flask or two being passed among them. She spoke in turn to each of them, saying, "Thank you," every few seconds, it seemed. And then there was another hand on her shoulder and she turned around, ready to listen to yet another worn cliché. But it was Aaron, and on his face was the most peculiar expression Olivia had ever seen. His mouth was all screwed up and he kept swallowing, his Adam's apple rising and falling, rising and falling. Every second or so his lips spread into a half smile and his eyes blinked rapidly. She peered into the clear green irises, so like her own, and yet now so very different. In them she saw both happiness and pride, but something else entirely different . . . fear.

She reached up and placed her hands on either side of her brother's face. Though he stood a good six inches taller, she still saw that part of him that was the adorable toddler who had followed her around, driving her to distraction when she had long grown tired of playing with him. It did not matter that others, including her own husband—*her own husband*—were looking at them, watching them closely. In that moment her heart belonged completely to her young brother. She intuited the emotions he was experiencing right then as surely as if they belonged deep within herself: his bewilderment, his confusion over how very much his life had changed in such a short time, even a sense of desertion.

Olivia's eyes brimmed with tears and she swallowed deeply. He was her own flesh and blood, and she would never, ever desert him. Of course, he would have been mortified if she had told him so here, in the presence of so many men, and so she simply held his gaze and squeezed her palms against the sides of his face, a gesture she had seen her own mother use so many times in the past.

"I love you, Aaron," she said, only loud enough for his ears. "We'll always be together. Don't you ever worry about that. It doesn't matter what I do or what happens, or . . . or whoever else is involved. You'll always have my support. I promise you that."

Aaron dropped his head for a moment, and she could see him making an effort to gather himself. He was learning so quickly! she thought, with a surge of love so fierce and compelling that it brought tears to her eyes. Then he looked up at her, his eyes clear and shining with genuine happiness for her.

"Be happy, sis," he said. Impulsively he planted a kiss on her cheek. "Be real happy."

He turned away suddenly, and someone shouted, "Hey, wanna ride back into Abilene? Maybe you could work up the nerve to actually walk in the front door of Sweet Sally's."

Laughter erupted and Aaron was quickly swallowed up into the crowd of teasing, jostling menfolk, eager to start the celebration.

Olivia was looking now at her new husband, but her eyes had brimmed over and she was swabbing her cheeks with the back of one hand. Francis took her hand and slowly wrapped his own around it. Though he had not heard what had transpired between his wife and her brother, he was aware of the emotional significance of their few moments alone. And suddenly he realized how very, very lucky he was, how deep and compelling was his love for this beautiful, brave young woman. He'd been made a very lucky man that day.

"Just don't forget," he said, leaning toward her. "Just don't forget that I love you, too. You'll never want for a thing, Olivia, never. I promise you that."

CHAPTER IX

December 1860

SMOKE billowed from the chimney of the little dugout house wedged solidly into a small bluff some three hundred yards from the banks of the Smokey Hill River. Beneath the clear blue morning sky, Olivia stood over the giant caldron of boiling water, into which was submerged a week's worth of clothing. A generous amount of lye soap had been added, and the odor was strong enough to cause the insides of her nostrils to burn and itch. Every once in a while she would slide the back of her arm back and forth against the tip of her nose, but the calico sleeve was wet and so drenched in its own share of soap that her entire face was beginning to react.

After a few moments she straightened, arched her back, and felt a distinct wave of nausea. The nausea, Francis had informed her only a few days ago, was not due to the soap or any other of the smells she had become so sensitive to over the past couple of weeks. She was very definitely, he had informed her, with child.

She had been shocked by his diagnosis of her condition, though really she should not have been. After all, she hadn't had her monthly for almost two months, and in addition, she had felt nothing like her normal self for quite a few weeks. By Francis's best estimation, she was some two months into her pregnancy.

Aaron had been dumbfounded when she had informed him, sputtering and blushing to the roots of his dark hair. Olivia had laughed, and he had reached out and hugged her, simultaneously planting a big kiss on her cheek.

She bent forward, gave the big paddle several more swirls through the dense soup of simmering cloth, and then withdrew it, laying it down on the small worktable Aaron had fashioned for her. There was so much left to do, so many tasks she hadn't even had the chance to get started today, and here she was, suddenly overwhelmed by a most intense desire to sleep. This had never happened to her before in her life; it had to be the pregnancy. Well, she couldn't indulge in a nap right now, but surely she was deserving of at least a few minutes of precious rest.

She crossed the trampled grass toward the huge walnut tree and sat down on the ground beneath it, resting her back against its trunk. It was an unusually warm day for December, which, added to the heat of the wash, only fatigued her more. But here, under the shade, the temperature was much cooler. She removed the calico sunbonnet hanging down the back of her dress and waved it in front of her face, sending a draft of cool air across her face and neck. Then she drew her knees up, leaned forward until her arms rested comfortably atop them, and glanced across the backyard toward the house. She looked at it for a moment, then lay her head back and closed her eyes; the soddy remained imprinted on the back of her eyelids as if she were still staring at it.

When they'd arrived the previous year in Salina, in the early part of September, they'd been fooled by the golden days of the Indian summer, which were warm and pleasant. Like most settlers, they'd made do with the Conestoga as a home, until such time as they'd made up their minds as to the type of home they wanted to build. However, with a few weeks' time, the rains had come, and they'd seen for themselves what they'd either heard or been warned of by fellow travelers and those they'd met thus far since their arrival. The rain itself was not so unusual either in duration or amount. What was different, however, was the amount and type of mud left in its wake.

Mud like none of them had ever seen before. It was a heavy, sticky compound and dangerously slick. It was an odd mixture of colors, red and black and clay, and it clung to everything: clothes, shoes, horses, wagons . . . everything. When it dried, it dried as hard as mortar. Fortunately, this proved to be its one saving characteristic. Using the right method of extraction, it could yield the most durable sort of brick one could want.

After talking to as many of the menfolk in the area as he could, Francis had decided they would be best off building their first house out of the sod. He'd seen many such homes, some of which had been standing for five years or more, and no doubt could go on for quite a while longer.

Olivia had been reluctant at first when Francis suggested building a soddy. "I don't want to live in one," she said firmly, shaking her head.

"Now Olivia," Francis had sighed in exasperation. "We've gone round and round over this and—"

"They're ugly, they're filthy, and it's not at all what I wanted." Olivia's brows were drawn together and her fists dug into the sides of her waist.

"But—"

"Francis, it's ridiculous. With all the land here, the timber . . ." she flung her arm out in a sweeping gesture.

"We cannot know the proper site to clear until we've been through at least one winter and spring."

Olivia had closed her eyes and dropped her head. It was useless. They'd gone over and over this so many times. He was right, she knew it in her heart. It would be better if they allowed some time to observe the lay of the land. To choose the wrong site for the frame house she wanted would be a huge mistake. She had seen a few dugouts, had been impressed that despite their crudeness they were perfectly functional. Often built into a bluff, they resembled nothing so much as a shelter for animals and she was determined not to start out her new life in such an abode. Since she couldn't have the frame house or the log house that she wanted, and absolutely refused a dugout, she'd have to settle on the soddy.

"All right," she agreed finally, smiling belatedly as Francis swooped her up in a big bear hug. Despite the lingering irritation of giving in to him she nevertheless revelled in the warmth of his body pressed against hers. She felt a small jolt of excitement at his touch, a mere hint of the enjoyment she shared with him in their bed. Soddy or frame house, one thing was certain; it would be the greatest pleasure of all to have a bedroom of their own—and soon.

The three of them worked hard on the soddy, along with the valuable assistance of their nearest neighbor Carl Vella. Vella quickly rounded up as many men as he could from the small town of Salina, and along with Aaron and Francis they all set to work.

Olivia was kept busy from sunup to sundown cooking over both her iron stove and a fire, keeping something always in the large cast iron caldron for anyone who needed a bite. Aaron used his hunting skills well, and brought in several rabbits and prairie chickens and squirrels. The stews Olivia concocted tasted heavenly to the men.

Francis seemed to love building the soddy more than anyone. He hung onto every word of Carl Vella's instructions, listening as the man explained and demonstrated the correct method for obtaining uniform thickness, strength, and levelness of the sod bricks. Olivia watched with admiration her husband's unshirted chest, the muscles glistening with sweat and dirt as he worked his spade into the soil, trenching furrows and cutting the sod into bricks thirty-six inches in length. She watched him load brick after brick onto the wagon, and then watched as Aaron slowly drove it toward the soddy site, saw the expression of satisfaction on Francis's face.

At night, after everyone was gone, and after he and Aaron had made a visit down to the river to wash, Olivia would await her husband inside the wagon, eager for him to crawl inside the coverlet and snuggle up next to her in the small space of the bed.

"I love you," Francis whispered as his rough hand tenderly stroked the side of her neck, his other pulling up on the hem of her cotton nightgown.

"I love you too," she whispered back, so grateful, so wondrous with the fact that she really did love him.

Aaron had taken to sleeping next to the glowing coals of the fire, instead of beneath the wagon as was usual, which gave them more privacy. Careful as they were to be discreet, muffled cries sometimes erupted from Olivia's throat, and try as he might, Francis had a losing battle on his hands trying to keep his own passion under control. Many were the mornings when Olivia avoided her brother's glance first thing in the morning, knowing he surely had heard the creaking inside the wagon the night before.

Slowly at first and then with increasing speed, the bricks went up, forming the walls of the house. Except for the spaces for windows and door, the bricks were placed side by side, cracks filled in with dirt, and then another layer added. Joints were broken, and every third layer was put down in crosswise fashion to insure a good binding. Carl Vella had suggested reinforcing the walls with wooden withes driven into each wall after it was completed, to which Francis agreed. After the windows and door were framed, attention was turned to installing a sturdy roof. Many of the poorer settlers made do with crude layers of brush and prairie grass, which, of course, were usually porous and had to be replaced often. Since they could afford it, however, Francis and Olivia were able to install a frame roof, over which thinner bricks of sod were secured.

It wasn't the most appealing sort of home, aesthetically speaking, Olivia admitted as she examined it that December morning fifteen months later. Nevertheless, it had served the three of them well. What it lacked in attractiveness, it more than made up for in practicality and efficiency. They had barely lived in it for a month before they were introduced to the harsh realities of winter on the plains. The sod house had remained impervious to the howling, unrelenting winds, the snow and frigid temperature. In the dead heat of summer, it provided an oasis of refreshing coolness. And its very nature eliminated the necessity of worry over fires from either the prairie or fireplace.

However, the house was not without its faults; that was certain. Though the roof was strong and reliable, rainwater found its way into the house, and many was the occasion Olivia had grown disgusted with the necessity of constantly shifting articles of clothing, furniture, and food from this place to that, in order to keep them dry.

Still, it was their home, and as time went on she had made it as cheerful and warm as she knew how. One day they would build a big, fine frame house, with enough room to house Francis's medical practice, which, he'd indicated, he wanted to resume on a full-time basis someday. Right now it was all he and Aaron could do to keep up with the place itself, to clear acres for planting and grazing, to care for the milk cows and a few sheep, which provided a good profit.

Thinking of them both, Olivia turned and gazed out across the grassy knoll where she knew they had headed early that afternoon. She couldn't see them. She felt a twinge in her throat and she wished with all her heart she could go to both of them this minute, tell them both how very much she loved them and wanted them near her. Increasingly she felt this sentiment. She supposed it was because of the long hours they were spending in the fields, mending the fences and checking on the stock, and seeing to the grazing heifers. But at least they were here in the evening and the morning. And of course, she thought, grinning smugly as she smoothed the slight mound beneath her apron, soon she would have less time to fret over her husband and brother.

Soon her days would be filled from sunup to sundown with the cries and demands of another little human life. She felt a surge of impatience, a need to clutch her baby—right now!—in her arms. She so longed to fill up their solitary, isolated lives.

She hadn't known what it would be like, really, living here permanently, and much to her gratification, she realized how much she had come to love it. The land itself was beautiful. Not like her parents' home, but beautiful still, in its own uniqueness. In and around her property were many ravines and creeks, and groves of tall, graceful trees of many varieties: elm, linwood, hickory, oak, and others she had no name for. And of course, the magnificent walnut she was seated beneath now. Most intriguing were the bluffs, earth formations she had never seen the likes of before. Many of them resembled cultivated terraces rising one above the other with some degree of regularity; others resembled distant fortlike structures. And then there were the mounds, small hills of land from the peaks of which one could gaze out across the miles and miles of undulating prairie. Olivia still marveled at the physical possibility of seeing across such vast distances.

Sounds, even the smallest, most insignificant of them, could be heard from so far away. And then, of course, there was the wind, ever faithful companion to the plains. It was a constant, an entity unto itself, and many were the days when she felt ready to burst from the tension the often mournful sound produced. But then, always unexpectedly, it would stop and there would be silence. A sweet, golden silence that left everything clean and fresh, and lifted spirits and hope alike. Olivia prayed for these moments, for try as she might, she never got used to the wind. Though she'd grown used to and loved the land, she lived for those times when the wind would stop and she could bathe in the glorious delight of its absence. It was a paradoxical existence, to be sure, but she'd long ago accepted it. She had chosen this path for her life to take. She had no intention of abandoning it.

January 1861

Francis sat at the table, his empty plate pushed back, a deep frown etched into his forehead as his eyes perused the slightly yellowed newspaper he held in his hands. From time to time he shook his head and muttered a deep grunt of concern, or let out a long sigh.

Olivia knew well enough not to ask him what he was reading, for she had done so often enough, and he never responded, so caught up was he in the words on the page. Anyway, she knew well enough what it was that had grabbed hold of his attention, and it was something that troubled her deeply. These days, anyone with half a claim to an intelligent mind had reason to be troubled, for the issues that so captivated her husband were captivating the entire nation. They were mostly economic concerns, but underlying most of them was the pervasive, divisive matter of slavery. Olivia herself had always considered the keeping of slaves an abhorrent concept, against everything she considered morally right. Her father had been adamant in his position that slaves were for those who were consumed with greed and shortsightedness. He'd felt the practice should be banned outright and had been among those who felt that Kansas should definitely be made a free state. Olivia could remember listening to hours of her father's discourses on this subject, and she'd always been in agreement. But she'd also always believed the subject to be one that concerned others. She could have her opinion, but it was just that: an opinion. She certainly never expected to be personally touched by the subject.

Until now. Now she was becoming increasingly troubled by Francis's preoccupation with the controversy centered around Kansas's acceptance into the United States. Reports were that by the end of the month, President Buchanan would finally sign the bill that would end years of often bloody skirmishes: Kansas was to be admitted as a free state. This was perfectly acceptable to Olivia, but Francis never seemed to let any issue just rest. More and more their conversations at the supper table concerned whatever articles Francis had just read, mostly those in newspapers that found their way to the tiny outpost town of Salina.

The uncharacteristic degree of emotion in her husband's tone was often disturbing, and Olivia tried to allay it as best she could.

"Francis," she said, setting a bowl of corn pudding on the table, "I'm confused about something."

Though he seemed preoccupied with his own thoughts, Francis glanced up at her from the newspaper he was engrossed in. "Yes?"

"Well," she said, taking her seat at the oak trestle

table, "I just don't understand why you go on and on about this. I mean, the matter of slavery, and the unrest in the South and such." She shrugged one shoulder, kept her voice light. "It seems to me that those things are far and away none of our concern here. I don't see why you are so affected either one way or another."

Francis stared darkly at her, his eyes unblinking as he peered deeply into her eyes. The look was so intense that Olivia drew back instinctively.

"You really don't have any idea, do you?"

"About what?"

"What do you mean, Francis?" Aaron piped up.

Olivia was surprised to hear her brother join in, for his attention at suppertime was normally focused on one thing and one thing alone—his stomach and anything and everything that could fill it.

"I mean," Francis said slowly, tapping the newspaper beside his plate with his index finger, "that both of you—yes, you, too, Aaron—have your heads buried in the mud. You're no different than a lot of other people, I'll grant you that, but believe me, a great change is going to occur in this country."

"What sort of change?" Aaron asked.

Olivia glanced at her brother, surprised by the genuine interest on his own face. Remarkably, his right hand, holding his fork, rested completely still beside his untouched bowl of pudding.

"I'm talking about war." Francis's tone was somber, filled with certainty.

"War?" Olivia exclaimed, pulling her shoulders and head back slightly. Her expression was one of incredulity.

"War? Really?" was Aaron's response. There was an unmistakable eagerness in his tone. Noticing it, Olivia experienced a rippling sensation in the pit of her stomach. She glanced quickly back at her husband.

"Yes, war," Francis said. "I don't know when, or

where, or how it will begin, but mark my word, this country is headed for it.''

"But how can you say that?" Olivia asked, clearly upset by now. "You don't know anything out of the ordinary, do you?"

Francis held up a page of the newspaper. "All you have to do is read; it's all here. It's obvious what is going to occur. Lincoln will replace Buchanan as president—I don't believe Douglas has a chance—and all hell will break loose. It already is breaking loose."

"How do you mean?" Aaron persisted.

Francis threw a hand outward. "The southern states are in an uproar. They feel their needs aren't being met—they speak of economics, but they mean slavery, of course. Their talk of secession is growing daily."

"Secession?" Olivia felt embarrassed, truly foolish over her ignorance.

"Yes. Secession from the United States. It will happen. Believe me."

Olivia put her fork down and shook her head. "That just sounds too . . . too . . . well, dramatic, for one thing. And ridiculous for another."

Her husband cast a scrutinizing look her way. "You really are living in an unrealistic world. So you think just because everything is relatively peaceful here—" he cast an arm in a wide arc "—that it's representative of the rest of the country?"

Olivia felt her face grow hot. "Well, of course not. I know there are problems and—"

Francis snorted disdainfully. "Problems! You should read the words of the gentlemen from Georgia, Mr. Toombs and Mr. Stephens, and you'll have a more realistic viewpoint."

"Look," Olivia said tightly. "I'm not arguing with you on this. I assume you know much more about the matter than I do. And of course, I should read whatever it is you keep your nose buried in all the time. But what does all this have to do with us? We're in Kansas, for heaven's sake!''

"Yes, and Kansas has been at the heart of many of the debates over slavery for some time now.''

"Yes, yes, I know all that. But we're going to be a state soon anyway, and things will just sort themselves out. I don't see any reason to get so upset about it. We've got our own lives to live.''

"And whatever life that will be, will be determined in large part by what is about to happen in this country.''

Olivia spoke in a gentler tone now. "But, Francis, really. You are too upset about it all. I do think we should keep abreast of what is going on politically, but I truly don't see that it concerns us personally.''

Francis lifted his chin and stared across the room for a moment. "My family is from Virginia, you know. My sister still lives in Richmond, and my brother has a home in South Carolina.''

"Well, of course, I know that,'' Olivia said, frowning. "But I don't see how that affects the way you feel now. I mean, you live *here* now. I'm from Ohio; I don't feel any particular allegiance toward that state. Not anymore.''

Francis hesitated for a long moment before responding. "I suppose we feel differently then.''

Olivia felt a jolt of alarm suddenly, and she could not remove her gaze from her husband's profile. He had picked up the newspaper and had turned it over and was reading it intently again. She swallowed deeply, felt the alarm quicken to something more akin to fear. Suddenly she saw her husband in a completely different light, was now privy to an aspect of his character she'd had no idea even existed before. She couldn't comprehend this part of his personality, this obvious passion toward a subject she had long since dismissed as being totally unrelated to her life. To their life together.

As she cleared the table, she watched him with a careful eye. Normally he read something after supper, as he was doing now; it was part of their routine in the evening, and she had come to think of his reading as a relaxing habit that he enjoyed. One that she enjoyed, too, at times. But now it had become more than a mere leisurely exercise.

Now, for the first time, she had a glimpse as to what it was he was actually reading and how he was thinking. Suddenly she was more scared than she'd been in a long while. What if he was right and there was war? What would he do? But there was something else she had noticed tonight, and it intensified the slow-building dread within. It was the look of eagerness on her brother's face as he leaned forward just now across the table and asked a question of Francis, something he rarely did while Francis was reading. Suddenly, as she watched the two of them, she saw not her husband and brother, but two men, concerned with worldly, manly events that excluded her, putting her interests very much in the background.

Painfully she turned away from the sight of them, bent toward each other in earnest conversation. Perhaps she was wrong . . . perhaps *they* were wrong. She could only pray and hope this was so.

Winter turned into spring gradually, and Olivia welcomed the change of season. Her belly grew as steadily and surely as the crops planted in early March. She felt awkward, yet better in many ways than she had in a long while. Her anticipation of the birth of her first child pulled her through the long, tiring days of cooking and cleaning and working in the vegetable plot. The harder she worked, the more restful were her nights. She was moving toward a wonderful event in her life, and the knowledge of this filled her with unsurpassed joy and anticipation.

In May, news came of the fall of Fort Sumter in the harbor of Charleston to the Confederate forces; President Lincoln had responded with the call to the Union forces to put down the insurrection. Olivia had read the news for herself; it was all Aaron and Francis seemed to talk about.

"What, I ask you, does Fort Sumter have to do with us?" she asked one night, as she and Francis were preparing to retire to their bedroom. Aaron was asleep in the loft above the kitchen; he'd gone to bed early that night after an entire day spent working in one of the fields of corn.

"It has everything in the world to do with us. We *are* part of the United States of America now, you know."

Olivia bristled at his sarcasm. "You don't have to use that tone with me," she said, yanking out a pin from her hair and wincing from the unexpected pain it caused as it caught hold of a strand of her hair.

He was silent for a moment as he pulled on his nightshirt. "I didn't mean to," he said finally. He sat down on the edge of the bed and looked down at the smooth plank floor. "But, Olivia, you can't deny reality. It does concern us. If not now, or in the immediate future, then surely in the months to come."

"But so what?" Olivia asked, still angry. "Why do we have to even talk about it, let alone worry so much over it? We have our place here—miles from anyone or anything, for that matter."

Francis sighed heavily. "There's really no use in our discussing this. I don't think we're ever going to agree anyway."

"Agree about what?"

He turned and gave her a tired look. "We have different backgrounds, Olivia. I cannot help but feel the way I do about the South. The same way you can't help but be concerned about your own home state, if you'll admit it. You're on the side that will win this war."

"That's ridiculous. There won't be a war!" She lowered her voice, surprised by her own angry outburst. "I just don't understand your stance, Francis. I mean, you hate slavery—the whole concept of it. We've spoken of it enough for me to know we're in agreement on that."

"Yes," he said slowly. "That much is true." Again he sighed. "It's more complicated than that, though. It's . . . well, it's a way of life for my family that's going to disappear."

"And it should!"

Francis gave his wife a sharp look. "There are things that will happen that will be devastating, things that you can't even imagine."

Olivia waved a hand in the air, dismissingly. "That is simply ridiculous. You can't predict the future any more than I can."

"Nevertheless, I have strong feelings about certain things, things that will determine my future."

Olivia raised her eyebrows. "My? You use the word 'my'?" She paused. "What about *us*?"

He didn't answer, just chewed one side of his lip as he stared out the window.

"Well?"

His voice was low, distant. "I will see to it that you are taken care of."

A shaft of fear riveted Olivia. "What does that mean?" Her voice sounded hollow, dumbstruck.

"It means . . . that I will be leaving within two weeks. I will travel east to check on my family in Virginia and South Carolina. I have to know how things are working out there. I . . . I cannot bear to be here when there is so much happening back home."

Olivia was so shocked, she reeled for a moment before snapping back, "Back home! All this time we've been married you never once indicated that you wanted or even cared to go back! You were headed for the gold fields in Colorado when we met. You said you were tired of being tied down to one place, practicing medicine—you wanted to help me make something out of this land. And . . . and now this?''

Francis was silent for a long while before answering. ''I know I said all those things. And I meant them. I just didn't know I would feel this way until now.'' He looked at her squarely. ''I have to go, Olivia. There is no way I could live with myself otherwise.''

Olivia found she was shaking by now. ''But how long will you be gone?''

''I have no way of knowing. It will depend on the travel time, what is happening in the cities . . . all sorts of things.''

''Like what?''

He took in a deep breath of air and let it out slowly. ''I intend to put my medical skills back into practice.''

''In what way?'' Olivia was staring at him wide-eyed, as if she could not quite believe what she was hearing.

''I will probably enlist my services in the Confederate army. I have no doubt there will be plenty of need for physicians. And I can be of use in other ways, too, I suppose.''

Olivia slowly got off the bed and began to walk back and forth in front of it. She ignored the twinges and kicks in her belly, ignored the way her swollen bare feet slapped against the planks of the floor. She stopped once and shook her head repeatedly from side to side.

''I can't believe you mean this. I can't believe it.''

Francis said nothing, simply remained where he was, staring out the window. He himself did not feel as if he were in this room, as if the situation unfolding now, one he had been dreading for some time, were really finally happening. It was every bit as bad as he had imagined it. He loathed himself for what he was saying to his wife, for causing her to feel pain and confusion, and no doubt fear, but he had gone over and over and over it, and there was nothing, in the end, he could do to change his own mind. For to remain here, in Kansas, when war was breaking out in the East, was impossible. He simply had to leave. It was an impulse as instinctive and compelling as taking his next breath. It had to be done.

"What about our baby?" Olivia asked, her voice higher-pitched and tremulous.

He lowered his head and spoke quietly, firmly. "You are healthy. You will do fine. I will see to it that Emma Vella will be here with you when your time comes."

"That's all? Your only comment is about our baby's delivery? What about him? Or her? Don't you even care if you see your own baby?"

"Of course I do."

"Oh, you do? Really? When? When will you see your own child? How do I know you will ever come back?"

Francis rubbed the back of his neck and then stood up. "I don't see any point in getting hysterical about all this."

"How . . ." Olivia started to shout and then lowered her voice immediately. "How dare you call me hysterical? You have just told me you are leaving. What am I supposed to sound like?"

He crossed the few feet separating them and reached out to her, intending to embrace her. But Olivia backed up toward the doorway and shook her head. "I don't need your solace. Not now."

"Olivia . . ."

She looked at him, wide-eyed. "Do you really mean it? Do you really mean you are going?"

"I just said—"

"I heard what you said. Do you mean it? I want to know."

Very slowly he nodded his head.

"You've been thinking this for a long time, haven't you?"

"I'm not the only man who has had to make such a decision," he replied quietly.

"*Had* to make a decision?" she retorted with heavy sarcasm. "I don't believe you had to do any such thing. No one is forcing you to go. You do it of your own free will."

"I don't know what else to say."

"Well then, that settles it, doesn't it?"

His answer was merely a look confirming his stand.

Olivia turned and strode quickly through the house to the door leading out to the small porch Aaron and Francis had added this spring. She kept on walking, straight onto the footpath and then around toward the rear of the house, headed toward her favorite retreat: the old walnut tree. She leaned against it and crossed her arms over her heavy bosom, barely aware that she was shivering in the night air that slithered up her cotton nightgown.

She stood for a long, long time, before sinking slowly to the ground, her head lowered to her knees. She never saw her husband watching her from behind the house, never noticed that he started to go to her, and then hesitated and retraced his steps back inside.

CHAPTER X

September 1861

THE hot, dry morning air was a mere hint of the endless day to come. Autumn, it seemed, was a long time in coming this year. Olivia stood in the doorway of the soddy, staring out across the acres and acres of land now dense with grass almost as tall as a man's head. The cows in the barn were lowing loudly, wanting their usual early morning milking. This, of course, in addition to the scores of other chores that needed her attention as soon as possible to avoid the more intense heat that would bear down on the Kansas soil in a mere few hours.

But today she could not move, could not begin to see how she could summon up the heart, let alone the energy required to set about her tasks. Her eyes narrowed a bit, she stared ahead, and it seemed that she had never seen any of the land before, as though she were a complete stranger on this land that she owned and had developed to what was considered by others as a successful venture. The only familiar thing right now was the sound of the wind.

Today, ironically, she was actually grateful for it,

grateful for its company. It was the only company she had now.

She was alone, completely alone. Francis had been gone for over three months, and only last night Aaron had left. She still could not believe it. She could not believe either one of them had left her here. Alone on the prairie, to cope with everything herself.

She let her arms unfold, and her hands drifted down the sides and front of her gown. They stopped when they reached her stomach, which was as taut and flat as a year ago. Her heart seemed to stop for a moment, and she lowered her chin, waiting for it to go on again. As always, it did. As sure as her baby's had ceased, hers had gone on, though for many, many weeks she had not wanted it to at all.

She had not thought her heart could break any further after the day Francis had left. It had been a chilly, windy day; the hot sun of the previous day had been obscured completely by dense clouds blowing down from the north. The wind whistled around the soddy noisily, sending showers of dirt descending downward from the roof. Olivia sat in the hard ladder-back chair near the fireplace, her nerves frayed, her mind sinking into depression as she heard, above the outside noise, Francis moving about in their small bedroom, checking the saddlebags he'd been packing all morning, making certain he had everything he'd need for the journey. Words formed inside Olivia's head, but she sat perfectly still, unable to utter any of them, knowing none of them would persuade him to change his mind.

"Olivia?" he said, stepping out of the bedroom, the bags slung over his shoulder, his roll underneath his other arm.

She looked up, said nothing.

"Don't fret so, darling," he said, his brown eyes glancing aside, unwilling to meet her own as normally they did.

She continued to sit in silence. She felt a kick inside and winced as she sat up straighter, her hand automatically reaching for the underside of her swollen belly. It was then that she saw the expression in his eyes change, then that she saw the fear, the concern, the possible regret for his actions. Her heart beat a little faster as she watched him carefully, praying he would stop the nonsense he was up to, would put down the bags and come over to her. But he didn't.

"It's just a twinge," he told her, as if she had asked him anything at all. Just then Aaron's loud steps could be heard coming toward the front door, followed by his loud knock.

"Saddle's on, Francis," he called out. "The mare's gettin' nervous standing tied."

"I'll be right there," Francis said after opening the door. The rain was coming down so hard he shut it quickly so as not to let much inside. He turned to Olivia, his hand still on the wooden knob. "I'll be writing you as soon as I reach Fort Leavenworth. If you want to send a message, send it there."

Olivia still sat mute, just staring at him, one hand on the edge of the chair, the other tucked beneath her belly.

A gust of wind rushed against the house, sending another shower of dirt downward. Francis reached up and wiped some of it off of his face. "I'd better go before this gets worse."

What's your hurry, Olivia wanted to ask. A man leaving in this type of storm must be in an awful hurry. But they'd already discussed that subject; nothing would stop him. Nothing.

He crossed the room quickly and, removing his hat, bent his head to press his lips against her neck. "I love you," he spoke in a low tone. "Please understand. I do love you."

Olivia turned her head to gaze back into the fire, hearing his retreating footsteps, the door opening and closing as he made his exit. She had not said one word of goodbye to him. Had not told him that she did understand, that she did love him too. At that moment she wasn't so certain that she did. It would be a long time before she could remove the anger and deal with the pain inside. Only then could she speak of love.

A mere three weeks after his departure, in mid-June, she had been stricken with pains in her belly so intense, so unrelenting, that she found it hard to breathe. Aaron was in the kitchen, tending to the dishes after the breakfast they had shared. Olivia had not eaten much, as her appetite had decreased over the past few days. She had settled down on the horsehair sofa with her bag of knitting when the sharpest pain of all hit her deep within, searing all the way to her back. She groaned and slumped forward, holding on to her thighs. Another pain followed quickly and she uttered a long, anguished, "Ahhhhh."

Aaron dropped the dish he was drying and it smashed into pieces on the hard earth floor. "Olivia? What's wrong?" he half-yelled as he sunk to his knees near her. "Is it time?"

She shook her head. "No," she grunted, blinded by the pain within.

"Should I get Emma Vella?"

"Think so," she managed between gritted teeth.

Aaron was out of the door in a flash, heading toward the corral where his horse stood grazing. When Olivia managed to lift her head, she spotted him jumping on the animal's back, a crude hackamore he'd fashioned from the lead rope all the control he had time to slip on the horse's head.

It was all Olivia could do to remain stationary, so great was the pain. She was completely unaware of the time it took for Aaron to return; it wouldn't have mattered anyway, however, since by the time the front door opened and Emma came rushing in before Aaron, she was already sure that the blood gushing across the sofa and onto the floor could indicate nothing but disaster.

"My God!" Aaron cried out at the sight of it, stopping dead in his tracks.

Emma Vella, a short, stocky, dark-haired woman known for her straightforward approach to everything in life, turned and spoke sharply. "Now don't stand there dumbstruck, son. Get to movin'. Get me some padding; sheets, towels, horse blankets . . . anything. And plenty of fresh water. Hurry."

There was no time for placing Olivia on the bed, so the birthing took place right there on the sofa. Despite Emma's valiant efforts to hurry along the delivery, it was still some two hours before the contractions were strong enough to manually assist the process, and by then Olivia was almost unconscious from the pain and loss of blood. The baby, a girl, was born with the cord wrapped tightly around her neck; she had been dead for at least an hour. Sadness etching her lined features, Emma cleaned up the dead infant, and started to cover her with a single linen sheet.

"Wait," Olivia whispered with as much force as she could manage. "See her."

Emma shook her head, hesitated, and then moved closer to where Olivia's head was propped up on a pillow at the end of the sofa. "She would have been a pretty little thing," she said softly, as she lowered the infant to her mother. Olivia remained dry-eyed as she gazed at the bluish tint, the wide, closed eyes, the shock of dark hair on the girl-baby's head. She turned her head and closed her eyes tightly, shutting out the image of her first-born, shoving aside the pain of yet another life which had been taken from her.

Physically Olivia had recuperated quickly, had been up and about within a few days. Inexplicably she had found a perverse sort of burst in energy. It didn't matter that the summer days were boiling hot, that she was inundated with chores triple her normal load. For Francis's leaving had placed on her shoulders most of the burden of running the place: overseeing the acres of corn and wheat, the few head of cattle that grazed on fenced pastures. And, of course, the vegetable garden, the stable animals, the poultry, the cooking . . . everything. It was a daunting amount of work for anyone, but to Olivia it provided release.

For in truth, she could not bear to think of what her life had become, how much she had lost. She'd lost the past before, and now she'd been deprived of the future, or at least the future as she had planned it. And if the thought of all this did slip through that firmly shut window of her mind, her heart felt its effects with a pain so searing, it took her breath away.

Somehow she had always managed to grasp on to that which had allowed her to come this far in the first place: her instinctive belief in her own strength. All that was required to maintain it was to place one foot before the other, to keep going, heading toward some goal or another, and when that goal was attained, to form another one quickly and set off in like fashion.

Right now, however, the thought of moving on toward any goal at all seemed almost unimaginable. She was having a hard time just keeping her thoughts set on anything other than what had occurred yesterday afternoon. Aaron standing before her, his horse's reins in his hands, hat held in one hand that he kept close to his side, his head hanging low as his eyes glanced up at her briefly and then quickly flicked away. Olivia, pleading with him, knew it was futile. Her brother had made up his mind a long time ago, probably when Francis had left. In truth, she understood why he was going. After all, what was there for him here on the prairie? He was eighteen years old now; adult life beckoned to him, and he was merely doing what most American men were doing. Going off to help fight for his country.

"I'm not sure what else to say, then," she said finally to him as he stood before her. "I wish you all the best."

"Thank you," he muttered.

"When are you thinking you'll reach Fort Riley?"

"I'm not sure. Within a few days, not much more."

Olivia reached up and rubbed her forehead beneath the brim of her calico sunbonnet. Her temples were beginning to ache fearfully, and she knew if she started to weep, it would get worse, much worse, very fast.

"I'm sure you'll be all right," Aaron said, in a suddenly forceful voice. "The Vellas aren't that far away and can help you out when you need it. And Sid . . . well, he hasn't been here long, but he'll catch on soon enough. You can ease back on some of the chores with him around."

Olivia let it slip by, though she was certain Aaron knew as well as she how that last statement was little more than wishful thinking. Sid Jones was a drifter who'd come by a little more than two weeks ago, asking for work. He was unwilling to state his age or where he was from, or how he had come to find himself in the middle of Kansas, especially now with so many men leaving, but Aaron had been taken with his apparent willingness to work. He slept in the loft in the hay barn, was up early every morning, and, after listening to instructions, plunged right into every task he was asked to carry out. His willingness to perform, however, was tempered by his persistent slowness. Rare was the task he started that was not finished by Aaron or herself.

"You must be careful," Olivia said.

Aaron glanced off into the distance; his fingers kneaded the reins laced between them.

"I know you don't want to hear this," she continued, "but I'll say it anyway."

"You don't have to worry about me," Aaron said, still looking off.

Olivia sighed softly. "Aaron, you can say that until the moon disappears and it wouldn't make a bit of difference. I've been worryin' about you since you were a baby. And I always will. But especially now."

"I never worry about you," Aaron said. "You seem so . . . so strong. No matter what."

"I wasn't so strong when Francis left. Nor when I lost the baby."

"But you kept going. You always do."

"And so you think I'll just keep right on going now, too? Like your leaving, Francis's leaving, doesn't affect me at all?"

Aaron winced, and she knew that she had pained him greatly with that last remark. But she was hurting, too, inside, and it was difficult not to want to express it.

"It's something I have to do, that's all," Aaron said, very quietly, sounding not much like the boy she knew him still to be, but like the man he wanted to follow.

She watched as he placed his foot into the stirrup and mounted the sorrel gelding he'd bought a month ago. "Will you try to write? At least to let me know where you are, how you are doing?"

"Sure. I planned on that."

"Good." She stepped back as the sorrel began to paw the ground, then swung his rear around toward her. He was a young horse, strong and healthy and plenty spirited.

Aaron drew his hat down low on his forehead and pulled on the reins, backing the horse a few steps and then sitting quietly until the gelding came to a halt. "Well, I need to be on my way."

Olivia felt the pressure in her forehead grow even stronger as the lump in her throat grew. She swallowed deeply, tried not to lift her hand to wipe the tear rolling down one side of her face.

She nodded rapidly several times. "Ride carefully."

"I can handle this fella," Aaron said, smiling broadly.

It was the smile that did it. Though he looked as handsome and as grown-up as any man she had ever seen, Olivia still saw only the little boy she'd loved since she was two years old. Tears were streaming down her face now, and she couldn't open her mouth to speak.

Aaron, seeing his sister weeping, frowned and started to dismount. But Olivia held up one hand and shook her head no. She wiped her eyes with the fringe of her apron and opened her mouth to say something, anything, but her voice would not cooperate with her intentions. So she lifted one hand to her throat and, amazingly, managed a smile.

"Good-bye, sis," Aaron said in a croaking sort of voice, his own eyes shimmering. Then his expression hardened and he pulled the reins sharply to the left, turning both the horse and himself away from Olivia. Within seconds, dust flew out behind the horse's hooves as he set out for the dirt trail that connected their property to the road that would lead him first into Salina and, from there, to Abilene and then on to Fort Riley. There he was to enlist in the Union army.

Olivia watched him until she could see him no more. If it hadn't been for Sid coming up from the hay barn and standing directly in front of her, patiently awaiting her attention, she probably would have gone on standing until she dropped right where she was. What was the point now? Why was she here, all alone on this farm . . . the vastness of the land making her feel so small, so inconsequential? She managed to answer Sid, though she couldn't recall later a word of what she'd said or what it was he'd wanted to know. There was hardly anything else she remembered about the long, sleepless night that followed, other than the deepening sadness in the center of her heart.

Now the morning sun was intensifying its glow on the horizon. The cows were quieter, and she assumed Sid was taking care of the milking. Thank goodness for that, she thought. Feeling a stab of hunger—she hadn't eaten since noon the day before—Olivia knew she should fire up the stove in the kitchen before it became too hot to cook anything at all. She turned at last and retreated into the sod house, walking into its dim, cool interior and over to the small, though much cherished, room that was her kitchen. Of all the efforts she had made in the sod house, the kitchen was the one that gave her the most satisfaction.

Blue and white gingham curtains framed the small window near the stove, and a thin white muslin sheer billowed slightly as currents of air infrequently brushed its delicately sewn hem. A few feet from the stove was the large trestle table Francis and Aaron had built for her from one of the black walnut trees they'd cut down on the property. It had made not only the table, but four nicely finished ladder-back chairs to accompany it. The surface of the table gleamed from the linseed oil Olivia painstakingly applied to it every other day. In the center of the table was a blue limestone crock she'd purchased in Salina, a poorly made product to be sure, but just right for the bunches of flowers she cut from her garden daily.

She had not yet begun to cut her geraniums, growing so profusely beneath the shade of the cottonwood tree near the vegetable and flower garden. When they thickened a bit more, she would select a few for the table. She measured out coffee grounds, added a pinch of salt, and then put the pot on to boil. Her movements stiffened as her husband's image flitted across the landscape of her mind as clearly as if he were right there, ready to join her at the table. Unconsciously she bit the side of her mouth, a habit she resorted to in times of stress.

Mustn't think of him. The refrain went through her

head for the hundredth time. But of course, she did, all
the while she was going about her morning routine. She
went out to refill the water pitcher with fresh water,
then stopped by the springhouse to select three large
brown eggs and a tub of butter. She'd make johnnycakes
and fried eggs for breakfast this morning, knowing Sid
would be much appreciative of her efforts.

Her eye fell upon the latest letter from Francis, which
was still lying on a cupboard shelf. It was worn by now,
much handled, much read. She had received it over two
weeks ago and still had not answered it. How could
she? After spending most of the summer in Richmond,
he was going on with his troop to a more active area of
the war that was breaking out all over the nation by
now. He would write her again when he reached his
destination, he'd informed her, but though his letter had
been kind, filled with questions about how she was
managing, various testaments to his love and longing
for her, she was filled with anger.

He could, by way of letter, pour out his heart to her,
release his feelings, and be done with it, but she was
forced to wait until the next time she received word
from him. And with every letter he wrote, he sounded
further and further from her own existence. Yes, he
probably did mean it when he said he missed her, longed
for her, but then she could only wonder how much. For
each letter grew more and more concerned with the
activities he was pursuing in his new life as a doctor in
the Confederate army.

And so she turned away from the small, light blue
envelope and made an effort to pretend it wasn't there.
But the pretense was not as effective today, for there
was no longer anyone with whom she could share her
feelings about the matter. She no longer had her brother,
Aaron, her confidant, her best friend. Emma Vella was
really the only other person she could rightly call a
friend, and she saw very little of the woman, usually

only during a monthly trip into town, or on the infrequent visits Emma made to see how Olivia was getting along. Feeling somewhat guilty, Olivia was helpless to do anything about her own self-imposed isolation. She was simply too sad, her mind too heavy to impose herself on those who, perhaps, would have welcomed her into their lives.

The day crept by torturously. Olivia wasn't sure why she even minded, though, for she hardly anticipated the onset of darkness. Her headache, she supposed, was why she was so upset. The heat, the pain of her brother's departure, the unending grief over the loss of her baby, the anger over her husband's determined participation in a lost cause; all of it came rushing up to the surface of her mind today until she felt overwhelmed by it, ready to just give it all up and . . . and what? What could she do with her life other than what she was now doing? And what exactly was she doing? She was making a life for her family . . . except there was no family anymore.

She spoke with Sid only a few times that day. He was busy in the pastures with the haying. The weather had cooperated, keeping the land dry long enough to cut the tall bluestem grasses, which would be bailed, loaded onto the wagon, and driven into town to be sold to the local feed merchants. In fact, one of the wagons was already loaded; Sid was to drive it into town directly after supper. As he often did of a Friday evening, he would more than likely stay in Salina overnight. Perhaps even two nights. Which, of course, left Olivia to manage alone. But then, at least he came all during the week. She was more often than not surprised when he'd show up again on Sunday evening.

She cleaned the house as she usually did, as always, despairing of the constant dust, which could never be completely managed due to the very nature of the house itself. She put on a kettle of stew to simmer until that evening, and then went outdoors to tend to the chickens and muck out the stalls where Mack and Jerry, the two draft horses, spent the night. Most of her work today, however, was centered around her garden, which was plenteous this year. It was all she could do to gather the ripened tomatoes and strawberries off the vines before the insects and birds made their claim. And she collected a wonderful batch of dewberries, too, mostly from along the creek banks that ran through one of the pastures. She'd had Aaron help her last week in setting up a small work area near the cottonwood so that she could do the preserving outdoors since it was such a time-consuming endeavor and she hated to be cooped up inside with it.

Sid came in late that evening from the fields, and as usual, had hardly a word to say, he was so busy ravenously consuming the plate of food she placed in front of him. A mere week ago she would have persisted at her efforts to draw him out a bit, to get him to talk more about himself, his past, what he had in mind for the future. Tonight she, too, was silent. What difference in the world could it make to her about Sid's future when her own was in such unexpected upheaval?

When he finished, Sid looked up from his plate and told her thank you. He was heavily tanned from the sun, but he looked exhausted, too, and so, despite the wish to just not say anything, she asked him about his day. Thankfully, he was as tight-lipped as ever.

"Went all right."

"Good. Do you have any idea when you'll be ready for the first delivery?"

Sid shrugged. "Soon enough, I suppose."

Normally his answer would have irritated her, but tonight it gave her the escape she was sorely in need of. "Well, then, Sid, if you don't mind, I'll just clean

up here and go on to bed. You look mighty tired yourself.''

Sid's chair scraped as he rose from the table. "Thank
you for the supper. Was good. Guess I'll drive that load
on in to Salina.''

"Yes. All right," Olivia replied, stacking her plate
on his and reaching for the empty bowls and platters.
In less than a minute Sid was gone. She cleaned up as
she always did, quickly and thoroughly. When she was
finished she felt more awake than she had the entire
day. She walked slowly around the rooms of the house,
feeling alone, so terribly alone. She had considered going outside and perhaps taking a walk, but a raincloud
had moved in, and rain was coming down slowly but
steadily by now.

She stopped in the middle of the front room, placed
her fists on her hips, and looked around. Truly she felt
ready to jump out of her skin. Her eyes tracked the
room more slowly until they rested on her meager col-
lection of books on the shelves Francis had built into
one of the walls. She looked at the books in despair. If
only she had more of them; if only she hadn't read each
and every one of them at least seven or eight times.
Maybe more. Francis and his newspapers. She'd always
chided him about those, and he'd always made com-
ments about her insatiable thirst for fiction. She'd noted
the hint of condescension in his tone, but it didn't bother
her, nor did it change her reading habits in any way.
She faced reality all day long; when she wanted something to read, she wanted something that would take
her away from reality.

Which was exactly the way she felt now.

She walked over to the shelf and raised her right hand,
letting her fingertips graze the spines of the leather-
bound books. Sighing, she selected *Pilgrim's Progress*,
walked to the horsehair sofa, and sat down near the
maple end table. She adjusted the wick on the lamp and

opened the book, willing herself to not only see the words she now knew by heart, but to let herself get drawn into them. It was the only thing she knew that could possibly relieve the emptiness.

There were sounds, unfamiliar ones she heard first within the context of a dream and which then slowly pulled her into a conscious state. Her eyes opened slightly and she noted that the room was gray, the way it always looked the hour or so before sunrise.

Olivia remained still, despite the fact that she had noticed immediately the uncomfortable position she was in—that of sitting almost bolt upright, her head fully back and resting on the back of the sofa, which had set up a powerful stiffness in her neck. She felt something in her left hand, which was flung in an outward position on the sofa, moved her fingers, and realized it was the book.

She started to move and then heard the sounds again. She sat very still. Living in the country, one got used to hearing all manner of sounds; this was something she couldn't begin to define. Listening very closely, she finally discerned some sort of scraping; wood against wood. And the sound of something rustling, then scraping again. The sound of booted feet moving about on the dirt drive that connected the house to the barns.

Of course, she thought, it's Sid getting an extra-early start this morning in order to escape the heat later on . . . and then remembered Sid had stayed in Salina last night. That thought was brought up short, however, when she heard the voices. Men's voices, none of them recognizable.

She pulled herself up hastily, rubbed her eyes with her fingertips, and then pushed back the hair that had escaped the pins at the nape of her neck. She moved quickly to a window near the front door and pulled back the curtain. The moonlight was bright, but she had to wait a moment for her eyes to register the scene taking place in her front yard.

She felt both astonished and confused at the same time. "What in the world . . . ?" She whispered the thought aloud. Some thirty feet away was a spring wagon, pulled by two mules who stood quietly muzzling inside feed bags tied around their necks. The back of the wagon was lowered, and three men were sliding a long, rectangular object off of it, one man at the end of it, the other two along either side. Whatever it was seemed to be costing them a good deal of effort. At last they had lifted it completely off the wagon and, taking a great deal of caution in doing so, turned toward the pathway leading up to the soddy. Olivia quickly stepped to the front door, slid back the bolt, and pushed it open. It was only when she stepped onto the front porch that she was able to more clearly discern what it was the men were carrying. Atop a makeshift stretcher was the body of a man, his head and face covered almost completely with a dark blanket.

Olivia's heart leapt into her throat. She felt the impulse to run toward the men coming down the path toward her, but her legs would not move. Absurdly, she was rooted to the spot. The man carrying the front end of the stretcher looked up, noticed her standing there, and came to a stop a few feet away. When he spoke, she recognized his voice vaguely. Someone she had met in Salina perhaps; she didn't know.

"Mrs. Burton?" he asked, his voice slightly breathless from his efforts.

Somehow she found her voice. She spoke slowly, succinctly. "Mrs. Olivia Sands Burton."

The man cleared his throat. "Ma'am . . . my name's Corporal Duncan Holloway." Again he cleared his throat. "Your brother is Aaron Sands. That correct?"

Olivia nodded. She stared, horrified now, at the sight of the blanket-wrapped head.

"Ma'am, we found your brother along Milky Creek early this evening. Took him into Salina, but there wasn't any doctor. Someone there told us he's your brother."

Olivia took a few quick steps forward, but her way was blocked almost instantly by Duncan Holloway's outstretched arm. "Why don't we take him inside first?"

Her eyes moved slowly away from her brother's unmoving figure to Mr. Holloway. "But . . . ?"

"I think it would be better if we got him inside before . . . well, before you . . ." He cleared his throat for the third time.

"What? What's wrong with him?"

"Ma'am, it'd be better if we can just get him inside."

Olivia turned suddenly and hurried back to the front door, opening it wide. Still carrying their burden as gingerly as possible, the men filed onto the porch and toward the door. It wasn't until they passed her that she saw the color of the blanket: a deep garnet red, glistening wetly in the pale light now seeping through the morning grayness.

Slowly, dreamlike, she felt herself sliding downward, her dress snagging on the handle of the door as she sunk into an oblivion of darkness.

CHAPTER XI

Topeka
1921

THE old woman's eyes seemed to glaze over. She was silent for several minutes, though she continued to rock back and forth in the rocker, slowly, rhythmically. Leah Rice waited, her pencil poised above the notebook opened in her lap. She watched as one of Olivia's hands reached up, as it did now and then, to stroke a strand of hair. It was hair as fine as a baby's, and as the arthritic fingers combed through it, Leah pictured how she must have looked as a young woman; she would have been striking, if not beautiful, Leah had thought many times, with dark, thick hair and, of course, her deep, luminous green eyes.

Olivia stopped rocking. She sighed lengthily.

"Do you not want to go on?" Leah asked softly. "We don't have to, you know."

Slowly Olivia placed both hands on her lap and shook her head. "No," she said in her surprisingly clear and youthful-sounding voice. "I don't mind. It's just that I haven't thought about that day in so long. Haven't let myself think about it, I suppose." She pushed on the rocker and let it rock a few times, turning her gaze back out the window again.

Finally she spoke. "He'd been scalped, you see. Not completely. Almost, though. For some reason the band of Pawnee who attacked him didn't see fit to finish the job. The men who brought him back to me were scouts with the Union cavalry. They brought him back to die, they said. They didn't think he'd last the night. Neither did I, as a matter of fact." Again Olivia fell silent for a while.

Leah waited and then chose her words carefully before speaking. The reply she received would provide yet another clue to an answer to the question that had haunted her for years and years. "And did he die?"

Olivia pursed her lips. "Eventually he did. But not that night. Not for a long while after that." She glanced at the younger woman. "Course, all of us have to go sometime, don't we? Don't really know why the good Lord hasn't called for me yet."

Because, Leah thought, feeling the excitement igniting within, because perhaps he meant for me to find you.

"Would you care to tell me about it? About what happened to your brother after he was brought home?"

Olivia drew in a slow breath. "There's hardly any way I could leave it out. He was . . . he was everything to me. And I . . . well, I was everything to him." She looked back at Leah and gave her a frank look. "He was my child from then on, you see. He was my brother, but he became the baby I never had, the child I was never given the opportunity to raise."

Leah felt a sinking sensation in the pit of her stomach, the uneasy doubt that perhaps she had made too many hasty assumptions.

"Of course," Olivia said, her gaze growing distant again, "of course, there was another child later. But that was different."

Leah swallowed. "How so?"

Olivia raised a hand and placed her palm against her cheek. "Oh, it just was. You might not even want to hear about that. Might not interest you."

"No! Not at all." Leah lowered her suddenly raised voice. "What I mean to say is . . . well, I want to hear everything about your life then. It will enrich my final rendition of your account of your early life here in Kansas."

"I understand. Well, then, we'll get to that part. Later. There was so much that happened after Aaron was brought back. I don't know . . . maybe you'll get bored with that part."

"No, no. Not at all. Like I said, I want to get everything down that you remember."

Olivia turned and gazed at the younger woman through narrowed lids. "Why is this so important to you and your organization?"

Leah laid her pencil down for a moment. "Well, you have lived a unique life. A most unusual one. It would be a shame if it went unrecorded. I mean, your story— your life—is an integral part of our history. We know everything about our men . . . very little about the women."

"Yes, yes," Olivia interrupted somewhat impatiently. "You did tell me all that. It's just hard to believe you wouldn't be bored by most of it. There wasn't much to that part of my life, you see, when Aaron returned, other than isolation. Loneliness. And work. Always that. That was about the extent of it."

"And your husband? When did he return?"

Olivia fixed Leah with a sharp look. "You're getting ahead of yourself, if you want to hear the whole story, as you say."

Leah smiled. "Yes, I suppose so. I should just let you tell the story as you see fit." She got up from her chair and crossed the room to the sideboard near the

door. Atop it, on a crisp white antimacassar, sat a tall
pitcher of iced lemonade. Two glasses were upturned
on either side of it. Leah filled the two glasses and
walked back across the room, placing both of them on
the small end table between the two chairs she and
Olivia occupied.

"My, that looks good," Olivia said, reaching out to
pick one up. But she winced from the pain of trying to
flex her stiffened wrist and fingers.

"Here, let me help you," Leah said, handing the
glass to the older woman.

"I once was the same as you," Olivia said, taking a
sip. "Could move around like I wanted. Picking up a
silly old glass was nothing."

"We all have afflictions at some point in our lives,"
Leah said. She took a sip of her own lemonade and
then, holding the glass outward in front of her, smiled
as she watched the droplets of condensation trickle
slowly down onto her fingers. She uttered a tiny, almost
imperceptible laugh.

"What are you laughing at?" Olivia asked.

"Oh, it's silly. I remember when I was little, holding
a glass of lemonade—or something, tea, perhaps—and
saying there were teardrops running down the outside.
Little bitty teardrops running down my glass." She
shook her head, still smiling, and glanced over at Olivia.
But her smile faded quickly as she noted the odd manner in which the old woman was staring at her; her
green gaze was riveting, and yet, in another sense, it
seemed she was looking at nothing at all. Then, slowly,
Olivia's head turned toward the window. She was
frowning, perplexity vivid in her features.

Olivia looked outside for a long while and then turned
ever so slowly back to face the woman who was watching her so carefully. "What a rather odd sort of thing to
say." Then, very cautiously, she placed her glass of
lemonade, hardly touched, back on the table. She looked

up. "Well? Where was I? You'll have to forgive my memory. Things just sort of come to me when they have a will to."

"That's all right."

"Don't know as it will help your note taking s'much."

"Really. It doesn't matter at all."

Olivia eyed the woman, nodded once, and then pursed her lips, ready to go on.

CHAPTER XII

NOTHING could have prepared Olivia for the shock of what she saw when the blood-soaked blanket was pulled away from Aaron's head. His face, his beautiful, handsome face, was unrecognizable, covered almost completely in the dark brown thickness of congealed blood. The top of his skull, his throat, and the lower part of his neck were also coated with it, as were the front and back of his flannel shirt. But far more stunning was the shank of hair protruding from the back of his neck; the dense clump of it was that which had been severed and peeled back from what had once been the meeting of his forehead and hairline.

He'd been gone only forty-eight hours when his unconscious body was found on the banks of the Kansas River, no more than ten miles outside Salina. Forty-eight hours since he'd left his sister and his past behind to pursue that which he believed to be his destiny; the life of a soldier, fighting like the man he knew himself to be. But it was a mistaken destiny. The band of Pawnee had tracked his movements from a bluff for only half a mile until they decided to strike.

It had taken every ounce of strength she possessed to maintain her composure, to hold back the wave of nausea threatening to overcome her completely. The cavalrymen, too, seemed extremely sickened from just looking upon her brother, but their corporal ordered them to give her some help. They set about gathering anything Mrs. Burton desired: fresh water, replenishment of fuel, stoking up a good, strong fire in the hearth. He then sent one of them back out to retrieve Aaron's saddlebag, which had been rifled through but otherwise undisturbed.

But Olivia had barely noticed any of the activity around her. Indeed, from the moment she had gathered her thoughts and begun the gruesome task of cleaning up her brother, she'd almost forgotten they were even there. She heard what they told her of the attack, or what they thought must have happened, but she did not appear to be really interested in the details. Finally something inside her snapped when the corporal said, in a sympathetic, somber tone, "I am truly sorry, ma'am. I'm certain he was a very fine young man."

Olivia turned to the man and said in a brusque tone, "I believe the present tense is more in order, sir. My brother, as you see, is still very much alive."

"Yes . . . yes, of course," the man faltered. "I didn't mean that . . . Please, excuse my rudeness, ma'am."

Olivia's tone softened a bit, but she could not afford to stand there, idly conversing with the man. "Thank you very much for getting him here. I am grateful to you for that. But as you can see, I've much work ahead of me."

There was no mistaking the incredulous expression on the man's face; he glanced long and hard at Aaron's motionless body sprawled on the horsehair sofa, and his thoughts were perfectly readable. As far as he was concerned, the young man was not long for the world; he'd been brought here to die.

Olivia, at once incensed and galvanized by the expression, made up her mind right then and there.

She immediately ushered the men from the room, ignoring their good-byes, and closed the door. She glanced back at her brother and stopped in her tracks as she heard what sounded to be a barely perceptible moan. Hurriedly she moved toward the small chest near her bed and fumbled through its drawer until she located the small vial she was searching for. She returned to her brother and knelt down next to him, almost repulsed by the sight of his head. Very carefully she smoothed the blood and matter away from his mouth, eyes, and what she could see of his forehead, and then placed her fingers between his lips to open them. Turning the vial upside down, she tapped until a few drops drizzled down the back of his throat, and then waited a few moments for the desired effect. When he was silent again, she pressed her head against his chest, hearing the weak though still steady beat of his heart, feeling the slight rise and fall of his chest.

She got up and looked toward the corner of the room near the front window, her gaze resting on the object hung on the wall stud, the only family heirloom that had been in the Sandses' household since before her birth: a fiddle, the one her father had brought with him when he married Amelia. To the surprise of everyone, her husband most of all, Amelia had learned in short order to play it well.

Olivia had taken it down frequently over the past year and a half since she'd lived here, practicing the chords her mother had taught her so long ago. It was harder than she remembered, but gradually she had caught on, teaching herself to play "Amazing Grace," and a few other hymns.

Francis had enjoyed her musical ability, urging her to play often. As she thought of him then, the husband she had not seen for so many months, her heart throbbed in sudden, exquisite pain. Often she could not summon his face to mind, nor his voice, the feel of him . . .

anything. Right now, though, it was as if he were standing here in this very room, watching her, beckoning to her, reaching out to her, smiling at her. Loving her. It was, she realized on an intellectual level, probably because of her extreme need of him that she was able to summon up his memory so well. But as her gaze was caught by the stack of white envelopes on the desk, all sent by her, all duly returned unopened and unread, she came back to present reality. He was not here; no one was here to help her. Certainly there was no time to ride over to the Vellas', her closest neighbors. And so there was no one else to consult with, no one from whom to obtain advice, even a word or two of comfort and solace.

One thing was absolutely clear: She had no time to mull over decisions. One must be made right then and there, with no turning back. Drawing in a fortifying breath, she took down the fiddle from its hook and carried it over to the trestle table. There would be no more music in this house, for she knew it would be virtually impossible to repair the damage she was about to inflict on the beautiful instrument. But her hands did not hesitate.

Selecting the most appropriate needle she had from her sewing box, she carefully threaded one of the catgut strings she had removed from the fiddle. She placed it on Amelia's old pewter platter, then spent several minutes assembling a variety of other items she would need. When all was ready, she moved to where her brother now lay perfectly still. His face, now reasonably cleaned of the crusted dirt and blood, was ashen. Olivia quickly checked the pulse on the inside of his wrist; it was so faint, she wondered for a moment if she were merely imagining it. But then she placed her ear to his chest again, heard the slow, steady rhythm of his heartbeat, and was reassured. The laudanum had rendered him unconscious. The worst thing that could happen would be for him to awaken during the procedure she was about to begin, so she reached once more for the vial of medicine and, taking pains that none of it spilled, sprinkled two drops on Aaron's tongue.

Finally, feeling both intensely nervous and yet somehow sure of herself, Olivia gently slipped her hands behind her brother's head and found the flap of scalp and hair that had been so crudely severed from his skull only hours before.

Though it took more than two hours, Olivia was unaware of the time as she set about methodically reattaching skin to muscle. Years and years of sewing, a skill learned at a very young age at her mother's knee, gave her the dexterity and stamina to endure the painstaking rethreading of the needle, the refastening and realigning of the torn tissue of her brother's scalp until it was completely reattached.

When he began to stir once, she swiftly administered more of the laudanum, making sure there would be enough left for the pain that would surely follow later. But at last she was finished. More weary than she could ever remember being in her entire life, she got up from her chair, half walked, half stumbled into the kitchen, and placed her hand on the wooden handle of the kettle. She picked it up and found there was still water in it, enough to heat up and make a good strong cup of tea. But then she noticed how blurred her vision was, how the floor at her feet appeared wavery.

"Shouldn't be that way," she mumbled aloud, vaguely aware that her thoughts were unorganized, blurred in their own way. Her hand dropped from the kettle, and she stepped back two steps and slid down onto the kitchen chair. Squinting back toward the sofa, she saw that Aaron was still in the same position, the huge mound of muslin swathing his head. She lowered her head and placed it inside the crook of her elbow, turning her cheek so that she had full view of him. His completely flaccid body appeared lifeless. She'd spent hours trying to save his life, and the impulse was still strong enough inside her to want to get up and walk back over to him, to see how he was, to listen to his breath once again, to place her ear against his chest to hear his heartbeat.

But her body needed attention now; exhaustion overwhelmed her. Her eyelids fluttered for a moment and then she was fast asleep, her brain quickly hurtling into that dark, unconscious state in which there were no thoughts, no dreams, only the sweet, restorative surrender of the body's own protective defenses.

The sound that awakened her in the late afternoon was eerie, instantly frightening. She'd grown used to all sorts of noises out on the plains: animal sounds, squeals of wind rushing around the corners of the exterior walls, the sometimes distant, though rare calls of the seldom seen Indians. But this sound, which came to her in her unconscious state first, was like no other she had ever identified. It grew louder and louder until she suddenly awoke, her head jerking off the table, her hair, half-released from its customary knot on her nape, askew and wild around her face.

She wasn't exactly sure where she was at first. But the sight before her eyes catapulted her out of drowsiness; she was up on her feet and rushing to where her brother was attempting to push himself up into some sort of sitting position.

Except it wasn't even that really; his upper body was slightly raised, and his arms were half-extended, palms outward as if to shield his face . . . his head. Olivia froze. Seeing the look of horror on his face, the wild, animal-like glaze in his eyes, it was as though the reality of his ordeal transferred itself, if only for a moment, to Olivia herself. She felt her body grow cold with raw panic, felt a sickness in the pit of her stomach that only the certainty of imminent death could produce. She knew then, with intimate certainty, the depth of agony her brother must have experienced, and suddenly, standing there, she wept. Wept copious tears of anguish and fear and panic and sickness and horror, and finally rage at what her beloved, beautiful brother had gone through.

It was then and there that she decided that nothing else mattered in her life except to make sure Aaron would receive the best care and attention she could give him. Her own needs and desires would be placed in the background for as long as it took to nurse him back to health. If he was to survive, it would be through her efforts alone. And she was determined to do it. No matter what the consequences, she would see him wake up one day and look at her, recognize her, speak with her, be once more the Aaron she had known all her life.

She shoved her hands roughly against her cheeks, pushing away the tears, then bent over, gently placing her hands on Aaron's shoulders, pushing him backward into the pillow. But surprisingly, he fought her, flailing his arms, hitting her hard once on the side of her neck. The blow almost sent her reeling, but she regained her balance quickly and reacted in a way that drew on the memories of her mother when she would call out to them in a moment of fear for their safety.

"Aaron! No! Stop it, do you hear me!"

He stopped, but suddenly his head began shaking left and right, left and right, and he began flailing his arms again. He uttered something unintelligible, his tone revealing a desperate panic.

"That's enough!" she said as loudly as she could, in a tone as much like Amelia's as she could make it. It worked, for Aaron suddenly ceased all motion and stared vacantly at her, all the fight gone out of him.

Suddenly his arms went limp and dropped to his sides, and his eyelids started to close heavily.

"That's good," Olivia said in a soothing, maternal tone, carefully pushing him backward.

Aaron's mouth moved, and what came out was a garbled sort of groan.

"Shhh," she half whispered, straightening and tightening the swathe of bandages on his forehead, and then tucking the blanket around his shoulders. Despite the cold, he was actually warm, and she feared fever. Indeed, she thought, it would probably be strange if he weren't feverish after such a wound. His eyes remained closed, and so she crossed the few steps back to the medicine drawer and rummaged around in it until she found a bottle of distilled feverfew. She would have to be sparing from now on, especially with the laudanum, for there was no telling when she would be able to ride into Salina and visit the mercantile. And even then, she was never sure there would be any medicinal supplies.

After administering the feverfew, she waited a few minutes, making certain Aaron was asleep. She noted now he did not sleep as before, as still as the dead; now he gave a twitch now and then, or a moan or groan or what sounded to be a half-formed word.

She was both astonished and relieved that her brother was actually alive. It had seemed so impossible that he would live through the day when she had first seen him, and now, amazingly, he appeared to be coming to, little by little, minute by minute.

During the evening, a cold front had blown through, dropping the temperature thirty degrees. Olivia had been totally unaware of it until now. She shivered involuntarily. The fire in the hearth had almost died out, and she needed chips to revive it. She'd have to fetch some from the woodshed, and, of course, take care of the morning chores since Sid was gone. She studied Aaron for a few moments and then, deciding that he was all right for now, reached for her heavy wool cape and threw it over her shoulders. Then she thought better of it, took it off, and retrieved the sheepskin coat Francis had bought her last year from its hook near the back door.

Trudging through the wind toward the barn, she was astounded by the drastic change in weather. It felt good, however; the previous weeks' heat had been almost unbearable at times.

As she stepped inside the barn, the odor of the uncleaned stalls was so sharp and strong that almost immediately a sense of depression descended upon her as the realization of her helplessness hit her squarely. How in the world could she do all of the work required here? It was impossible. How had she done it before? She stood stock-still in the middle of the aisleway and knew that if she had ever had the answer to that, she no longer knew what it was.

Somehow, she was able to perform what needed to be done, however. After pitching fresh hay into each animal's stall, she filled each trough with as much water as she could manage to carry. Her breathing was so rapid from the effort that the air around her head was white with vapor.

The cleaning of the stalls, she decided, would have to wait. Not so much because of her weariness, but because she needed to hurry back to the house to check on Aaron. She prayed God he hadn't awakened. But the thought that he may have panicked her, and she left the barn quickly. The woodshed was on the way back, and she quickly gathered up as much wood and as many buffalo chips as she could fit inside the burlap sling fastened around her shoulder and hanging against her hip.

When she reached the house, she hesitated only as long as it took to remove her boots before hurrying on to the front room. She noted with profound relief that

Aaron was still asleep. Indeed, he was in exactly the same position as when she'd left him. She stood by him quietly, observing him, and then she bent forward to place her hand against his cheek to check his temperature.

Her hand had barely made contact with his skin before his eyelids flew open. From his mouth erupted a primitive cry that was born of horror. Olivia jerked her body backward, the hand that had been touching his face now clutched tightly at her side, as if singed.

"No." The word came from his lips, garbled and foreign-sounding to her ears. This was not her brother's voice, was not anything like she remembered. His beautiful eyes were glassy, completely blank of any recognition that she was his sister, that he was here, back in the house he had left less than two days ago.

Throughout her life, she would ever remember that one instant as the moment when she knew he was lost to her. When she knew that whatever happened, however much he might improve, he would never be the same.

Her heart leaden, everything in her life, all that it encompassed, the work, the depression that hung like a pall over her from missing Francis and losing the baby—all of it played across her mind's eye in the unforgiving light of reality. And now Aaron.

She could not do it all alone. It was pure foolishness to imagine she could.

CHAPTER XIII

February 1868

THE fire barely flickered in the hearth, and the room was growing almost frigid. The wind howled outside, whistling around the eaves of the soddy's roof. The noise of it was grating, distressing, more than enough to drive one to madness. Olivia, shivering beneath the multiple layers of clothes she wore—which consisted of just about everything in her entire wardrobe—wearily got up from the sofa and walked over to the fireplace. She glanced at the dwindling pile of buffalo chips; it was woefully small. Wouldn't last much longer than a day and a night, if she intended to keep a steady fire going. But the thought of going outside now, braving her way through wind and snow to the woodshed, was daunting.

Stooping over, she stirred up the small fire and then, seeing it was about to go out entirely, threw another couple of chips on it. Snow or no snow, she'd have to go out shortly anyway to see to the animals in the barn. She would gather up another supply of chips on her way back.

Standing up straight, she crossed the room slowly

toward the kitchen. It was so cold, her whole body ached with the motion of her efforts. Nevertheless, she had to get the stove fire going, too, if there was to be any breakfast this morning. In fact, it seemed odd that it was actually morning. The days lately had become indistinguishable from the nights, the heavy, dark snow clouds blocking out virtually all of the sun's rays. The effect of this type of weather could be overwhelmingly depressing. Work, constant physical work, was the only antidote. However, Olivia thought grimly, there was really no choice about that anyway. If she didn't see to the stock, make certain they were watered, grained, and hayed twice a day, once in the morning and once in the evening, then it wouldn't get done. Likewise, if she didn't see to the fire in the hearth and the preparation of the meals, they would simply go cold and hungry. It had been four months since the last hired man, McKinney, had announced he was leaving. Going on to Abilene, he'd said. Nothing more than that; just that he was leaving in the morning. Sid had come and gone up until a year ago. She hadn't heard from him since, and doubted she ever would. Just as she knew nothing of her husband; where he was, why he had not returned.

Now she worked every day, from sunup to sundown, not believing sometimes she'd hold up till nightfall. But she did, managing to care for Aaron, too. She'd had to reduce the hours of sleep she got, of course, but she slept more soundly than she ever had, and her health remained tolerable. At least McKinney had waited to leave until after they'd finished with the final harvest. With winter setting in so early, most of her attention was focused on either the animals or the house. And, of course, Aaron.

She put on a kettle of water to boil for coffee and was about to replace her house shoes with the heavy work boots she wore outside, when she hesitated. Might as well check on him, she thought. He'd had a particularly bad night and had only slipped into a restless sleep an hour ago.

Warmed up a little by her movements in the kitchen, she hitched up the hem of her skirt and slowly climbed the ladder to the loft. Before she even reached the top, she could hear his soft snoring. She felt relief at the sound of it. Still standing at the top of the ladder, she peered through the dim light toward the bed on which her brother slept. He lay on his side in a curled-up position, both of his hands clasped together and tucked just beneath his chin. His hair, his beautiful chocolate-brown hair, hung down in his face and spun out over the blanket that covered his shoulders. Even in this state of dishevelment, his handsomeness was unmistakable. She let her gaze linger on her brother's sleeping form for a few more seconds, then slowly backed down the ladder. She would never, it seemed, lose the feeling that his mere presence was a miracle. How could it be otherwise? But how could she sustain it much longer? Help was what she needed. Help with just about everything.

March 1869

Luke Coyle arrived on the property one afternoon in early March, a month of strong, unrelenting winds howling across the vast, rolling bluffs, lowering the lingering winter temperatures at least twenty degrees. He rode at a walk the last fifty yards or so and gave the horse, a stout gray gelding, a loud ''Whoa'' when it reached the hitching rail. Olivia was bent over, scattering feed to the few hens picking about in the front yard. The weather had improved considerably over the past forty-eight hours. It was still cold, but the wind had slowed some, and the sunshine felt good on her head.

Olivia had heard the horse from far off, and when she'd glanced up and saw nothing, she knew that if horse and rider were coming her way, it would be a good ten minutes before they arrived. She went about her business of gathering chips and wood and strapping it all across her upper back and then began to feed the chickens, not looking up from her work until she heard the horse snort as it entered the yard.

"Hello there," said the man, his voice rich in tone.

Olivia nodded, her eyes squinting slightly as she appraised the man atop the horse. She couldn't make much of him, for he was covered from head to foot in a huge, dirt-mangled, hooded fur coat. She wondered briefly at her lack of fear, but only briefly. What did she have to fear? She'd already been through three lifetimes of fear.

"Anybody else around?" the man asked, his mouth still moving as he finished the question. Tobacco, Olivia noted; of the chewing kind. One awful habit that Francis mercifully never had. "A man?"

"No." Olivia said the word tightly.

The man looked at her, and his frown deepened. The woman did not frighten easily; that was certain. Well, out here in this godforsaken country, it stood to reason that a woman on her own would be possessed of gumption and grit. His saddle creaked as he turned his entire body away from her in order to spit, gentlemanly, out of her line of vision.

Olivia noticed what he was doing, and appreciated his attempt at good manners, but winced nonetheless. She was faintly amused to see that when he turned back around again, puffs of dust arose from his coat and hood.

"Why not?"

"Why not what?" Olivia asked, shifting the load of fuel to her hip.

"Why's there no man? Why are you out here alone on the prairie?"

"I live here."

He nodded and pursed his lips. "Yes, ma'am, I can

see that much.'' He looked directly at her. ''How long?''

''How long what?''

Luke Coyle drew in a deep breath and let it out slowly. ''Ma'am, I'm real sorry to be intrudin' on you like this, but I mean no harm.''

Olivia stood her ground, watching him, waiting. Then she, too, took in a deep breath and asked, ''Why is it you ask so many questions, Mr. . . . ?''

''Coyle. Luke Coyle.''

''Mr. Coyle. Well?''

''Just tryin' to be friendly is all, ma'am.''

''You've come a long way to be friendly.''

Luke chuckled, a deep-throated, soft sound that Olivia found somehow immensely pleasing. How long had it been since she had heard anyone laugh? Anyone at all, including herself?

''I'm lookin' for work,'' he stated. ''Any sort of work.'' He paused. ''You surely could use help of some sort. Don't see how you could take care of this place all alone.''

''Amazingly enough, that's exactly what I've been doing,'' Olivia said, the barest grin curving the corner of her lips.

It had been three years since the end of the war now, and still she had not heard from or about Francis. She had no idea whether he had survived, though most of the time she gave in to doubts that he had. Aaron had recovered outwardly, almost to perfection. The only remaining sign of his wound was a scar on his forehead at the hairline, where one of the stitches had become briefly infected.

He helped out at times as much as he was able to. She didn't push him. Amazingly, after all he'd been through, Aaron was unusually good-looking. This was confirmed by those infrequent occasions—in town, mostly—when women were in his presence. Invariably they were taken with him, would stare in open, unlady-like fashion. But Olivia took pains to keep him away from social encounters, for she was loath to be put in the position of explaining to others why he was such a recluse, why he didn't respond as most men did. Only she understood his tormented mind, and that was the way she preferred it.

And so she struggled on, living alone, working day in, day out, to provide a life for the both of them. She refused to look into the future—three, four, or five years from now. Life had to be lived one day at a time; that was the only way to look at it.

Luke Coyle's eyes widened considerably, unbelievingly. "That so?"

"Yes, it is so."

He gave a nod of his head. "Well, then, I suppose a woman as capable as you doesn't need to be talked into anything." He picked up his reins, which were lying on his horse's neck, and started to turn the horse around.

"I didn't say I wouldn't like any help, did I?"

Luke hesitated.

Olivia shifted her load once again, and sighed heavily. "As a matter of fact, I very much do need help." At just that moment, sounds could be heard from inside the house; Aaron was calling out to her.

Instantly Luke Coyle's expression became wary. "Thought you said there wasn't any man around."

Olivia had turned immediately to start toward the door; suddenly the full implication of her words previously hit her. Indeed, she had said there was no man around, and she had meant it. This was a strange yet accurate realization that had the power to stir up all sorts of pain and regret, but she quickly put it aside in order to deal with the moment at hand.

She opened the front door and stuck her head inside. "Just a minute, Aaron." A garbled answer came back to her, and she added, "I'll be right there."

She turned back to face the visitor and said, "Yes, I did say just that. The man you hear inside is my brother. He's somewhat . . . ill."

"I see. What's wrong with him?"

Irritation flashed for an instant within her, but she simply answered curtly, "I'm sorry, but I must attend to him."

"I'll wait."

She looked back at Luke Coyle for a brief second, before turning and jerking open the front door. Inside, she found Aaron pacing the room, walking rapidly toward one end, standing there for a moment, and then returning to the opposite side. He'd been having a bad day since he awakened that morning.

"What's the matter, Aaron?" she asked, hurrying over to him.

But his only answer was garbled, nonsensical; she knew, from past episodes, he was fighting off his demons again.

She led him back to the sofa, gave him a cup of chamomile tea to soothe his agitation, and smoothed his hair gently as he rambled on and on until he began to relax. "Relax" was a rather dubious term when referring to Aaron, for it simply meant that Aaron remained quiet, his body stock-still as his eyes focused unseeingly straight ahead. Sometimes—most of the time, actually—he could maintain such a position for over an hour at a time. During that time he would be completely unresponsive to any attempts on her part to speak with him. But speak she did, often keeping up a nonstop chatter, hoping he would hear at least some of what she was saying to him.

Except now, it would have to wait. She needed to take care of the stranger outside first. But he was nowhere to be seen when she came back outside, though his horse, reins tied securely around his long, fuzzy neck, was now nibbling on the sparse shoots of grass in her front yard.

Olivia was wondering where the man had disappeared to when he rounded the corner of the house, headed toward her, in his arms a large stack of kindling. His great cloak whipped out all around him in the wind, but the hood had fallen onto his back. She could see the dense dark blond hair on his head, which no doubt would be a few shades lighter after a good wash or two. And she noted, too, that his face, underneath the grime and unkempt beard and mustache, was somewhat handsome, in a rough sort of way, of course. As he walked toward her, she had a sudden, unexpected memory of Francis, rounding that same corner, carrying something or other, striding toward her with much the same self-assured step. So completely was she taken up with the vision of her husband—whom she had been unable to conjure up in her mind's eye for a very long time—that she was unaware for a moment that Luke had stopped directly before her.

"Thought this might help you out a bit."

Olivia swallowed. "Well, yes. It will." A stiff gust of wind almost blew her bonnet off her head, and she reached up quickly to secure it. But as she did so, she saw his gaze follow her hand. Quickly she tucked her hair inside the calico bonnet and retied the lappets. She stared at the much-needed wood in his arms.

"What would you like me to do with it?"

"Oh . . . well, I keep it near the hearth. But . . ."

"This'll be fairly hard to carry inside yourself."

"No . . . I'm not sure if . . ." Her voice was vague and indecisive.

"Why don't you just let me take it inside for you?"

"No," Olivia said hastily. "Why don't you just put it here, beside the door . . . and I'll bring it all inside later."

"All right, then." He did as she asked and then

straightened, slapping his hands together to rid them of the bits and pieces of wood and dirt. "I didn't mean to be offensive," he said, nodding toward the house. "About your brother, that is. Been told I'm nosier than I should be at times."

Olivia's features relaxed a bit. "It's all right. He was injured years ago in an Indian attack. He's . . . he has his good days and bad days. Today's a bad one."

"You takin' care of him alone?"

Olivia nodded.

"And there's no one else around?"

"No," she admitted. "We have neighbors a few miles away. But no one seems to have leftover time for visiting." She smiled wryly. "This is not exactly city living."

Luke Coyle's amazement deepened. The woman who stood before him was young, strong, and a darn sight more pleasing to look at than most women he'd come across in several years. Her place—all of it—appeared to be well kept. The soddy was straighter than any he'd come across, and a far sight tidier. The windows were well scrubbed, and fresh tieback curtains hung inside them. Even the barn was respectable, what he'd seen of it. It seemed impossible that she could manage all this alone. What in the world was such a nice-appearing woman doing here, out in the middle of nowhere?

He wondered as much to her aloud.

"Well, Mr. Coyle, I'm here because I own the place. And, as you see, I manage just fine. Of course, it's winter now and there's not much to do with the fields or the gardens."

"What will you do come spring?"

"I'll get to work on whatever needs doing." She was slightly amused by his bemusement with her situation, and as they stood there talking, she realized she was becoming more and more comfortable with the man. "I'll just strap on the harness and plow to my mule and get to work planting seed. Like everyone else in these parts.''

"Corn?"

She shrugged one shoulder. "A few acres of wheat also. But not too much since it's less reliable. Mostly corn and bluestem for hay.''

"Mmmm,'' he muttered. He gazed off for a moment, thinking about that. It was something, a woman alone, out here on the prairie, doing tasks he himself found daunting. Tasks that had driven him to leave his home, seek out another life altogether. He'd settled on the life of a wrangler, had spent several years driving herds from his native Texas to Abilene, and sometimes beyond. He mulled over the situation he was in now once more and then turned back to the young woman.

"I've got an offer for you.''

She crossed her arms over her chest and waited. As he spoke, she noted that his features were not nearly as old as she had at first thought. And his eyes . . . a distinct, clear blue. Red-rimmed from the cold and fatigue, emphasizing the blue even more.

"Since you need help real bad, and I—''

Her response was quick. "I don't need help 'real bad,' sir.''

He raised both eyebrows. " 'Sir'? That's more formal than I'm used to. Look, I don't see how you can say that. Certainly you need help. A woman alone, caring for an ailing man . . . It's not right.''

She had to smile. "Right? Listen, I've been here alone for a long while. It may seem strange to you but I don't think there is such a thing as right or wrong out here on the prairie.''

He wanted to ask her just what *were* her reasons for being alone out here, but that could come later perhaps.

"And besides, I can't pay anyone anything right now. I don't have the cash reserves for it.''

"I'm not interested in money. I only want a place to

stay. Just till early summer. I just need to bunk down somewhere for the rest of spring. So . . . I'd be willing to stay, work as a hand for you, do anything you need until then. That's my offer.''

Olivia's eyes narrowed. ''In exchange for room only?''

Luke raised one eyebrow. ''And grub, too, of course.''

Olivia was silent for a moment. ''Just why do you need a place to stay, Mr. Coyle? And where will you move on to in the spring?''

''Abilene.''

Olivia nodded several times. ''Where do you come from?''

''Texas. North central part.''

''And what is it you do for a living?''

''I'm a cowhand. Been drivin' herds up North and back for a few years now.''

Olivia raised both eyebrows. She looked down at the ground and moved the toe of her boot back and forth in the dirt, mulling over this information. This man, a complete stranger, could be telling her nothing more than a pack of bald-faced lies. He could be a criminal, for all she knew, a murderer on the run from the law. After all, he was from Texas. That fact alone said plenty. But then, the truth of the matter was that she could use help. If her chores alone were cut in half, it would free up her time so she could be with Aaron, who needed her attention increasingly every day. He was improving, certainly, but there were times when he needed her as he worked his way through the sporadic battle against the nightmares that visited him day and night.

But the fact that she would not have to hand over any of her cash reserves—which had diminished considerably over the past few years—was a compelling aspect of Mr. Coyle's offer. And he seemed at least as capable as anyone else she might have sought to help her out.

The idea crossed her mind, too, that it might not be a bad idea to have a man around for Aaron's sake. She wasn't sure why exactly this might be so, but it might be worth a try.

"All right," she said suddenly. "You can stay. The barn loft is plenty warm in the winter."

He seemed surprised by her answer. "Thank you." He gave a sideward nod of his head. "I'll just take my things then and go on back."

"All right."

Aaron called out again, and she turned to open the front door.

"Uh . . ." He cleared his throat.

Olivia stopped. "Yes?"

"I was hoping there might be some grub."

"Supper is usually at five o'clock. That's only an hour away."

"All right."

Olivia saw the glimmer in his eyes, and she had to wonder when it was he had last eaten anything of substance. But that was the last she thought of it, for Aaron was yelling now, and so she turned and went back inside the house.

The arrangement with Luke Coyle worked out far better than she could have imagined. On the very first night, as Olivia lay in bed pondering the wisdom of her decision to let him stay on, she nevertheless realized that she was actually worrying about it far less than she may have at another time. Oddly, she felt more secure than she had in a long, long while, and finally, as she drifted off to sleep, she realized the reason was that, finally, there was someone here other than herself to shoulder at least part of the burden. It wasn't Francis, but then, Francis was rapidly becoming a mere memory that she only occasionally pulled up into her everyday thoughts. Wishing him back home had long since become a fantasy she could no longer afford to indulge in. Indeed, all she wanted now, all she expected, was to find out the truth about what had happened to him.

All she knew, at this point, four years after the War between the States had ceased, was that he had made it safely to Washington by early July 1861. All of her efforts to learn more—and indeed, she had written to as many government agencies as she'd reasoned might be able to help her—had produced not one shred of information as to what had happened to him. She considered the prospect that he was still alive almost implausible.

Each and every night, she said a prayer for his safe return, though in her heart she realized the futility of those brief moments of spiritual indulgence. Tonight she did not indulge. Tonight her thoughts and feelings were focused elsewhere, and mercifully, she felt no guilt whatsoever. Only a small degree of dread that this new security, this new focus . . . this new man, was but a temporary situation and nothing more.

As slumber overtook her, Luke Coyle was the last image on her mind.

Not once, in the entire time he stayed with them, did Olivia regret her decision that March afternoon. Luke Coyle settled into the routine of helping run the farm as if he were as much owner as was Olivia herself. He worked as hard as she had ever seen any man work. At last, she did not have to concern herself with the care and feeding of the animals, and that alone was a welcome relief. But he also saw to it that the fields were plowed and seeded, once even riding into Salina and hiring additional help for three days to complete the job.

Olivia was enough of a realist not to take the situation for granted. He'd said he was going to leave in early summer, and as the weeks wore on, he said nothing more about it. Sometimes she forgot that he was there temporarily. She would quickly shake herself mentally and return her attention to the details of the work that consumed her time from morning until evening.

In spring she always made soap. Now, for the first time, she actually enjoyed it. She had saved up grease and scrap trimmings since autumn, and one evening, after preparing a fire beneath the soap kettle in the backyard, she dumped them all in, leaving them to cook until well done. The next morning, she turned the gloppy mess in to a wooden tub of rainwater and left it to cool and separate into debris and grease. The next day she skimmed off the grease and dropped it back into the kettle, which now contained boiling lye that she'd collected from the wooden hopper she always kept supplied with ashes from the fireplace or stove. It was a delicate, time-consuming process, but when it was completed, when the mixture had been poured into more water in which it would cool and solidify into soap, Olivia felt a sense of pride in her efforts. She would enjoy the fruits of her labors for several months.

In the winter she had made a trip into town and purchased bolts of unbleached muslin. Now, with warmer weather, she was able to color the cloth: logwood for black, madder powder for red, and dark brown from walnut bark she collected herself. She imagined the dresses and skirts she would make, and her spirits lifted. It didn't much matter, of course, what one wore from day to day on the plains, but she couldn't help longing for a bit of color to add a measure of cheer to her daily routine.

She spent a great deal of her time cooking, but it was with unusual pleasure that she did so now. Luke was a skilled hunter, as it turned out, and barely a week went by that he did not bring her a supply of fresh meat or fish. She applied all her skills to preparing the varied array of wild game he brought in: deer, wild turkey, quail, prairie chicken. With the fresh vegetables from her garden, she was able to produce meals that were some of the tastiest she'd had since moving to Kansas. Corn was the main staple of the Kansan diet, and she, like most every other settler she knew, had long since grown weary of the interminable list of corn recipes that dominated everyday fare: cornbread, grits, mush, hominy, samp, corn dodgers, corn on the cob, griddle corn cakes, corn muffins . . . and for a change, white pot, a mixture of milk, eggs, and corn meal, topped off with either sugar or molasses—usually the latter. She longed dearly for wheat bread, but since her wheat crop was so valuable, she sold it all whenever it was harvested.

But Luke, declaring he couldn't live more than a month without at least one or two flour biscuits, had somehow managed to rustle up a supply of wheat flour, which was almost miraculous given the fact that the wheat harvest the previous autumn had been severely limited. Olivia took advantage of the coveted staple, and using her mother's old recipes, she baked her dough in the old iron baker that had been in the family since she was a child. A three-legged contraption, it was placed on a bed of coals in the hearth, and its heavy iron lid was covered with more coals. The first time she made biscuits, the smell of them baking was enough to catch Luke's attention halfway to the barn. His compliments and thanks for her efforts were profuse and sincere.

It was nice enough to have such attention directed toward her efforts, but Luke Coyle's presence helped out in another, even more important way. Aaron became increasingly capable of sustaining long periods in which he remained unagitated, almost calm. Though he did not speak more than two or three sentences all day long, he was the first to be seated at the table at mealtimes, and it was obvious his mood improved drastically the moment Luke took his own chair. Olivia decided quickly that whatever the real story of Luke Coyle's life, nothing could negate the positive effect he had on her brother.

Luke seemed to take all of it in stride; though he never said anything to Olivia about his attentions toward Aaron, she recognized the fact that he knew exactly what he was doing. Somehow he sensed just the right way to draw Aaron into a discussion, having infinite patience with Aaron's halting manner of speaking. It had often driven Olivia to distraction; she'd had to force patience to deal with his stutter, his frequent confusion over what was being said or asked of him, and his even more frequent inability to finish a thought. But all of this seemed not to bother Luke one whit, and it never ceased to amaze her that he was so kind.

As the weeks went by, Aaron seemed to almost flourish. He ventured out of the house for longer periods of time, and eventually began to go along with Luke. Sometimes Olivia would follow along at a distance, pretending to carry on about her work, but with the sole intention of discovering what went on between the two of them. Surprisingly, there was hardly any more conversation than that which took place at mealtimes, perhaps even less. But there was an undeniable bond between the men, dependent, it appeared, upon the activities both of them engaged in. Whatever Luke did, Aaron tried to do too, albeit at a much slower, somewhat uncoordinated pace. In a matter of a few weeks, he was able to perform almost all the tasks in the barn, from simple mucking of stalls to cleaning the leather tack. Olivia was both amazed and immensely pleased by the change in her brother; inevitably, she began to feel an emotional pull toward the rugged, capable stranger who had entered their lives.

But, she mused early one morning as she hung out freshly washed sheets, he really wasn't a stranger anymore. A sensation went through her then, as sudden as the erratic gusts of wind whipping out the sheets, as if she, too, were being affected by the shifting, ever-changing wind patterns.

She frowned and reached for the last of the items in the clothes basket, a pair of jeans . . . Luke Coyle's only extra set of pants. Olivia's hands kneaded the damp material for several seconds until she realized what she was doing. It was a completely ridiculous action, seeing as how she'd been washing his clothes for several weeks now.

"Silly," she muttered, shaking her head slightly. Finished, she picked up the basket and headed toward the back door of the house. Inside, where the light was poor, her vision was temporarily dimmed, and so she did not see at first the tall figure standing near the kitchen wall.

"Oh!" she cried out in surprise as she practically ran into the man. One hand flew to her throat, and she sucked in her breath. It was only Luke, coming inside for his breakfast before he headed back to tend to the myriad chores awaiting him.

"Did I frighten you?"

"Yes," she half laughed, giving a shake of her head. "I didn't see you standing there." She placed the basket on the floor and said, in a much more sprightly tone of voice than she would have normally used, "I'll have breakfast on the table in just a moment."

"That's fine," he said, slowly leaning into the door-post with one shoulder.

Olivia hurried about the kitchen, placing tall glasses of fresh milk on the table and then adding platters of fried grits and scrambled eggs and day-old biscuits. She felt his eyes on her the whole time, making her uncharacteristically self-conscious. She'd never felt this way in her own home before; she was instantly confused and filled with vague resentment.

"Well, then," she said crisply, "I guess it's all

ready." She glanced around the room. "Where's Aaron? Was he with you in the barn?"

"No, he didn't come out today."

Olivia frowned. These days Aaron was often up before she was, already mucking the stalls in the barn. "He hasn't done that in a while. Let me just see. . . ." She walked across the adjoining parlor toward the stairway that led up into the loft. As she climbed the stairs, she could sense Luke's eyes continue to follow her, and she grew even more disconcerted than before. Before she even reached the top of the stairs, she heard her brother's gentle snoring. Then she saw him lying in the bed, his back to her, the covers pulled up to his chin. A feeling she hadn't known in a long while hit her full force, and suddenly she felt deflated. A tinge of something else rippled through her veins, something she had thought was behind her: a sense of despair, of hopelessness over her brother's condition. She'd been fooled by the seeming progress of the past couple of months, reasoning that the positive changes she'd witnessed in her brother every day were permanent, perhaps the beginning of what would eventually become a complete return to normalcy.

And now here he was, curled up in the fetal position, childlike once more. Of course, it was still early in the morning, and perhaps one could say he was merely tired and needed more rest. But Olivia knew instinctively that that was not the case. She'd seen him too many times like this in the past. He was simply regressing once more to the one place he'd always found respite from the pain of his thoughts, his memories. Inside himself.

Slowly she descended the stairs. Luke was watching her, but his expression changed when he saw her own.

"What's the matter?"

Olivia turned her head and gazed out one of the front windows. "He's asleep."

"That's all right. He needs rest, is all. Felt like sleepin' in myself this morning."

Olivia crossed the room to the sofa and sat down. "It's not that."

"What do you mean?"

He had walked across the room and was standing near her, and somewhere in the back of her mind, Olivia took note of the fact that this was the first time Luke had entered the front room. His visits to the house had thus far been confined to the kitchen.

She sighed softly. "He's slipping backward. He's all curled up like a baby. When he gets like that, he'll stay that way for hours and hours. Won't even wake up to eat." She sighed again, heavily this time. "He hasn't done it in so long." On the last word her voice broke, and she turned her head away quickly.

Luke's boot scraped the floor as he shifted his weight. "He'll come out of it. Just give him some time."

"He's had so much time already." She looked up at Luke, her eyes liquid, her emotions barely in check now. "You don't know what he's like at his worst. Since you've been around, he's been the best he's ever been since the attack. I can't believe he . . ." Suddenly she felt weary beyond measure, as if all the efforts of caring for her brother were rested squarely on her shoulders like some enormous weight she couldn't be rid of. And she did not think she could be the brave person she always was right now, did not think she could endure another measure of the fear that had lurked in her mind all this time: that all her efforts to help Aaron had been for naught.

She felt Luke's fingers unlocking her clenched hands, and as she slowly lifted her pained gaze to meet his, she knew a deep-felt sense of gratitude for this man's presence in her life. At once she recognized both the security of his being there and a dread for the pain that was sure to come when he left. For it was only now that she admitted how truly difficult her life had become, had been for a long, long time. It was one thing to feel self-sufficient, to convince oneself that a life of solitude, of loneliness, was worth it.

Luke pulled her to her feet so effortlessly that she felt as if she were gliding, up off the sofa, and toward him, toward and into his opened arms, which encircled her, gently yet firmly embracing her. She opened her mouth to speak, but the lump in her throat was too thick, too much on fire with unexpressed emotion.

"Shhh," he whispered, pulling her closer into his arms.

Her breast pressing against his chest, her cheek resting on his collarbone, she drew in a shallow breath. He smelled of the mingled aromas of soap and dirt and feed and hay, and instantly she felt her will catapulting into a reality she knew had been waiting for her all along. She no longer had need of justification for the physical pull she felt for Luke Coyle, no longer saw the necessity of denying such a feeling. What would be the use of doing so anymore? What was the point in denying herself the fulfillment of her own desires?

And so it was quite a natural thing that happened next, her lifting her chin upward the way she did, not closing her eyes but watching his lips as they parted ever so slightly. She tilted her head back even further, and his lips met hers finally. For a moment her gaze remained locked with his, and she knew that he, too, could no longer find reason or logic to keep from doing that which he had wanted for a long, long while. She closed her eyes then, relishing the feel of his lips brushing and pressing against hers until she opened her mouth and felt his tongue slide within.

Suddenly she was kissing him with a ferocity that was every bit his match, as if she no longer could continue starving herself of that which her body craved. She heard her own sounds of passion, and somewhere in the back of her mind was astonished by the intensity of sensation washing over her. When one of his arms cupped the back of her knees, his other wrapped around her shoulders, and he lifted her up off the floor, it seemed merely the most natural thing in the world. Though she had never seen an ocean, she had read of white-crested waves, knew that what she felt now must be the same as the experience of being lifted high up onto one, of being carried forward by an unstoppable, inevitable physical motion.

He placed her on her own bed, in the small bedroom that she had shared once with her husband but that had been her own for much longer. Her hands went behind her back, releasing the ties of her apron before returning to the buttons at the neckline of her dress. Their figures—he standing before her, slowly removing his own clothing, she sitting on the edge of the bed—were in semishadow since there was but a tiny window in a west-facing wall. But each could clearly see the other's features, and desire reached a fever pitch for Olivia. When he had finished undressing, her gaze wandered slowly down the hard-edged curves of his work-muscled body; her insides felt liquid and hot . . . and more than ready.

She said not a word, and as Luke slowly dropped to one knee on the braided-rag rug, he, too, remained mute. Olivia shivered, for the cool air was quickly slipping inside the opened front of her dress. Luke saw the shiver, and she thought she noticed the faintest expression of satisfaction on his face. His hands tugged on the sleeves of her dress until her arms were released and the dress fell, unrestrained now, to her waistline. He gingerly removed her chemise, and at once her entire body tensed as the backs of his hands slowly grazed her naked breasts. She could do nothing but wait, for she was overcome by the intensity of sensation she had not felt for too, too long.

Luke continued to lead in this lovemaking dance, playing it his way, and yet, instinctively perhaps, her way, too. As he lifted the hem of her skirt, pushing both it and her slip up into an unwieldy ball of material, she sensed the sudden impatience within him, felt a shudder ripple across the surface of his skin where her own fingers grazed. With his left hand on her left shoulder, he pushed her backward until her head lay on the bed. His right hand continued to wrestle with the yards of calico until at last he shoved the mass of it upward, over her head, tossing it aside roughly.

Within seconds he was above her, grazing her mouth with his kisses as he slowly united his body with hers. She had not known physical intimacy in such a long time that she was astonished at first by the greediness with which she not only accepted him, but pulled him even closer inside, wanting more than she had ever imagined it was possible to want.

They had, she realized, been preparing for this moment from the very first time they met. As their bodies blended, melding into a solid union of uninhibited passion, Olivia felt the hot sensation within her build to a feverish pitch. And as she reached, then descended from, that pinnacle of her body's response, it became clear to her that she had been filled with something other than physical satisfaction and pleasure; she had begun the process of filling the emptiness within her soul, a deprivation she had not realized until now was so shattering, so wanting.

CHAPTER XIV

1921

LEAH Rice felt a warmth spreading across the smooth, pale features of her face. She lowered her head and scribbled busily, willing away the unwanted blush. But she looked up when she heard the old woman's lighthearted chuckle.

"I . . . I didn't catch that last thing. . . ."

But Olivia Sands lifted one arthritic hand and waved it dismissingly in the air. "Oh, pooh. You're just embarrassed. But you wanted to hear everything, didn't you?"

Leah bit her lower lip and sat up straighter in the ladder-back chair. "Yes, of course. Anything you care to tell me."

"But you sure weren't expecting me to admit such a thing, were you? An affair with a man I wasn't married to. Scandalous!"

"No. I'm not here to form any sort of judgment about your life—or your life-style. Whatever happened . . . well, it happened." Leah raised a shoulder and smiled ruefully. "The truth is, I blush very easily. Always have.

Since I was a little girl actually. I was always told it made my eyes look even greener.''

Olivia's eyes narrowed and her gaze was strangely penetrating as she leveled a scrutinizing look at the woman before her. Something . . . something she just said, Olivia thought, makes sense somehow. She thought on it for a moment and then decided it wasn't worth the effort. How many times had she had the train of a thought and lost it completely? Ah, well, just another price one pays in growing old.

Still, though, that comment about blushing reminded her of something . . . but of what? Olivia shook her head slightly and said, ''You want to know if I was in love with him, though. Don't you?''

''I . . . I . . . Well, it's none of my business really.''

''Well, I wasn't. Oh, I tried to talk myself into believing I was, and for a long time after he left, I really believed I had been in love.''

''When did he leave?''

''Oh, that very summer. He'd said he just needed a place to stay for a while, and he was true to his word.''

''I see.'' Leah hesitated, then clearing her throat lightly, asked, ''How did you feel? About him leaving, that is.''

''Oh, I absolutely hated it! Thought I would die. I mean, you see, there still had been nothing from Francis. Not a word. I was still trying to get information from the army, but I heard nothing but 'We don't know.' '' Olivia shook her head slowly from side to side. ''It was a horrible time for me.'' She looked off into space for a long moment and then added, very quietly, ''And then there was the baby, too.''

Leah's hand paused above the notepad. ''The baby?''

Olivia seemed not to hear for a moment. ''I was pregnant, you see. When he left. I didn't know, of course, until several weeks later, and it was only a few weeks after that that I lost it.''

Leah was silent.

"I couldn't believe it had happened to me again. I really thought that perhaps having Luke's baby would somehow put it all to rest. What had happened between him and me, you see. But . . . it wasn't meant to be."

The room was quiet for a long while as Olivia became lost in her memories, and Leah made note of the sad facts being related to her. Just as she finished, there was a single knock at the door and a nurse peeked around it. "I've brought more iced lemonade, if you would like. Gingerbread, too."

Leah placed her notepad on the table and stood up. "That would be delightful." She took the pitcher of iced lemonade from the nurse, and the plateful of iced gingerbread cakes. Olivia was still gazing out the window.

"Would you care for some lemonade?"

Olivia turned her head and looked at Leah as though she had forgotten where she was, or who Leah was. Then her clouded gaze cleared and she said, "Yes. That would be very nice."

Leah poured the sweet lemonade into the two tall glasses on the nightstand and stood near the window next to Olivia as they both sipped slowly of the refreshing liquid.

"Tastes good," Leah said. "Can't seem to get enough of it today."

"Mmmm," Olivia mumbled. Something about the inflection in her tone alerted Leah, and once more she found her thoughts focusing on something from the past, something she could not identify. She winced and fought back the sense of extreme frustration that overcame her at times like this. Many had been the times throughout her life when she'd seen something, or heard something, or smelled something that triggered a feeling deep inside her: a half memory. Of what, she could never pin down. But none of those feelings or half memories were like the agitation that plagued her whenever she experienced the dream that had haunted her for as far back as she could remember. It was a very mundane sort of dream, and yet it had recurred with such unrelenting frequency all of her life that she knew there had to be at least minor significance to it. As she grew older she had queried her mother about it, asking her what she thought such a dream could signify. But her mother, until the end of her life ten years before, had always had the exact same reaction. "What could a dream about grass mean about anything? Don't be silly, child. I'm tired of hearing about it."

The statement, however, did nothing to assuage Leah's curiosity. How could a recurrent dream about anything be insignificant? she wondered. Dreams didn't just come from air. And so she continued to ponder the reason for her dream about tall, moving grass, grass into which she would run and be swallowed up, and through which she would keep running, feathery stalks brushing against her cheeks and arms and legs as she went. Her hands were always in front of her, pushing through it, as if she were swimming. Swimming through waves of grass. And she was laughing. Always, always laughing. She would awake from the dream with the most incredibly happy sensation, sometimes finding she was actually smiling. And then the smile would fade and she would wonder, again, what it all meant. It was at such odds with everything she'd known in London, where she had spent almost all of her childhood, that she was forced to surmise she must have read about the grass in some book or other. Though that did not make much sense either since she'd been having the dream since before the time she learned to read.

Olivia spoke up, and Leah rapidly returned from her reverie. "It was good," the old woman said, handing over the glass, held tentatively in both gnarled hands.

"Oh, my, yes," Leah said. "It is very good."

"You didn't drink it," Olivia pointed out.

Leah smiled and returned to her chair. "I will, though. Now. Would you like to continue some more for today?"

"I've nothing else to do."

"I thought you might be tired."

Olivia uttered a half laugh. "Tired? No, I don't think so. How can a person be tired sitting all day? No. Boring is what it's like living here." She paused and then went on. "You know . . . I can honestly say that I've never in my life been as tired as I was when I was in my twenties. Seems like it'd be different, I know. Getting old and all . . . Age is supposed to catch up and make you unable to do the things you did when you were younger. Which is true, of course. But what people today don't know, don't realize, is how much pain a person had to endure back in those days. Nothing was ever done with, and so you were always tired. Always."

"What about your brother? Did he help you out after Mr. Coyle left?"

"Took him a while, but yes, eventually he did. Luke taught him a lot about what he'd forgotten he already knew. I comforted myself after he'd been gone a while with the thought that God sent him to help out Aaron. And he did do that."

"What happened to him? Luke, that is."

"Never did hear a word from him." She cast a wry glance at Leah. "You're thinking I didn't have much luck with menfolk, aren't you?"

"Well, I . . ."

"You'd be right if you did. Well, there was another one, so the story's not over. Of course, I didn't meet him until seventy-two, no, seventy-three, I believe it was. Early summer, if I remember right. Yes, it was, because I remember the heat so well. Lord, it was hot."

Leah shifted in her chair. "Was he someone new to Salina at the time?"

"Salina? Oh, no. Moved away from there in the summer of 1873. I tried, Lord knows I tried to make a go of it alone, but it just wouldn't work anymore. I never could manage to get the help I needed on a regular basis, and after the Kansas flooded out one spring, I just decided it wasn't much use anymore tryin' to keep something going that wasn't going to work out. I think I'd always believed that if I stayed there long enough, Francis would come back. It was silly, really, thinking as long as I stayed where he left me, he'd always want to come back at least and see what happened to me." She paused. "Of course, that never happened. Pure fantasy. And, Luke, he never came back either. So . . . I decided to sell. Had an offer that was quite good, and it didn't take long for me to make up my mind."

"I know you went on to Hays," Leah inserted.

"Yes. I did." Olivia shrugged one shoulder. "Can't really remember the reason I went there, to tell you the truth. Except that I just knew I had to go west. I knew I was never going back east again."

"What did Aaron think of that decision?"

"Well, he didn't have too much to say. You have to understand that Aaron didn't say much about anything, anytime. He still had the nightmares, and he seemed to lose more of his remembering as time went by. He'd forget things . . . little things. If I told him I was going to bake custard the next day, he'd ask me all day long when it would be ready. He must have asked me a million times what happened to Luke. A doctor I took him to once said his head had probably been damaged inside during the attack."

"Was he part of your reason to leave also?"

Olivia thought for a moment. "Yes. I thought it might help him somehow. Might help him forget at least part of what had happened to him. Well, anyway, it seemed a good idea at the time to head toward Hays. Mostly I'd just heard about it through others traveling through

Salina. From railroad promoters, land agents, and the like. Well, so I just did it; sold the land and bought a quarter section, which was all I thought I could handle at the time. I'd have to wait and see, of course, if I was able to make a go of it.''

"You bought the land sight unseen? Just as your father did?''

Olivia's eyes fixed on Leah. "That's right, I did. Did exactly as my father did.'' A tinge of irony was in the soft smile on her face as she remembered yet another similarity. "And just like Father, I decided that we would make our way west in a railroad car. Only that time, it was Aaron who was unable to travel any other way.''

Olivia scratched the top of one hand with the gnarled fingers of the other and was silent for a while. Then she let out a gentle sigh and said, "But it couldn't have been more different when we got there. The only comparison to be made was that it was still Kansas.''

"What was so different?'' Leah probed.

"Well . . . for one, it was a more desolate looking sort of land—at least it appeared so when we first arrived. But that was changing rapidly, though at first we weren't aware of why, or what was happening.''

"You're speaking of the settlement in Victoria?''

Again Olivia's gaze was sharp as she studied the younger woman taking notes beside her. "That's right. You've really done your homework, it appears.''

Leah smiled and dipped her head to one side. "To some degree, I suppose. I've read a little about all parts of Kansas around that time period. Victoria was mentioned once in one of the books I was reading; it seems to have one of the more interesting histories of towns that sprang up then.''

"And later died,'' Olivia added wryly.

"But it did come back again. I mean, it exists now.''

"Oh yes, that's true. But at the time no one would have ever guessed it might come back."

"Can you describe it?"

With that question, Olivia's features began to gradually soften, and to Leah, watching quietly, it seemed as though the layers of years were peeling back one by one, revealing a stunningly vivid glimpse of the young woman whom Olivia had once been. It seemed as though a particular light had settled round the old woman, and as she began to speak, even her voice sounded lighter, younger . . . filled with renewed hope.

"There was nothing like it," Olivia said, her voice close to a whisper. "At least nothing like I'd ever seen before. Our quarter section was just a few miles outside of Hays, and even less from the new town of Victoria. With the money we made from the sale of the farm and soddy, we were able to have a frame house built. It was small, only two and a half rooms at first, but oh, was it grand compared to that house made out of bare earth. Not having to contend with the dirt alone felt like heaven."

Olivia paused and then blurted out, "That new house was magnificent in comparison!" She placed a shaky hand over her mouth and seemed momentarily overcome with emotion. "It was—at that time—everything I ever wanted, everything I thought I could ever have. And it was enough, more than enough. But . . . soon, to my true amazement, there were scores of just such houses as ours cropping up here and there, dotting the prairie as fast as a spreading wildfire. Well, it turned out this was the new settlement that Mr. George Grant had organized. He was the Englishman who purchased fifty thousand acres from the Kansas Pacific. Wanted to found a new city on the prairie for his people. Englishmen mostly." Again she paused for a long while, and Leah waited patiently for her to go on.

When she didn't, Leah prompted, "What were they like? Did you know any of them?"

Olivia raised both eyebrows. "Oh, that I did. It would have been impossible not to know them really. There were so many of them in need. . . ." She shook her head and smiled ruefully. "So many of them had absolutely no idea what they were doing, how they were supposed to live in the land they'd traveled so far to settle. I felt sorry for them. Don't know how a few of them would have managed as long as they did without my help."

She shook her head and sat up straighter in her chair. "Of course, there were all sorts of other immigrant colonies at the time. There were the Swedes over in Lindborg, the Scottish families up in Scottish Plains on the northern border. The Mennonites, and all the German-Russians in Munjor and Herzog and such. But . . . nothing so fascinating as the Brits. In my opinion, at least." Suddenly she broke off and looked over at her visitor. "You've got a sort of accent yourself. Are you American?"

Leah swallowed and was taken aback for a moment. "Yes. I am now. But I was an Englishwoman for a part of my life."

"Which part was that?"

"Oh . . . mostly my younger years."

"I see."

"I came here," Leah offered, "when I was twenty-three. America is my home now."

Olivia nodded and then looked down at her fingers, which were now entwined. They didn't hurt so much right now. Maybe this talking was doing some real good after all.

"Well, I don't intend to say anything unfriendly about your people or—"

"Please," Leah interrupted, "don't censor anything

you want to say. I just want to hear your story. Your personal interpretations of what happened back then.''

Olivia smiled. '' 'Back then.' Seems like yesterday, or no more than the day before that. Well—'' she leaned back ''—all right then . . . I suppose the reason the Brits were so eager to settle the territory there was because of their founder, this Mr. Grant I told you about. He was a real promoter. But, too, I do think he truly loved the land. There was a lot to love about it at that time, really. Most people would have told it just the opposite: that it was barren no-man's-land. Same as they said about Salina, or any other place in Kansas. Still called it 'bleedin' ' Kansas and all that. But it wasn't the case. There were hardships—plenty of them, and real terrible ones, too—but it had a beauty all its own. The plains were just endless, rolled on and on and on as far as your eye could see. And in the spring it just seemed like someone spread an enormous carpet of flowers across it all. So colorful! It's still beautiful, but there's nothing to compare to the way it looked back then—no fences, no windbreaks; nothing except the land and the sky.''

Olivia shrugged. ''Might sound a tad sentimental to you, perhaps, but it was true. That's what it was like back then. Well, this Grant fellow fell in love with what he saw spread out before him. He made his purchase and went back and organized his colony, and before you could believe it, the first of them were headed into Kansas toward the little town that he named Victoria.'' A grin lit Olivia's face. ''Lord, was that a sight to see!'' She paused and then turned to look at Leah, who was waiting expectantly. ''That was the most interesting period of my life, I guess you could say. Though when I got there, it seemed like the very worst.''

''In what way?''

''Oh, the change, the uprooting and all that. It really affected me in ways I didn't expect. It was just plain starting all over again. So . . . I guess the irony of what happened soon after made it all the more difficult.'' She paused and then said, ''That was when I finally found out what happened to Francis.''

CHAPTER XV

1873

The not-so-distant howling of a band of coyotes sent a familiar sense of loneliness through Olivia. The sound always made her want to go back inside the house, but she didn't want to leave her comfortable chair on the front porch of the new two-bedroom frame house she and Aaron had moved into a few weeks before. It was August, and the heat lingered into the night now, stirred only by the continuous, though gentle southerly winds.

Aaron was asleep already, and she was glad for that much. The trip west two months ago had been difficult for him. He'd been very frightened of the train itself, had sat the entire trip with his back as straight as a ramrod, his eyes, panic-stricken, focused on the passing scenery outside the window. Olivia's attempts to soothe him had been for naught, since he barely seemed aware of anything at all other than his own fear. She'd felt badly for him, hated having to put him through such misery, and could only trust that she was indeed doing the right thing for the both of them.

Now that they were here, in the house finally, it

seemed that things might finally have a chance of becoming normal again. Although for the both of them, the term *normal* wasn't exactly typical. By now she knew Aaron would *never* recover from the attack that had done irrevocable damage to his mind. She no longer expected any change for the better, and so she had come to accept who he was and what he was capable of . . . and no more than that. And if anyone ever attempted to comment about him, or criticize his oftentimes slower mannerisms, she was lightning-quick in her response. She would not tolerate any sort of advice either, no matter what the circumstances. Of course, it was infrequent that such encounters occurred anyway, since she kept Aaron away from any sort of public scrutiny for the most part. She would always live away from the mainstream, she reasoned, for that very reason. She could not bear to witness her brother ridiculed, could not bear to watch him as he struggled so ineffectually against that which was overwhelming to him, and that which he could no longer understand.

All he could deal with now was their situation, his life with her, the only person he could understand or communicate with. It could have been different if Luke had stayed on. But by the time she arrived in Hays, she had managed to put that part of her life behind her. Luke Coyle had been but an aberration in her life, and she'd best forget him completely.

The little house they were now living in had gone up in less than three weeks, a feat that had amazed and thrilled her, for it meant that their days living in the hot, airless hotel in Hays were cut short and she was able to more quickly move Aaron into a stable environment. And, indeed, he'd improved rapidly as soon as they were out of the public eye. Though it took him a while to become used to the new house, with Olivia's patience and help, he had managed to do so. In time they would build on to the shedlike structure that had come with the property, an abandoned squatter's shelter, making it into a proper stable for the two young horses she'd purchased from the army post stable in Fort Hays. All the stock she'd owned in Salina had been sold along with the property, leaving them with the necessity of having to start completely over when they arrived at the new place. They had the house now, and there were plenty of available men willing to hire on when she was ready to start turning the soil and planting the acres of wheat and corn she intended to farm. She already had her two mules, two milk cows, a sow that had already produced a litter, three goats, a flock of hens, and one rooster. She'd gotten them all for a good price in Hays shortly before moving onto the homestead. She'd have a late harvest, but hopefully an adequate one.

Thus had begun her new life.

But now, looking down at the folded sheet of paper on her lap, Olivia considered the wealth of emotions stirring inside her chest at that moment, all of them laced with the keen sense of irony that the information she now possessed was the *real* new beginning.

That morning she had ridden into Hays. She needed items from the general store, and when she was done, she stopped by the army mail office as a matter of course more than anything else. Upon her arrival in Fort Hays, she'd spoken with one of the officers, had related her story to him about her inability to obtain information about Francis, fully expecting him to just shrug and commiserate with her plight. They all did that much; but sympathy she'd had enough of over the years. However, the man volunteered to write to Washington on her behalf, and though she'd been surprised and grateful, she'd assumed that he was merely being kind to her. She expected nothing to come of it.

She had received government letters before, all consistent in content: there was no available information on what had become of Francis. And so as she had opened yet another light blue envelope this morning, she'd experienced the same sense of futility she'd developed over the years. But as she began to read the sentences printed on the onionskin paper, she was stunned beyond measure. Quickly she had glanced back up at the top of the page and confirmed that, yes, the letter was indeed addressed to her, and as she read on, that yes, there it was, his name, Major Francis Joshua Burton.

Her fingers gently and repetitively stroked the page now, a single-page letter she'd never expected to receive. By now she knew every single word of it, for she had read it at least twenty times. Her husband, the words went on in terms of compassion and respect, had died in Culpepper, Virginia, in the spring of 1862. He'd been working in a Confederate hospital and had contracted typhoid, presumably from one of his patients. He himself had spent four weeks as a patient and then had died, not having recovered from the unconsciousness he'd slipped into during the third week. The temporary hospital, the letter mentioned, had been taken by the Union later, and patient records had been lost. Unexpectedly, some had been rediscovered within the past year. The army expressed its extreme regret for the inordinate delay in relaying information about her husband, but hinted that perhaps if Dr. Burton had been more inclined to support his brethren in the Union, the situation would have been different.

A lone coyote howled from some distant bluff as Olivia gazed off across the starlit expanse of land, her entire being acutely aware of that which she'd thought was long since left behind. But, of course, it was still out there, always had been. It seemed she could just get up and start walking, step by step, across the prairie that stretched out boundlessly until it met with the horizon, journeying to that point in time that was her past. And there she could simply walk up to him, her husband, her lover, the father of her first conceived child, and stretch out her arms to him. Again she would feel the secure strength of his arms wrapped around her, and her world would be as once it had been.

Another coyote's plaintive cry joined the first, and she was brought out of her reverie. She glanced back down at the letter and slowly began to fold it into a tiny square. It was a distraction, but a useless one, for she was still possessed, to the very root of her being, with the presence of him, the reality of his existence. It was overwhelming; despite the warmth, her body shuddered as chills spread from her head to her feet. She yearned to cry, desperately so. She longed for someone to be with her right now, someone to place an arm around her and tell her that it was all right. But this was the most childish feeling of all, she realized, a fantasy that had no basis in reality.

There was no one there, and she had no choice but to confront what she had confronted too many times before in her thirty-two years of life. Another death . . . another loss. At least she'd found out about him, a small voice whispered in the back of her head. But another, stronger one asserted itself also. Despite the relief she was certain would come from finally knowing what had become of him, some part of her had never quit believing that surely he might one day return. Even while in the throes of her passion for Luke, she had known this much about herself. As long as she had not found out anything bad, there was always the possibility that Francis was still alive, that he would be coming back to her. He was out there *somewhere*.

She swallowed, with difficulty, for a lump had formed in the back of her throat. What was so difficult now, what was so painfully difficult to recognize, was that he had been gone—had been dead—almost from the very beginning. Less than a year after he'd left, he'd died. And she'd spent eleven years wondering, hoping, sometimes *believing*, that he was still alive. This was the part she found most difficult to reconcile. When she'd thought things were one way, they were, in fact, completely the opposite all along.

She swallowed again and heard the paper crinkle as her fingers dug into the tiny square of it. The coyotes picked up their plaintive call again, and the sound seemed to soar upward, into the midnight-blue sky, an echo of the sound ripping through her heart.

The sound of grief, deep, penetrating grief that could find no release, no solace.

The hot, arid summer air turned quite chilly as autumn made an earlier than normal appearance that year. With each passing day Olivia felt the pall of grief easing up in her mind and in her heart. The more she worked, she discovered, the more she was able to cope with her long-delayed, but much-needed time of mourning. Aaron seemed to thrive with each passing day, and as he did so, he began to take an interest once more in things outside himself. He even, Olivia noted with welcome relief, began to talk more than his usual limit of six or seven sentences, and those only consisting of a few words each. Indeed, on a few occasions she was able to engage him in semidiscussion, though it was still much like talking with a small child. It was as though, she earnestly believed now, God had intended for him to be the child she had never had, the child she had wanted with all her being. Not many people could understand such a sentiment, but she didn't care what other people thought. She understood her own heart, and that was all that counted.

"Aaron," she said one bright, cool morning as she cleared away the breakfast dishes, "I'll be riding into Hays this morning for a few things. I'm going to talk with that man I told you about before. Remember the man I mentioned last week?''

Aaron shook his head back and forth slowly, a crease etched deeply into his broad, handsome forehead. His green eyes were as clear and beautiful as they'd always been, but they darted rapidly around the room, as if he were searching for something. This was a tic that had started two years ago, and of all his aberrant mannerisms, it was the most disturbing to Olivia. Much as she forced herself to ignore it, she worried about it, wondered what it could mean. She would not take him to see a doctor about it, of course, for she feared yet another diagnosis of insanity. But more than the fear of diagnosis was the fear of recommended treatment: that Aaron be sent to an asylum. She'd been advised in such a way once before, by a particularly self-righteous and judgmental doctor in Salina, and had vowed to never, ever get herself, or her brother, into such a situation again. She and she alone was his caretaker, and no one, no doctor or any other given to unsolicited advice, would ever mention such a possible ''solution'' to her again. She'd commit herself right along with him before she'd allow Aaron such a horrible fate.

''You don't remember?'' she asked again. Gradually Aaron's eyes stopped darting about and focused on her face.

''The cutter?''

Olivia smiled gently as she wiped a dampened rag across the dark-stained oak table. ''Yes, that's the one.'' She straightened up and neatly folded the dustcloth. ''His name is Cutter Singleberry. Kind of a silly name, isn't it?''

Aaron, who was standing now near the front window, his favorite place in the whole house, nodded once or twice.

''I think so, too. I think he said he was a woodcutter once, didn't he?''

Aaron shrugged. His arms were crossed, his hands tucked inside each armpit. From his stance, Olivia could tell that this would not be one of those times when he would join her in conversation. So she simply went on talking, explaining what she had in mind for the day.

"Well, anyway, I've thought it over, and I think we should hire him. We have to begin work on the shed; there are just too many problems with it as it is."

"Need another fork," Aaron said, turning his head suddenly toward her.

"Yes, that's right. We do need another pitchfork. That's what we've been talking about all week. What else did we decide to buy?"

Aaron stared straight ahead for almost half a minute and then his eyes met hers. "Soap. Some soap."

"That's right. Some saddle soap. The special kind that smells so good. The one you like to use."

Aaron nodded rapidly and then resumed staring out the window.

Olivia untied her apron, removed it, and then hung it on a peg in the corner near the stove. Her heavy calfskin boots were near the back door on a rag rug, and she picked one up and began unlacing it. "You'll be all right if I just ride into town for a short visit, won't you?"

Slowly he nodded, though she could see that his eyes had begun their darting motion again, this time darting about the landscape, looking, always looking. His eyes, she had long since recognized, were the source of the fatigue that overcame him so early every evening. He could not stop looking, searching, waiting. He would never stop.

But he was learning to tolerate her absences if she could manage to assure him that he was safe if he remained inside the house. There were only the front door and the back, and adequate bolts reinforced both. But she had added a locking mechanism to the windows also, and along with these mechanical precautions, had never once failed to return when she said she would. Her efforts had paid off, for he was, if only very slightly, a little less dependent on her.

"I'll saddle up Rainy and set off then, all right? Might as well get an early start."

With the sound of her opening the back door, Aaron suddenly swung into action, hastening his inspection of the front door bolt, the windows, and then finally, coming behind her, closing the door as she left. She heard the heavy wooden bolt slide into place almost immediately.

She walked swiftly toward the shed, for though her dress and coat were of good, strong quality, the wind was stiff and chilly, and cut through the fabric of both. Rainy, a mixed-breed gelding, was foraging about in his stall for a bit of hay among the bed of straw. There was hardly a piece left, for he'd long since eaten what Aaron had tossed in earlier that morning. Rainy was the name he'd come with, and so Olivia had kept it, but she'd often thought a more apt name would have been Ravenous, as he was certainly the fastest and most voracious eater she'd ever encountered. He'd eat as much as she would give him, and that in the span of a mere few minutes, for he seemed to be constantly hungry. He had trouble keeping on the weight he had, so she did give him extra rations, but the necessity of doing so was rapidly driving up her feed bill. Nevertheless, his good side far outweighed the bad. He was the kindest, most well-broken horse she'd ever ridden, his gaits as smooth as molasses.

She brushed Rainy thoroughly, ran the steel comb through his mane and tail and then tacked him up. She mounted him easily, for he'd been taught to inch forward with his front hooves, thereby lowering himself to accommodate her lesser height. Each and every time the horse did this, Olivia patted his neck and cooed as one would to a baby, and then prayed fervently for his continuing good health.

The ride into Hays did not take long usually, for she was only five miles beyond its outer skirts. She could not resist slowing the horse down, however, as her eye was caught by the activity going on in the distance. Smack-dab in the middle of the endless stretch of prairie, there were now newly built houses dotting the brand-new settlement called Victoria. Olivia had heard of the land purchase by the Englishman, Sir George Grant, the previous year, but she had not believed anything would really come of his stated plans to start a colony there, mostly of English settlers.

But, as it now appeared, she, along with many other homesteaders in the area who'd believed as she had, had been proven wrong. In May of that year the first of the colony arrived, and within weeks the sounds of building could be heard across the prairie. As Olivia rode on toward Hays, she could clearly see some of the houses, most of them designed as two- or three-room clapboards. There were others, though, far larger and grander in scale, the most well known among them Sir George Grant's two-story manor house, which Olivia had seen on a couple of occasions.

As she traveled the newly forged roads that ran through the skirted Victoria, she passed several horse-drawn carriages. From across the prairie, she heard the clarion notes of French horns, followed by the yelping cries of scores of hounds. Rainy pricked up his ears instantly and reacted with a quickened pace as he both heard and felt the pounding of horses' hooves setting off across the bluestem in pursuit of whatever prey had been chosen for the day's hunt. Across the plains Olivia caught sight of the group of them, men and women alike, racing their mounts in a close pack. The men wore tan or white riding breeches and scarlet jackets, the women forest-green or dark blue riding habits. The latter she'd seen up close once before, and had marveled at their construction, admiring their flattering design yet at the same time disdainful of the dangerous, ground-sweeping length of the skirt.

Olivia shook her head, and watched the party disappear onto the other side of a bluff. As she dismounted and secured her horse's reins to the hitching post in front of Hinkley's Hay and Feed Supply, she was still thinking of this new element in her world, one both fascinating and disconcerting. So immersed was she in her own thoughts that she almost crashed full tilt into a woman coming down the steps of the tin-roofed building.

"Excuse me, but I . . ." Olivia began, and then stopped, her mouth remaining open, her eyes narrowing curiously as she stood face-to-face with the woman before her. She knew the woman, recognized something in her facial expression, the large dark brown, piercing eyes.

Slowly the woman, her face heavily lined and sundarkened, surveyed Olivia's own features, perusing them in an embarrassingly intense manner. Olivia took a step back and started to speak, but the older woman preempted her attempt.

With a hand held outward, forefinger pointed directly at Olivia, she said, "Summer of fifty-nine. You traveled overland with me and my family, didn't you? Your name . . . Audrey . . . no, Olivia. Right?" The woman's face broadened into a big grin, revealing an incomplete set of teeth.

Olivia was dumbfounded. It was the woman she had gotten to know so well on the wagon train from Atchison to Salina. The only woman in attendance at her wedding. But she couldn't remember her name! Redness flooded her cheeks as she smiled back. "Yes. That's my name. But, I . . . I can't remember . . ."

"Leona. Leona McGill. And let's see; your last name

is Sands. Or was." The woman shifted the bulky burlap bag she was carrying, resting it against the opposite hip. "And you had a brother, name of Al . . . Allen . . . no, no, was it Aaron?" Noting Olivia's nod, the woman went on, in a loud tone, completely unaware that other customers were standing nearby, watching the exchange. "And let's see here, you had a couple of horses—enormous creatures. Names were Sampson and Whiskers." She snapped the thumb and forefinger of one hand and said, "Right?" Her eyes were filled with delight at the display of an obviously prodigious memory.

"I can't believe . . ." Olivia half whispered. "I can't believe you remember all that."

"Oh yes. And the man." At that point Leona winced, chewing one side of her mouth. "Now, don't say a word. . . ." Suddenly she snapped her fingers and blurted out, "Francis Burton. The good doctor. You two were hitched up before the party left Salina. That was some wedding."

At that, Olivia's eyes began to tear up and she lowered her head. Then she looked back up and uttered a half laugh through the tears. "You haven't missed a thing. I can't believe you're . . . well, you're there. Here, I mean. I mean it seems impossible after all these years. . . ."

Leona leaned down, placed the sack against the railing, and said, "Honey, let me tell you somethin'. Nothing's impossible in this crazy world. Why, I guess it must have been written in the cards for us to meet up again." She took a step downward and stretched out her arms. "C'mere. Give me a big hug. I was your matron of honor, for heaven's sake."

There on the steps of Hinkley's, Leona McGill pulled Olivia into her arms and hugged her as tightly as if she were her own long-lost daughter. Oblivious to the customers watching the mini spectacle, Olivia hugged her back, not even attempting anymore to hold back her tears. Though she had thought often of the woman in whom she had confided in those awful days after her mother's death, had longed for just such a friend again, she had never in her wildest dreams imagined they would meet up again. But the tears were more than that; they were also representative of all she had worked so diligently these past few months to put behind: the memories of her youth, the days of Aaron's innocence and good health. And, of course, those early days of getting to know Francis, her wedding beneath the cottonwood tree on the banks of the Kansas River.

She did not realize that her entire body was shaking until Leona, patting her on the back, said softly, "Shhh. It's all right. We can talk about it."

Olivia pulled back and wiped her eyes with the underside of her thumbs. "Sorry."

"No need to be sorry. I think I gave you a severe fright is all."

"No, you haven't frightened me at all. Just . . . well . . ."

"What are you here for? At the store, I mean."

"Oh, just a few items. I really came to talk to a man about helping out on my place. It's . . ." Olivia looked around as if trying to regain the ground that had been suddenly pulled out from under her.

"You go on inside and get whatever you need, and I'll put this in Mr. Ellison's wagon and come right back and meet you."

"Mr. Ellison?"

"The man I work for," Leona explained, looking off to one side and then giving a roll of her eyes. "He's havin' his 'cuppa' right now at the Section House Depot."

Olivia frowned in confusion, and Leona went on, "Mr. Ellison's a Brit, and you know how they are.

Fussy about their tea and crumpets and all that sort of stuff. But he's one of the nicer ones . . . a real looker if you ask me."

"Well, I . . ."

"Look, I'll just do as I said, and be right back. I'll explain more when I come back. Unless you're in a big hurry?"

"Well, I do have to get back to the house before noon."

"Then I'll be quick about it. And you do the same."

"All right then."

Leona smiled again and hustled down the steps out onto the gravel sidewalk, leaving Olivia to stare at her retreating figure. Then, noticing that a woman and her two young daughters were watching, having actually stopped dead in their steps a few feet away, Olivia hurried up the steps and into the feed store.

She was finished with her transaction in a mere five minutes and then went around back to meet with Cutter Singleberry. The man, lean and wiry and somewhere in his early fifties, was sweating profusely as he tossed bales of hay into an overhead bin. His hair, almost completely white, was threaded with the fragrant light green stalks of hay, and as he talked with Olivia, he continuously picked pieces of the stuff off his face and eyebrows, occasionally turning his head and spitting out a strand or two onto the dirt floor.

"Yes'm, I can get started any time you want. All you have to say is when."

Olivia, startled by the eagerness of his acceptance of her offer, had to consider for a moment her answer. "Well then, how about tomorrow? Is that too soon?"

"Nope. Be just fine."

"There won't be a problem with your job here?"

"Nope. I work when I feel like it here. And I don't feel like it one bit anymore. You need some buildin' done; that's my thing. Second to loggin', of course, since I done that since I was a youngun, but there sure ain't no loggin' business out here.''

"That's true enough," Olivia agreed. She had met Cutter on several occasions before, and now had to stop and think what had taken her so long to decide to ask him to work for her. She had taken a liking to the codger since the very first.

"All right then," she said, giving him a big smile. "I'll see you at your convenience in the morning. You know how to get there, don't you?"

"Sure do," Cutter said, then bent to the side and spat. "Know just about every house in these parts. Yours is not hard at all to find."

"Well, good then. I'm looking forward to it, Mr. Singleberry."

"Cutter. Just Cutter."

"All right, Cutter. Good-bye, then."

Leona was waiting for her in the front lot of the feed store, and she moved quickly toward Olivia as she saw her coming.

"Are you all finished?"

"Yes," Olivia said, pulling the drawstring on her reticule.

Leona held out a small cheesecloth bag and said, somewhat sheepishly, "I had another idea. Might seem silly, but see, I usually bring myself something to eat while Mr. Ellison is inside the Depot." She shrugged. "Guess I feel kind of silly going in the place for a sit-down meal when my employer is inside having his. Doesn't seem right to my way of thinkin'. Anyway, I'd be happy to share this with you."

"In what capacity are you employed?" Olivia asked.

"I'm Mr. Ellison's housekeeper. It's not bad, actually. He's got a cook for all his fancy dinners, so for once in my life, I don't have to do anything over a hot stove. Just keep house is all."

"But," Olivia said, appearing confused, "I don't quite understand. . . ."

"How it is that I'm a housekeeper for some Englishman bachelor? Well," Leona said, sighing heavily and placing the palm of one hand on the small of her back, which she arched delicately, "it's a heck of a long story."

"I don't mind listening," Olivia said. "And I'd love to share with you whatever you have. I don't want to go inside either. Let's find someplace to sit down. Over there, near the maple. We can just sit on that log."

The two women crossed the feed store yard and took a seat on a fallen birch that no one had bothered to move, and that was as smooth as hewn wood. Leona began removing bread and cheese from the bag, and turning to Olivia, smiled ruefully and said, "But I'd wager you have a lot to talk about yourself, don'tcha?"

Olivia nodded, feeling the lump rising in her throat again. At last, she thought, grateful for the relief that washed over her in comforting waves. At last here was someone to talk to. Someone who knew her from years past. Someone, she recognized instinctively, who would understand. She'd been alone for too long. She hadn't realized until that moment how much she longed for female company.

Impulsively she reached for Leona's hand. "Yes, I do have a lot to talk about. But really, it's enough just seeing you, Leona McGill. That's the truth."

Leona placed her other hand atop Olivia's and squeezed. She knew exactly what the younger woman meant. She'd come across lots of women over the years, stranded alone on the plains. Some of them went out of their heads eventually. It was difficult enough coping with the harshness of daily life, but to have to do so alone was simply cruel. She could see still the girl she remembered so vividly from the journey west some fifteen years ago. But not much of her was left. It was inevitable, of course, but still it seemed sad.

"Well, let's both get started, then," Leona said cheerfully. "Food first, talk second."

"All right," Olivia agreed, smiling as she accepted the chunk of cheese Leona handed her.

CHAPTER XVI

THE acrid odor of ammonia assaulted Olivia's nose as she entered the shed barn. Aaron, though he had been helping all along in pitching hay, graining, and mucking stalls, had quite clearly been less than effective in his efforts.

But Cutter seemed oblivious to the smell. Indeed, he appeared to relish his new work, for today, like every day for the past two weeks since he'd been working for Olivia, he whistled continuously. He did not whistle idly, but in a clear, melodic tone, utilizing specific tunes that he had perfected. The sound was pleasing to the ear; Olivia had gotten to where she expected it. The improvements he'd made on the shed were remarkable; altogether, Olivia could hardly believe her good fortune in obtaining his services. She'd learned more about him since he'd arrived. A widower, he had lost his only son at Bull Run; his wife had died twenty years before. In '58 he'd traveled to the Pacific Northwest and eventually become a logger; he'd loved the occupation so much, he still thought of himself as such. He reiterated this point on several occasions. He'd come back east only to find his son, to see if he'd come back to the Northwest with him, become a partner, but Fort Hays was as far as he'd gotten. It was there that he found out his son's fate. So he'd just stayed on, having lost the heart to return to where he'd left.

He appeared happy enough now, at least as far as Olivia could ascertain. With her permission he'd built, in addition to four additional stalls, a room for himself. In the span of a week he'd decorated it with a variety of pelts and various heads of animals he'd killed, stuffed, and mounted himself. Olivia had seen the room once, and had expressed her amazement, which Cutter took to be the highest of compliments.

Cutter was good to Aaron. Like Luke, he harbored no prejudice toward the young man's deficiencies, and from the start, demonstrated a remarkable patience with him. Little by little, Aaron seemed to be emerging from his shell. He woke up early now and was in the barn with the older man before breakfast, ready and willing to gain instruction from him.

Now she could see Aaron and Cutter together, finishing up the last of the deep mucking job that had been ignored for so long. Cutter had already saddled up Rainy for her, and the horse pawed the ground where he stood tied to a wooden hitching ring in the middle of the newly added barn addition.

Olivia untied the reins and said in a loud voice, "I'm leaving now, Cutter. Aaron."

Cutter stepped out into the aisleway and wiped an arm against his brow. "You headin' over to Mr. Ellison's place again?"

"Yes. To see Mrs. McGill."

Cutter nodded. "Well, be careful then."

"I'm not certain how long I'll be gone."

"Me and Aaron'll take care of ourselves just fine."

Olivia grinned and then tugged on the reins, leading Rainy toward the mounting block Cutter had built for

her. It wasn't really necessary, especially since Rainy
was such an accommodating animal, but Cutter had insisted. "Cain't have all these highfalutin Brits around
here with their fancy Thoroughbreds and such and not
even have a mounting block. Why, you're as pretty as
all them other 'ladies of leisure'; you sure deserve a
mountin' block at the very least."

Olivia, thinking it was a silly notion, had nevertheless let him go ahead with it. Now she used it every
day and was glad for it, along with all the other little
conveniences Cutter provided, things he could make
but were too expensive for her to purchase. He'd put
together a few items of furniture already, but that which
she loved most, for it was by far the most useful, was
the clothesline he constructed. No more stringing rope
between trees, always having to hitch it back up again,
and hoping the wind wouldn't wreak too much damage. Now she had a twenty-foot clothesline, good-
quality hemp rope nailed and stretched nice and taut
between six-foot solid oak posts driven two feet into
the ground. It made wash day a great deal easier; that
was certain.

The ride to the Ellison place—"estate," according to
its owner, Mr. David Ellison, whom she had not yet
met—was a mere two miles. As soon as she rounded
the left-hand turn in the road about three-quarters of a
mile from her own place, she could see it. The house
was a one-story affair, containing four rooms, had a
twelve-foot porch all the way around, and behind it was
an equally well-constructed carriage house. Both build-
ings were painted pastel blue, and latticework had been
added along the eaves, which gave it a most charming
effect.

Olivia always shook her head at the sight of it. Such
a house for just one man! It was preposterous! Down-
right wasteful, in fact. But that was an envious thought
and so she quickly chastised herself for having it. But

to think that Leona lived there now, as a housekeeper
. . . well, it still seemed not right, even after all these
weeks. It was simply incredible to Olivia that the older
woman's life had come to this. Her husband had been
killed in the war, and with her children she'd gone
west to start a new life in Oregon. Leona had gone
back east as far as Fort Hays until she got word of her
husband's fate, and when she learned of it, had not
had the energy nor gumption to leave, much the same
as Cutter had felt after learning of his son's death. Her
daughter, young as she was, had married a man twice
her age, and Leona's son had moved in with them.
They all seemed to be perfectly happy. Leona told
Olivia she just couldn't see traveling west again, joining up with a son-in-law near her own age and his new
family, which used to be *her* family. So she had just
stayed on, working in the hotel for a while and then
as a clerk in the general store, living in a rooming
house all the while.

She'd applied as housekeeper for Mr. Ellison last
spring and had been hired immediately. So far, so good,
she'd told Olivia, but she admitted she still had no idea
who her employer really was, what he thought, or why
he had chosen to travel all the way to the heartland of
America, giving up all he'd left behind. And apparently
he'd left quite a lot behind. It didn't make one iota of
sense to Leona.

Each and every time she saw Olivia, Leona would
harp on this one subject. And today, it appeared, would
be no exception.

Olivia found her on the front porch, broom in hand
as she swept. As Olivia dismounted, Leona called out,
"Glad you came. I'm 'bout ready to lose my sanity."

Olivia looped the reins over the hickory hitching post
and made her way down the pathway toward the porch.
"What's the matter?"

"Him. That's what."

Olivia frowned and placed a finger over her lips. "Shhh. You'll lose your job if he hears you talking like that."

"Hah! That man? He doesn't hear a word I say. All I hear is, 'Mrs. McGill, how are you today? Good evening, Mrs. McGill.'" She imitated, hilariously, her employer's accent. "He couldn't care less what I actually do around here."

"Then why do anything at all?" Olivia took a seat on the wicker divan.

Leona stopped sweeping and leaned an arm on her broom handle. "I couldn't stand livin' here and not earnin' my keep. And if I didn't do anything, the place would be a shambles in no time." She shook her head. "You've seen these people. Don't have a hair of an idea about where they really are. Think they're off in Cornwall or some such place."

Olivia laughed outright. In her own, not particularly articulate, manner, Leona had put her finger exactly on the character of the English colony living in Victoria. They really did spend all of their time acting as if they were off on some wonderful safari. It was amazing, truly amazing. In town one glimpsed this by observing the new settlers who arrived daily, bringing with them all manner of luxury items from home: fine clothing, high-bred livestock, including sheep, Thoroughbred horses—used primarily for the "hunt"—and cattle. Everyone, it seemed, was determined to mimic the city's founder, Sir Grant, whose typical day of social engagements involved games of cricket, high tea, and lavish dinner parties.

"They're over here every evening, I tell you. Never seen so many visitors in my life."

"Like who?"

Leona waved a hand in the air. "Oh, I don't know all their names. Mr. Ellison's cronies, is all. Brits, all, that's for sure."

Olivia grinned. "You wouldn't have any prejudice against the British, now would you?"

"Course not. I think they're a fine people. Real pleasant, actually. All that proper talk and all. You get to where you like it."

"Then why do you sound so exasperated?"

"Oh, because I just think they're *too* nice. I mean, you can see it for yourself, can't you? They don't do anything really productive at all. Oh, it's all been said before and . . ." As her voice trailed off, both of them looked out across the rise of prairie to the north of the quarter section of property. Four mounted riders crested the small hill, and then, coming down over it, bounded forward in a headlong chase toward the house.

The horses were huge, sleek Thoroughbreds, and the sight of them racing neck and neck, their riders leaning forward, spurring and cropping them onward, ever faster, was truly a sight to behold. Indeed, it was a form of horsemanship that Olivia had certainly never seen before, and one with which she'd become increasingly fascinated. She could not pull her sight away from the four riders; and grudgingly she admitted a sort of envy. It didn't make sense, she told herself; she had a wonderful horse herself, and he could race like the wind, if she chose to put him to the test. But it wasn't the horse; it was something far more compelling than that.

As the riders neared the house, one of the women threw back her head and uttered a laugh, a beautiful, melodious, infectious laugh. It was that more than anything that clarified for Olivia what intrigued her so about the group of Brits. It was but another demonstration of their carefree, lighthearted attitude toward their lives. Not since she was a child had Olivia been so nonchalant, so heedless in any pursuit. And it seemed, very clearly, that these people, adults all, had never been anything but thus.

The group directed their horses to the hitching post where Rainy stood tied. A groom approached quickly from the side of the house and began speaking with the tall, blond man in the group.

Leona placed her broom quickly against the wall and began smoothing the knot at her nape. "That's him. Mr. Ellison."

Olivia stood up and said, "You didn't tell me he would be here. I don't want to hold up your work."

"I didn't know he'd get back so early. He's usually gone the entire day on Monday." She turned to look at Olivia, who was red-faced and still staring at David Ellison. "Now, look here, don't just run off. That's silly. I'll introduce you to him. Intended to all along." She reached back and gave a good jerk on the ties on her apron. "Do him a sight good to meet a red-blooded American woman."

"Leona!" Olivia half whispered. The horses were being led away toward the stable, and Mr. Ellison and his guests were heading up the pathway toward the front porch.

"Ah, Mrs. McGill, you're here," David Ellison said as he mounted the steps. "I do so hope you have a refreshing bit of drink prepared for us. We're absolutely dry all round."

"Would you care for lemonade?" Leona asked. Olivia was astonished by the lightning-quick change in Leona's manners. Gone was the critical attitude; in its place was a cheerful, subservient one. As Leona turned to fetch the refreshments, she suddenly remembered Olivia standing there.

"Oh, Mr. Ellison, this is my friend, Olivia Burton. She lives up the way a bit. Been meaning to introduce you two, but you've never been home when she's called."

Olivia was embarrassed by the last statement, but she simply smiled and said, "Hello. Nice to meet you, Mr. Ellison."

"Delighted," the man said, grinning broadly. "But please, do call me David. We all go by first names, right, Morris?"

The older man, standing between a woman his age and another some twenty years younger, nodded. "Righto."

David Ellison held one hand outward toward his friends. "These are my good friends—and possibly your own neighbors—Morris and Anna Talbott, and their daughter, Meredith."

Hellos were exchanged, and Olivia noticed that Leona had already hustled inside the house. "Well," she said, "I'll be leaving, then. Very nice to have met you all. Perhaps we'll meet again soon."

"Please," Ellison said earnestly, pulling more wicker chairs out from against the wall and placing them round a small glass and wicker table. "Join us, won't you? We need to meet our neighbors. I'm sure there's plenty of lemonade for all of us."

"Yes, do stay," Anna Talbott said, smiling winningly. "We'd love to talk with you. Actually," she said, taking a seat, as did her husband and daughter, "we know very few Americans. It's odd, I suppose, but we've only been here a short while. The only people we know are the ones that were in our party coming over, and, of course, David, who arrived before we did."

"It's true," said Meredith, reaching up to remove the pin attaching her velvet riding hat onto her thick mane of dark auburn hair. "Father keeps us too isolated. It's ridiculous."

Morris grumbled in an affectionate manner, "Pshhhh. Ridiculous. Rubbish. Always place the blame on good old Father. Doesn't matter what the subject's about."

David Ellison pulled over another chair and, standing behind it, gave a beckoning tilt of his head. "Please, Olivia, have a seat."

Olivia smiled and relented, taking her place in the proffered chair. "Thank you very much."

Leona returned in no time, it seemed, the cook following behind her. It struck Olivia as odd that she had come merely to visit her friend and was now being put in the position of being served by her. However, Leona seemed to take little notice of the change in social arrangement, cheerfully going about the business of serving her employer and his guests, fussing over all of them equally.

It seemed that almost instantly Olivia fit right in, and she was pleasantly gratified by this. She stayed far longer than she'd originally intended, but every minute of the visit seemed worthwhile. Much of the conversation was about the cross-country ride the Talbotts and Mr. Ellison had just returned from, with many anecdotal references as to the peculiarities and advantages—or disadvantages—of each individual horse. Olivia listened politely, thinking that for all the declared interest in discussing things American, the four of them seemed quite content to keep the conversation centered on themselves. And, of course, their equine friends.

She was starting to grow quite bored when David Ellison finally said, "Enough about our horses. We'd like to hear about Olivia here, wouldn't we?"

Questions were asked as to Olivia's life on the plains, and all eyebrows were raised when she revealed that she was not married, had not been for over a decade since her husband was killed in the War between the States. But despite the proclaimed interest, Olivia noted that it was mostly polite inquiry, a certain form of decorum with which she was unfamiliar. She did not give prolonged answers, and before long, Meredith made yet another remark about her horse, and the conversation reverted to its former topic.

Something about their unconcerned display of self-absorption did not sit well with Olivia, and so she finished her lemonade and pushed her chair backward. "Excuse me for interrupting, but I really must be on my way."

Instantly David Ellison stood up and said, "We're no doubt boring you senseless with all this chatter."

"No, not at all. I really am expected back soon."

"We've enjoyed meeting you," Morris Talbott said, and his wife and daughter murmured their agreement. "Since we're neighbors, we'll no doubt meet again. Soon, perhaps."

"Yes. I hope so."

As she walked toward the porch steps, with David Ellison following her, Leona was just coming through the doorway with another pitcher of lemonade and a plate full of crumpets. She stopped and said, "You're not leaving, are you?"

"Yes, I must," Olivia replied. "Come over when you get a chance."

"I daresay I haven't been lenient enough with your time, Mrs. McGill," David said. "You should have told me you had such a good friend. Any time you'd like to visit Olivia—any time—feel free."

"That's very kind of you, Mr. Ellison." Leona spoke sweetly.

Again Olivia was astonished by the almost fawning manner her friend employed toward Mr. Ellison. But admittedly, she couldn't help being impressed with the man himself and was flattered when he took the trouble to accompany her to where her horse stood. He was a truly handsome man, and she had to confess an undeniable attraction toward him.

She was further impressed with his directness when he said as she swung up into the saddle, "I would very much like it if you would visit again, Olivia. I enjoyed your company tremendously. We all did."

"Thank you. I'm sure we'll meet again."

"Very soon, I hope." His warm brown eyes held her own gaze a moment longer than was really appropriate, and suddenly she was flooded with a feeling she had not experienced in a long while: the sense of her body coming alive, an acute awareness of her femininity.

She smiled, thanked him again, and pressed her heels into Rainy's sides, urging him forward. She was reluctant to leave and yet eager to get away. She put Rainy into a slow trot and then a smooth canter, until he seemed winded and slowed down of his own accord. For the last half mile toward her house, the horse resumed a leisurely walk. She pulled the brim of her sunbonnet down low over her eyes to shade out the midday sunlight. Had she misinterpreted the little scenario with David just now? "David," she chastised herself. She was already thinking of him on a personal level.

"Silly me," she muttered aloud. Best to forget about the man, she told herself firmly. But why? a small, urgent voice questioned. Because he was different from her? Because in all likelihood he viewed her as nothing more than a friendly neighbor? But what did that matter if she liked him and he liked her?

"Good Lord," she muttered louder this time, causing Rainy to pick up his ears. Even the horse was responding to her strange mood.

But still, even as she rode toward the barn, even as she dismounted Rainy and gathered his reins to lead him inside, the image of David Ellison was with her. And, as it turned out, remained with her for the rest of the entire day.

* * *

She received word from him two days later. The Negro groom she had seen at his place rode up to the house to personally deliver a message in letter form. She thanked the man, watched him ride off again, and then slit open the top of the letter with her fingernail. Inside was a brief correspondence, followed by an invitation to a dinner party the following Friday evening. If she did not respond, he indicated, he would take it she meant to come. He would truly appreciate her attendance and was very much looking forward to seeing her again.

Olivia was hit by a tremendous surge of excitement as she read the invitation. At once she was flattered, excited, and nervous. How long had it been since she'd attended a social? Except for one or two back in Salina, she couldn't recall. Of course, she would attend, she immediately thought, and in the next second realized with a sinking sensation that she had absolutely nothing to wear to the affair. At least nothing of the sort that the other women would be wearing. At once she recognized that this was a long-since-abandoned reaction on her part also: the desire to parade her own femininity as much as the next woman. After years of living a totally practical life, one in which clothes were merely a necessity and nothing else, she felt that something had been awakened in her, something that had never gone away completely, but had merely lain in dormancy for well over a decade. Years of behavior, even thought patterns based solely on matters of sheer necessity, suddenly were crumbling in the face of this one small, insignificant invitation.

But of course, it wasn't at all insignificant, was it? The truth was, she could no more deny the anticipation she felt than she could deny the wind across the prairie. There was no question as to what she would do. Her decision had been made the instant she read the last sentence of David's letter. For months she'd observed these people from another land, who quite obviously were of far better means than she had ever known. Though she could never profess to understand them, the undeniable reality was that their enthusiasm was infectious, and enviable. It was almost impossible to observe them, or, as she had two days ago, to be with them, and not desire at least a part of their seemingly carefree outlook. Life on the plains was difficult and trying enough as it was. The need for distraction was almost overwhelming at times, and here was the chance for it. She would be foolish to decline the invitation.

But still, there was the matter of dress. What in the world could she do? There was absolutely no time to stitch up anything on her own, and it was impossible to ride into Hays and have a dressmaker whip something up in short order. No, she would have to do something else.

But she had no idea what.

The answer came in a most unexpected manner, and from an equally unexpected guest who arrived that afternoon. From the garden, Olivia heard hooves clopping along the drive that circled round to the stable. She was kneeling down, bent over burgeoning rows of strawberry plants that she was weeding, when she looked up, curious as to whom the visitor might be. Aaron and Cutter were at the back of the stable, working on the new tack room.

Olivia was startled to see that the rider was none other than the young Talbott woman. Completely surprised, Olivia stood up and dusted the dirt from her hands and arms.

"Hello there," Meredith called out from where she sat atop her mount. Once more Olivia was enchanted with her unusual melodic voice.

"Hello," Olivia returned the greeting. "What a nice surprise to see you."

Meredith grinned and cocked her head to one side. "I do hope you won't consider it an imposition that I just rode up like this. I've been out putting Moritz here—" she patted the sleek gray Thoroughbred on the neck "—through his paces. He must be worked daily or he's no more fit than a snail. Anyway . . ." She raised one shoulder. "I saw this house and thought it must be yours. Mr. Ellison's housekeeper told us after you left what it looked like. So . . . I decided to drop by. I hope it's not horribly inconvenient for you."

"No, not at all," Olivia said, pulling back a wisp of hair that had blown directly across her eyes. She felt like a pauper compared to the beautifully attired young woman. Dressed in a dark green wool riding habit, Meredith looked absolutely stunning, her perfect posture in the sidesaddle setting off to glorious advantage her slender, yet softly rounded figure.

"Would you like to come inside? I have coffee from midday. Or I could make a pot of tea, if you prefer."

With graceful, catlike agility, Meredith dismounted her horse. "That would be wonderful. I'm tremendously thirsty." She stood with the reins in her hand and glanced around, as if expecting a groom to emerge from somewhere.

Olivia approached her and said, "Unfortunately, there's no one here to help with your horse. Will he stand tied?"

"Oh, of course. He's got wonderful manners, despite the fact he's so terribly spoiled." Meredith handed the reins to Olivia, who led the horse a few feet away to the hitching rail. She tied the reins loosely while Meredith loosened the girth and removed the saddle, propping it several feet away on the same railing.

"Come inside, then," Olivia said, leading the way toward the back of the house.

Inside, it did not take long for Meredith to make herself at home. As Olivia set about boiling a kettle of water, the young woman drifted about the kitchen and parlor, talking as she let her gaze survey the furnishings and artifacts of this decidedly American household.

"Quite a nice little place you have here," she remarked, turning to face Olivia. "A real charmer."

"Thank you," Olivia said. "Why don't you sit down?"

But Meredith seemed so out of place sitting at the oak trestle table in all her finery that Olivia had to stare for a moment. Then she went about setting cups and saucers down and pouring the tea into each.

"Mmmm," Meredith murmured as she took a sip. "Very good. Scotney's?"

"No. But I like this one very much." Actually, Olivia had no idea what brand it was.

"Mmmm." Meredith set her cup down and then, with her elbows on the table, linked her hands together and cupped her chin atop them. Her large, gray eyes focused directly on Olivia. "It's very odd, you know."

"What's that?"

"Your living here alone. Must be quite difficult with your not being married and all." She clucked her tongue, smiled, and added, "I apologize. That must've sounded quite intrusive—rude—to say the least. It's a fault of mine that Mother and Father never tire of reminding me."

"Well," Olivia replied slowly, "I don't really mind. It would seem odd to some, I suppose. But as a matter of fact, there are many women who live alone out here. Many of us lost husbands and other family members in the war."

"Yes, I've read about all that. Ghastly war. Ghastly."

"What about yourself, Meredith? You seem to be of marriageable age."

The young woman laughed, not without a tinge of irony. "Ah, yes, indeed. How very right you are." She picked up the cup and peered at Olivia over the brim. Then she set the cup down slowly. "I was to be married this fall, as it were."

"What happened?"

"Well . . . he called it off." She snapped her fingers. "Just like that. But," she added cheerily, "what can one do?"

"Move to America?" Olivia raised one eyebrow as she grinned jokingly.

Meredith laughed. "Indeed." She sighed and toyed with the rim of the saucer. "There was someone else for him. An old story. Quite boring."

"Do you still love him?"

"Him? No, never! If someone tells one he loves someone else, well then, it doesn't make much sense to grieve over such a thing, do you think?"

"No, not really. But . . ."

Just then the back door opened and both women turned to see Aaron walking inside. As was his custom, he immediately removed his hat, hung it on its peg, and then the light jacket he'd worn outside that morning. As he bent over to untie the laces of his work boots, Olivia said, "Aaron, we have a visitor."

Aaron looked up quickly, and his eyes shone briefly with fear. It faded, however, when he glimpsed the young woman sitting with his sister, but he said nothing.

"This is Meredith, Aaron. Meredith Talbott."

"Hello," Aaron said haltingly.

"Meredith, this is my brother, Aaron."

"Hello, Aaron," Meredith said in her sweet, dulcimer-toned voice. "Olivia, you never mentioned that you had a brother."

"No, I didn't. I don't know why. . . . Just slipped my mind, I suppose."

Aaron was still standing in the doorway, unmoving, but his eyes were focused intently on Meredith. Olivia relaxed somewhat, for this was the way he looked at Cutter. This was a good sign; obviously he felt no threat from this beautiful young woman sitting at the table.

"Are you and Cutter finished yet?" Olivia asked.

"Almost. I thought . . ." He swallowed, his eyes still fastened on the visitor. "I thought dinner might be ready."

"Oh," Olivia said, standing up hurriedly. "I forgot I told you it would be earlier today. What a fool I am. I completely forgot. Here, let me fire up the stove, and it won't be but another half hour or so."

"It's all right."

"Would you go back and tell Cutter?"

Aaron nodded and reached for his hat. As he did so, Olivia, who was already placing the kettle on the stove, caught a glimpse of Meredith, surreptitiously studying her brother from behind the cup she'd lifted to her lips. Well, thought Olivia, what normal red-blooded woman wouldn't direct a good look at Aaron? He was a handsome man. A very handsome man.

Aaron turned and left, but Meredith continued to stare at the spot where he'd been standing. "Your brother is quite a nice man," she remarked. "Quite handsome, too."

Olivia banged the wooden spoon she was stirring the slightly congealed leftover stew with against the side of the iron kettle. "He's always looked the same. Since he was a baby."

"I'm surprised he's not been caught already."

Olivia glanced at her questioningly.

"Married. I'm surprised he's not married. You know, being quite the looker and all."

"Oh. Well, he's not. Actually, he never has been. He lives with me. We help one another out."

"Have you two always lived together?"

"For the most part," Olivia answered, replacing the kettle lid and wiping her hands on her apron. She did not care for the direction the discussion was taking, which was rapidly becoming a shade too personal. "Would you care for some more tea?"

"No, thank you," Meredith said, pushing her chair back and standing up. "I'm sure my horse must be getting restless by now. I've enjoyed your company very much." She started to pull on her gloves, then stopped. "Oh! You did receive the invitation to David's dinner on Friday night, didn't you? He said he was going to invite you."

"Yes, actually, I did."

"Marvelous."

"Ummm . . ." Olivia ventured, "I wonder; exactly how formal an affair do you think it will be? I'm concerned about the proper attire."

"Oh, I think something nice would be suitable. I've an ecru lace and chiffon gown I'm partial to. I think I'll be wearing that."

Olivia gave a nod of her head.

"Why do you ask?"

Olivia gave a half laugh. "I don't really think I will quite fit in with your crowd. I don't have as nice a dress as that at all. In fact . . . I have no idea what to wear. I mean . . . well, out here there has never been a need for anything resembling lace and chiffon."

"I've an idea," Meredith said in a sprightly tone, raising her eyebrows and clapping her hands. "I have the perfect gown for you. It's a lovely shade of green. Oh, it would match your eyes splendidly, and—"

"Oh, no. No, thank you," Olivia interjected hastily, waving a hand in the air. "I didn't mean to give the implication that I'm asking for a favor."

"Don't be silly! I must confess, there is a bit of something the matter with the gown, which is . . . Well, you seem to be a good deal thinner than I am. Mother says I've been sneaking too many sweets of late." Meredith pursed her lips and raised one eyebrow. "I have to admit she's probably right."

"But still . . ."

"I won't take no for an answer. I'd love for you to wear the dress. I'll bring it by tomorrow. You can try it on and have plenty of time to make changes to it if you need to. And you don't have to worry. I haven't worn the thing since we left London." She lifted her shoulders and then cocked her head to one side, smiling brightly. "So, there it is. A perfect solution, don't you agree?"

Olivia sighed and looked away, uncomfortable and yet grateful for the offer. What, really, would be the harm in accepting? It would solve the problem. And she did want to attend the dinner.

"All right, then."

"Great." Meredith slapped her crop against her skirt. Olivia opened the door for her and followed her outside.

"Thank you very much," Olivia said as the younger woman swung up into her sidesaddle with youthful agility.

"I'll be back the same time tomorrow, then?"

"All right."

With a great, big smile then, Meredith pulled on the outside rein and urged her horse forward.

Olivia, watching her retreating figure, was inexplicably bemused by the unwelcome idea that she had somehow just been roped into something. She wasn't at all sure as to what that might be, only that it definitely had just happened, and she would be well advised to keep on the alert as far as the beautiful Miss Meredith Talbott was concerned. It was an awful, almost mean thought, and she couldn't fully understand the reason for it.

Then she turned and went back to the house, vowing to rid herself of a notion that was probably founded in an emotion she'd never liked and hadn't experienced in a long, long time: plain old envy.

CHAPTER XVII

Cutter pulled on the reins with a gentle "Whoa, there, now," and the mare came to a stop. The spring wagon creaked and groaned as the rusty wheels ground against the axles. Olivia, sitting next to Cutter on the driver's seat, clung tightly with one hand to the handrail, and with the other clutched at the small velvet hat perched atop her hair. Eyeing the array of fine vehicles assembled closer to the fenced-in front yard, she closed her eyes and let out a rush of air.

Cutter leaned way over to the side and issued forth a stream of thick brown tobacco juice. Normally, Olivia would have cringed, for she did so hate it when he disposed of the stuff in her presence, but on this night she was far too nervous to pay attention to anything other than her own nervousness, her heightened sense of anticipation.

Wiping his mouth with the back of his shirtsleeve, Cutter gave her the once-over, much the same as he might eye a horse to gauge its soundness. "You'll do," he declared, and then hopped onto the ground. As he handed her down, Olivia answered dryly, "Thanks, Cutter."

"Now don't be ornery-soundin'. You look mighty fine. Pretty actually."

Olivia raised her eyebrows and the corner of her mouth lifted in a grin.

Cutter clapped his hands and pointed his index finger at her in a rapid-fire gesture. "There you go. Now you're lookin' real nice. Smilin' makes you look . . . well . . ."

"Yes?"

"Not so danged teacherly."

At that Olivia burst into laughter. Aaron's head popped up in the back of the wagon; he'd come along for the ride but had fallen asleep once he'd laid his head back onto a sack of feed. "What?" he muttered.

"You all right, Aaron?" Olivia asked, running her hands across the fabric of Meredith's dress, smoothing it out as much as possible. Meredith had been right; the green velvet garment, once taken up a nick or two here and there had turned out to be indeed quite flattering on Olivia's slender figure.

Aaron nodded. "How long?"

"I'll only be gone a few hours. Cutter is going to take you back home, and you can help him with the tack. That all right?"

Aaron nodded his agreement.

Impulsively, Olivia turned and pivoted in a full circle, spreading the skirt out as far as her arms would extend. She laughed when she stopped, since the motion had made her slightly dizzy, and said, "What do you think, Aaron? Do I look pretty?"

Aaron nodded very slowly, but there was a small frown etched on his forehead. Olivia knew she looked entirely different to him; it was so rare that she dressed up, he was unused to it.

"Pretty," Aaron said softly, and Olivia suddenly stood stock-still, hearing her father's voice as clearly as if he were standing right beside her. It was uncanny that for one fleeting second it felt as if perhaps her father was giving his much-treasured approval of her through her brother.

"You better get on inside," Cutter said, breaking the spell. He dusted off his hat against his thigh and then slapped it down firmly on his gray head. "Now act proper and all that, but mind that you are you. You ain't one of them high-livin' simperin' types, and you could teach 'em a thing or two in your own right. Hell's leather, for that matter you could teach 'em just about everything. Appears to me they don't know which way the sun rises and sets they're so danged—"

"I understand, Cutter," Olivia interrupted, humored by the lecture. "Truly, I do."

Cutter climbed up back onto the seat and picked up the traces. "All right, then. I'll come on back in about two hours then, like you said."

Olivia winced. "I'm not even sure if I should stay that long. Or maybe less . . ."

"Well, no matter, if you're not done we'll just wait out here. It's a nice night anyhow." Cutter flicked one of his hands outward, saying, "Get on with you. I'm not budgin' till you do. You'll get your skirts all coated when these wheels start movin'."

"All right," Olivia said, picking up the loop on her skirt to lift it as she walked toward the house. Might as well get over the nervousness, she thought. She had handled herself through far, far more unnerving situations than this one. After all, this was just a party!

David Ellison's attention was captured by a couple who were talking to him in earnest, but when he saw Olivia standing in the doorway to the great room, he swiftly excused himself and crossed the room to greet her. Olivia was completely captivated; he was a sophisticated, polished man of strong masculine good-looks.

His eyes, hazel, seemed slightly glazed as he bent toward her, picked up her hand and shook it in a way she'd never had done before. He lowered his head toward hers and spoke in his very British accent, "Absolutely delighted you came. I consider you my hostess for the evening. Indeed, I demand it!" he emphasized gallantly.

"Thank you," Olivia said, noting the definite but not offensive smell of liquor on his breath.

"You look absolutely ravishing," he declared, letting his eyes take in the full length of her. "Smashing dress."

"Thank you very much," Olivia muttered, flattered and embarrassed at the same time. When had she ever heard such lavish praise? She could not recall a time ever.

"Olivia! There you are." Meredith appeared at her elbow. "I agree with David. You do indeed look smashing. Where on earth did you find such a gown?" Her eyes twinkled and she smiled. Noticing Olivia's look of confusion, she added, "No, don't tell me, it's the one from Kansas City that you ordered."

Olivia said nothing, but smiled back and nodded her head very slightly.

"I thought so."

"Well, I must say," David added, "you have exquisite taste. Come along, I'll introduce you to a few of the ladies and chaps here. They'll be delighted to meet you. I think you must be the only true-blue American here." With that he tossed back the rest of the contents of the brandy snifter he was holding and then chuckled heartily.

She was introduced to so many people that evening, she quickly gave up trying to memorize names. Everyone was British, everyone was extremely polite and interested in meeting her, everyone remarked in some form or fashion that as an American she was truly "different,'' a remark she couldn't quite classify. And, with the exception of a handful of guests, all were interested in what sort of animals she raised, in particular the breed of horses she owned. She merely sipped at the brandy David provided for her, but as the night wore on, she was well aware of the increased imbibing among the other guests. Cigar smoke wafted up toward the ceiling in great clouds, and she was slightly sickened by the pungent aromas of the various blends of tobaccos being used.

She longed to escape outside to the veranda, and when finally she did so David followed. ''Are you all right?'' he asked, reaching for her hand and holding it within both of his own.

''Just a little hungry,'' Olivia answered, smiling up at him. His eyes were glassier than before, but they peered into her own with a frank sensuality that sent quivery sensations throughout her insides.

''Cook is a bit late,'' he said, pressing her hand, dipping his head a bit further toward hers.

Forcing herself to avert her gaze she stepped back a bit and looked downward. ''That's all right. I was a little dizzy too. I'm not used to all the smoke.''

''Ah. I see.'' Pivoting a bit he said, ''Perhaps we should have all the doors opened wide. Yes, of course, that's the thing for it. I'll see to it.''

''Oh, it—''

''No. Can't have anyone getting ill simply because of the cads inside who are behaving so thoughtlessly.''

Olivia frowned and smiled at the same time. ''Cads? I thought they were your friends.''

''Oh, they are. They happen to be cads nonetheless.'' His attention caught, he snapped his fingers and called out, ''Stewart, see to the doors, will you. Open them all up, let out that ghastly cloud in the room.'' He turned to Olivia. ''Truly miss your friend Mrs. McGill since she's gone to visit her daughter. Stewart couldn't hold a candle to her common sense."

But within moments the deed was done, and Olivia marvelled at how quickly her wish had been granted. It must be so wonderful, she thought, to simply call out one's wishes and have them carried out with immediate dispatch. A tinge of envy flickered within but was over-ridden by the smug realization that it had been she who had caused such an action on David's part. When she went inside with him to be seated for the dinner she felt better, more certain of herself.

The dinner was spectacular by Olivia's standards. She, who had never eaten on anything finer than her mother's old, cracked pottery, of which there were only a few pieces left by now, found herself holding gilt-edged bone china and sterling flatware. As inconspicuously as possible, she took it all in as the five-course dinner was served; the lace table-cloths, gold candlesticks—of which there seemed to be dozens—the delicate French satins worn by the ladies, the English tweeds sported by the gentlemen, all as casually as the calico and denim of those of lesser means. Fine wines flowed as platters of roast pork, baked pheasant, and rainbow trout were served. Everyone ate lustily, and when the trifle was presented in an enormous lead crystal bowl, Olivia didn't think she could put another bite in her mouth. But she did so, if only to avoid contributing to the one subject of conversation that had dominated the entire evening; the equestrian hunt. Anything and everything to do with the hunt, for that matter; the stock, the prey, the routes, the obstacles.

Almost three hours had passed before she felt it appropriate to indicate to David that she would like to leave. The party was in full flower by then, the drinking had not stopped, and more than one person had stumbled heavily against her back. Once a man had thrown his head back in a loud guffaw, and as he did so his heeled shoe landed squarely on the top of her own left foot. She cried out involuntarily, but the sound was drowned out by the noise all around. By the time she stood on the front veranda, her foot was throbbing, but David was holding her elbow and her mind was distracted from the pain.

"I do wish you could stay longer," he said, moving ever-so-slightly closer to her side. She could feel the material of his jacket against her hand; for some reason it sent shivers up and down her spine. There was an urge within her to turn to him, to encourage him to envelop her in his arms, to feel his embrace, his lips upon her own. It had been so long . . .

But she did nothing of the sort. Instead she said in a firm tone of voice, "I'd love to, but Cutter is here to pick me up and take me home."

They both looked toward the stable area where Cutter had parked the wagon; his slumped appearance gave the impression that he had fallen asleep. "Guess I'll have to wake him up," Olivia said. She turned then and said, "David, thank you so much for the invitation. It was a fine evening."

"No thanks are necessary. Just promise me this won't be the last one."

Olivia smiled and nodded. "All right then. I promise. Good night."

She walked down the paved walkway, stopped halfway and with another smile on her face turned to issue one more thank-you. But the porch was empty. David had gone back inside. Well, she thought, he did have other guests to tend to; she certainly wasn't his only concern.

She woke Cutter when she climbed up onto the wagon seat; Aaron remained sound asleep in the back. Cutter rubbed his eyes forcefully, and yawned uninhibitedly. He glanced at Olivia, bent down to pick up the traces and clucked softly to the mare. Olivia yawned in response to his and reached down to rub her foot which was still aching.

"Must've been one hell of a party," remarked Cutter as he set the mare at a walk.

"It was nice," Olivia said.

Cutter gave her a sidelong glance. "How soon you plannin' on taking off that garment?"

Surprised, Olivia said, "What?"

"Cigar smoke don't set well on the thing. You went in smellin' like a dandelion, come out stinkin' like a boxcar."

"Thanks a lot!" Olivia said, amazed at his audacity.

"Thanks ain't necessary. It's a fact."

"Cutter!"

"You tellin' me you ain't itchin' to shuck that thing off?"

Olivia hesitated for a moment and then burst out laughing. "Yes, I am in fact!" The relief she felt in that moment was welcome; she hadn't been aware she'd even needed any until that moment. Cutter was right. She was tired, overwhelmed by the evening, and the first thing in the world she needed right now was the privacy of her own bedroom, and her own precious feather bed.

"Put her into a trot, Cutter," Olivia said. "It was fun, but all I want right now is to get home."

Despite the awkwardness of that first social affair, the relationship with David Ellison intensified. It marked, for Olivia, a completely different phase of her life. Despite her marriage to Francis and her all-too-brief involvement with Luke, she found herself formally courted for the first time, and by a man of sophistication, of refinement. His culture, so vastly different from her own, was fascinating, almost enchanting.

* * *

Hard, grueling work had been and would always be a part of life on the plains, and she had long since come to accept this way of life, not only for the present but also the future. Kansas had seen the exodus of thousands of its settlers since she'd arrived, and though many were the times when Olivia had found everyday life almost impossible to endure, she had never once truly considered leaving. Something about that very hardship, surviving the adversities that had been her constant companions for almost fourteen years, had had the effect of hardening her resolve to stay, to endure. And it seemed that she had succeeded to a great degree. But one matter was paramount in her consideration to stay put: her love for and concern for the plight of her brother. As time went on, she could not imagine removing him from what had become familiar, what felt safe to him now. He would not thrive in any other place than here. It was that simple.

And so it was rather disturbing to recognize the feelings, unwanted as they were, that were provoked by her relationship with David. His way of life, however impractical beneath the surface of it, was nonetheless undeniably appealing. Just thinking of it brought on self-pitying thoughts. She had the right to be tired, didn't she? She had the right to wish for a life filled more with joy and relaxation than with unrelenting work. And she had the right to find such a sophisticated, elegant man as David Ellison attractive and desirable. Yes, of course she did.

For three months their relationship grew and, seemingly, flourished. David invited her frequently to his house for dinners and other social functions, and always it was clear that the two of them were a couple. Olivia felt she had been starving most of her life for the culture, the refinement and social graces, to which he introduced her. Now, at last, she was actually partaking of the way of life that she had only read about in novels.

It was all wonderful, so wonderful that she soon learned to ignore the vague disappointment that crept into her thoughts at times, the disappointment that the relationship she and David shared, though fulfilling in most ways, was missing some significant element. Indeed, at times there were feelings of emptiness, the vague sense of going nowhere at all. As if perhaps, the unwanted voice inside insisted, as if this were but some mere interlude in his life.

He never spoke of his past, though she knew he was the son of a titled country gentleman in England, that he had never been married, and had very much enjoyed his bachelorhood of thirty-five years. He had no need of money; thus he could afford to merely exist on this land his father had invested in, could manage well enough without having to actually "do" anything. This sometimes bothered Olivia, for she had never in her life been able to simply "exist." Nor had anyone she had ever loved or with whom she had been closely associated. Nevertheless, she could not resist the lure of comfort he offered her, the lofty, carefully worded allusions to the possibility that she herself might also be a part of his world.

He was certainly a romantic figure: handsome, charming . . . all the things one would imagine a refined country gentleman would be. He spoke elegantly, complimented her frequently, filled her time as it had never been filled before. And yet . . . and yet, there had been no real exhibition of physical interest toward Olivia. Though she responded to his strong good looks with a great deal of inner desire, she waited impatiently for a demonstration on his part that he felt the same. Oh, she knew it was not proper for a gentleman to make advances the way Luke had, or even Francis, for that matter. But she would have been more than willing to dispense with propriety. She longed for a touch, a kiss, a mere caress, and as weeks went by, only felt an even greater longing for that which was not forthcoming. Why? she often wondered. Why had he never even attempted to touch her, to hold her hand or place an arm around her shoulders?

The longer he did nothing, the greater her frustration built up, until there came a point at which she could think of almost nothing else. She was consumed with David; she dreamed about him, had even begun to feel stirrings of anger that she knew, and feared, might propel her into initiating action that she might someday come to regret. She grew more and more irritated, partly because of her obsessive thoughts, which dominated all others, and partly because of a lack of sleep. She snapped at both Aaron and Cutter and began to grow resentful of the normal daily routine. It was an affront to the new life she was being introduced to, nothing but a hindrance and a sore irritation.

As she became more focused on such inner turmoil, she began to grow neglectful of other matters in her life, matters of great consequence. Meredith Talbott's presence in Olivia and Aaron's life had become something of a constant, ever since that first dinner party at David's house. Her impromptu visits became so frequent that Olivia, who never lost her liking of Meredith's sweet, enchanting voice, or her uplifting, cheerful, personality, missed her sorely on those days she wasn't around.

Since Meredith took her horse for a cross-country ride every morning in order to keep him fit for the hunts she participated in, and since Olivia's place was so convenient to her parents', she simply worked it into her schedule to arrive at Olivia and Aaron's on her way home from such outings. As a result, Olivia quickly became used to a midmorning cup of tea instead of her usual coffee. Often Aaron joined the two of them. He did not stay long, and had little to say, but he was polite and seemed to listen well to his sister and her new friend's conversation.

Meredith was an irrepressible raconteur, and Olivia frequently wondered how in the world she managed to find so very much to talk about when, in fact, her world was now quite limited in scope. Nevertheless, though her own mind frequently wandered as Meredith chatted on, she noticed that Aaron was visibly relaxed by the patter. For that alone, Olivia would have endured hours of the young woman's presence.

A few times she returned to the house from a trip to town to find Meredith already there, conversing with Aaron outside the barn, or sitting with him on the porch, both of them seated and sipping tea that Meredith had made. Observing them thus pleased Olivia immensely, for just seeing Aaron so relaxed, his appearance so normal, was heartwarming and reassuring. To see him smile now and again, to hear his gentle, soft laugh . . . she would have paid any amount of money for it. And so she welcomed Meredith's attention toward her brother as much, if not more than, that which he'd received from Luke, and now Cutter. All of them had offered support and had given back to her brother at least some of the happiness that had once been his completely.

She was still at loose ends as to her feelings about the rather mysterious relationship she and David shared, but to have this one, very important part of her life improving was a much-needed relief.

One November afternoon, she stood staring out one of the front windows. It was a rainy, miserable day that saw the fields of grass flattened beneath the continuous daily drizzle, the sky closing down on the land with dense, leaden clouds that had shown no sign, for over a week, of dissipating. There was nothing much that could be done outside, as the ground had turned to mud, and the damp cold was bone-penetrating. Olivia had busied herself with preserving some of her late-harvested strawberries, and when she had finished that, she pulled out her sewing and darning basket and set to work, mending long-neglected items of underwear, socks, shirts, and sweaters that were now much-needed with the onset of winter.

She worked swiftly but with an edge of impatience that no amount of diligence would diminish. She had not seen or heard from David in over a week. The weather was to blame, of course, for it was practically impossible to travel the roads, which were in such soggy condition. Therefore, she couldn't imagine David risking taking his fine carriage out if even for the short ride over to her place. And neither could she risk her own trap or Rainy's legs in such unpredictable mire. Be patient, she told herself firmly.

But it was her worst trait of late, this lack of patience where David was concerned. She missed his company terribly, missed the nearness of him, the sound of his voice. But as soon as this admission was made, it was countered by another, more practical thought. Wasn't there more behind this unshakable impatience? Was there doubt? Doubt as to the seeming lack of reciprocity of those same feelings on his part? The answer, she admitted ruefully, was yes.

Oh, she thought that afternoon, she was about to leave her senses! She jerked hard on the needle that was jammed into a woolen sock, and when it came through, it went straight into her left thumb. She uttered a yelp of pain as immediately blood began to pool up.

"Damn!" she said aloud, annoyed with the uncharacteristic profanity as much as the prick to her thumb. Busy cleaning the small wound, she did not at first hear either the footsteps on the porch or the

knock on the door. The rain, though not heavy, had
kept up a steady pummel on the roof of the house,
muffling most other sounds. As she returned to her
chair, the bleeding stopped finally, and she finally
heard the knock.

Her first thought was that perhaps it was David, having braved the elements to see how she was doing.
Wishful thinking, the inner voice reminded her, just so
she wouldn't be disappointed as she opened the door.

She was shocked to see a very wet, very distraught
Meredith standing there, her lovely face reddened and
puffy, especially around the eyes.

"Meredith! What is it?" Olivia's voice was raised in
alarm. "Has something happened?"

"Can I . . . come in?" Her lovely voice held a nasal
quality; the corners of her mouth were drawn downward.

"What is it? Is your father all right? Your mother?"

"Yes, they're fine. Can I come in?" she repeated.

"Yes, of course, of course," Olivia said hurriedly,
pulling the door open wide. "Here, let me take your
cloak. It's soaked!"

Meredith stepped inside. "Yes, I know." She handed
Olivia the coat, then commenced to intense shivering.

"And you're cold, too. Go stand by the fire, for heav-
en's sake. Goodness, there's not much left to it. Here,
wait a moment and I'll put on another log."

Hastily Olivia built up the fire and then turned back
to her friend. "Now, come here. Don't move. It'll warm
you while I put on water for tea." Suddenly she stopped
and said, "Or perhaps I should offer you a bit of
brandy."

Meredith shook her head, but Olivia paid the gesture
no mind and did exactly that. Into a small glass she
poured a generous measure of aromatic brandy and
handed it to Meredith. She shook her head as Meredith
started to speak and said, "Not another word until you

calm yourself down somewhat." Meredith took a sip, and Olivia said, "Some more. More. A big swallow. There, that will do."

Meredith looked down at the floor and handed the glass to Olivia. "You sound like my mother."

"I take that as a compliment."

She returned with a blanket from the chest in her bedroom and draped it across Meredith's shoulders. "Now," she said, "sit down. You look exhausted. I can't believe you came all the way in this weather."

Slowly Meredith sat down on the end of the sofa, closest to the fireplace, but not in her usual casual fashion. She sat perched on the edge of it and kept her head toward the fire. Suddenly she glanced at Olivia. "Is he here? On the farm?"

Olivia frowned. "Who? Aaron?"

Meredith nodded.

"Yes, of course."

"Where? In the house?"

"No," Olivia said, perplexity in her tone. "He's in the barn with Cutter. They're stitching up broken tack."

"Are they almost finished? Will they be coming inside soon?" Meredith's gaze focused on the back door.

"No, they'll be there for several more hours probably. They have other things to do also." She paused. "Heavens, Meredith, what is all this about?"

Meredith swallowed hard and took in a deep gulp of air. When she spoke it was in a sudden gush of words, as if she decided to just get out what she had to say as fast as possible. "I just got back from Hays. I rode directly over here. I thought at first I should go home, and then I decided, no, I need to come here. I have to—"

"Meredith," Olivia interrupted, "are you telling me you rode all the way in this horrible weather to Hays and back? Why on earth would you do such a thing?"

"That's what I'm going to tell you." She swallowed, took in a deep breath.

"Yes?"

Meredith looked up, and her luminous gray eyes were puddled with tears. She spoke now in a whisper, her voice breaking, "I went to see Dr. McGuinness. I . . . I'm . . . oh God, this is so hard to say. To tell you."

Olivia stared at the distraught young woman, her heart beating somewhere in the vicinity of her throat. A sense of depression descended over her like a fog, and like a prisoner hearing the clank of the bars behind him for the first time, she awaited the words this woman was about to utter with a sense of foreboding. Stop, she wanted to say, don't say it. Please don't say anything. But she heard herself say aloud, "Go on, Meredith. What is wrong?"

Meredith placed the fingers of one hand over her lips, and through them said, "Yes, that's certainly an appropriate way to put it. 'What's wrong?' " She dropped her hand and stared directly at Olivia. "I'm pregnant. With child. Whatever you wish to call it."

Olivia shook her head in dismay. "What? . . . I . . . I don't know exactly what to say, Meredith. I mean . . ." She looked down at her lap and then back up at Meredith. "I mean, why are you telling me? You should be telling your mother, don't you think? She loves you very much and . . . Have you told her?"

"Aaron is the father."

The words hung in the space of air between them with a heaviness that matched the leaden atmosphere outside.

Suddenly Olivia was unaware of her heart beating at all. She continued staring at Meredith; her face had gone completely ashen.

"I know it's a shock to you, but—"

"Would you repeat what you said, please?"

"I . . . Are you all right, Olivia? For God's sake, you're so white suddenly, and—"

"Would you repeat what you said?" Olivia spoke woodenly, her tone devoid of emotion.

"I said . . . I said, Aaron is the father of the child I am carrying."

"That is a lie." Olivia spat out the words.

Meredith drew herself upward and directed a steely gaze at Olivia. "I beg your pardon."

"You are lying."

"I am most certainly not! I would never lie about such a thing! Ever! How can you even think I would lie about it? How insulting!"

"Keep your voice down."

Meredith threw off the blanket and stood up. "I am not lying to you, Olivia. I realize this is a shock, but it is the truth. The absolute truth."

"But how can it be? Explain it to me, please."

Meredith turned slowly and moved toward the fireplace, positioning herself so that she stood sideways to it, half facing Olivia, half facing the back door. "We've been intimate," she said after a few moments of silence. "Twice. Only twice. It was a mistake on my part, but it . . . just happened."

"When?"

"Sometime in early October. You were at David's having lunch . . . the first time, that is. The second time you were at the dinner party I was supposed to attend with Mother and Father. The one I said I was too sick to come to. I was here instead. I started feeling ill the middle of this month. Mother suggested I see Dr. McGuinness, but I kept putting it off. I already knew, I just didn't want to hear him confirm it."

"Where?" Olivia spoke again, her eyes fixed on the floor beneath her feet. "Where did it happen?"

"What difference does that make?" Meredith flung

one hand upward. "Upstairs, in his bed, if you must know! But that's not what I came here to discuss with you. I wanted to tell you first, before I tell him."

Olivia looked up then, her green eyes filled with anguish. As unwilling as her mind was to accept what she'd just heard, her heart recognized the truth in Meredith's words. The sense of betrayal was as deep as it was raw; she felt as though a knife had been plunged deep into her chest. She found it extremely difficult to speak, but somehow she heard herself doing just that.

"You haven't told him?"

"No." Meredith began to fidget. "I can't. I mean . . . I don't really know how."

"Why not? You've obviously spent a lot of time with him." Olivia could not control the heavy sarcasm in her tone.

"I know. I know." Meredith began twisting her hands together. "But . . . you know him yourself. Aaron's not very communicative. I know he loves me, and I love him dearly, but, well, it just seems that it's been me who's done most of the talking ever since I've known him. He . . . well, you know, he's just not a man of many words."

"Go on."

"I asked him, you see, about marriage, but . . . but he wouldn't give me an answer. Nothing . . . he said nothing at all. Yet I know he loves me. He has to."

Olivia stared at the woman for a moment before commenting, "That is what you want to believe."

Meredith turned her head sharply. "How can you say such a thing?"

"Oh, I can say it. I can very well say it." Olivia paused and fixed a pained expression on the young woman now facing her squarely. "Meredith, you have deceived yourself. Aaron doesn't love you; he never has and never will. And the very thing you tried to do to secure his love—and you did do that, didn't you?—well, it failed. Utterly failed. As it was bound to.''

Meredith's eyes blazed with sudden fury. "How beastly of you! You know nothing of Aaron. He may live here with you, but you know nothing!''

Now Olivia's gaze mellowed a bit with compassion, for she saw that there was no turning back now, no place for anything other than the truth. All this time and Meredith had never once noticed anything different about Aaron, or if she had, she'd interpreted it merely as part of his personality, an eccentric one perhaps, but one for some reason she had become enamored of, had turned into something else. Comparisons to her relationship with David crossed her mind, but Olivia pushed them aside.

"Sit down, Meredith. Please, just sit down.''

Very grudgingly the young woman did so, and for several minutes the two women just sat and stared at each other. At last Olivia spoke, the anger in her voice replaced now with empathy and sorrow.

"Aaron is not who you think he is, Meredith. He never has been.''

Meredith frowned in innocent bemusement and waited. "I don't . . .''

"No, you don't understand. There is no way you ever could have. I will tell you everything then, so you will understand.'' Olivia leaned slightly forward, and her eyes were deep pools of anguish.

"Aaron is mentally unbalanced,'' she said softly. "He's not been normal for many, many years. You see,'' she went on slowly as she watched the look of disbelief spreading across Meredith's face, "you see, at the time when the war began—back in sixty-one—he was injured in an Indian attack. He was savagely beaten, and three-quarters of his scalp was removed and left dangling from his head. Then he was left for dead. He was brought back to me by army officers. It happened not far from our home near Salina. They brought him back home to me . . . to die. But—'' she paused, swallowing, remembering now the events of those days with an acute sense of immediacy "—of course, he didn't die. I would have done anything to keep him from dying. I loved him, you see . . . I've loved him all my life. I could never imagine not loving him and caring for him.

"When he left me—after Francis did—I thought, naturally, that I would be the one to die. Because I could not bear the fact that they both left me alone. I thought they would never come back. And . . . I was right in one sense. But Aaron did, only not in a way I ever imagined.''

She paused for a long while. Meredith said nothing, just sat staring directly at Olivia.

"Anyway,'' Olivia went on, "I mended him eventually. Other than losing my father, burying my mother, and losing my first baby, it was the most difficult thing I ever went through.'' She pursed her lips and raised an eyebrow in reflection. "I suppose going through all that might have something to do with my staying on in a land where so many have left. What could I go back to, really? Oh, I know, you all think it quite a lark to be here, but you really know nothing. Nothing at all.''

Meredith blinked several times, and Olivia said, "But, of course, that is not the subject of this discussion. I will say it directly to you, Meredith. Aaron is quite incapable of loving anyone, let alone being able to take on a wife and child.'' She paused. "I must ask you one thing. Was your . . . lovemaking . . . was it romantic? Did he speak to you, tell you he loved you? Did he make promises to you?''

Meredith shook her head almost imperceptibly.

"I did not think so.''

Meredith said nothing.

"And he probably never mentioned it to you again, did he?"

Again Meredith said nothing, but her silence revealed that Olivia had guessed the truth.

"That is because he doesn't remember it. You see, he suffered some sort of brain damage, according to one of the doctors who saw him. Of course, it is impossible to tell what sort, as those things cannot be determined, but I know, after years of living with him, that the way he is now is probably as good as he will ever be."

Finally Meredith spoke, her voice shaking almost uncontrollably. "Are you saying he is crazy?"

"He is mentally ill, Meredith. He is simply not normal . . . in the sense that we think of it."

Suddenly Meredith stood up, her features stricken with panic and horror. "Then that means the baby . . ." she whispered, her hand suddenly jerking upward and covering her mouth. "The baby . . ."

Olivia started to get up. "I don't think there would be anything to worry about in that regard, Mer—"

Suddenly Meredith was rushing across the room toward the front door, yanking it open and then running headlong across the porch, down the steps, and through the rain to her waiting horse, who stood, tied to the hitching rail, with saddle and bridle still on. Meredith jerked the reins free and threw herself into the saddle, almost sliding off into the mud before pulling herself up and securing her position.

Olivia called out to her, but the rain had intensified and her voice was drowned out anyway. She watched as the horse picked his way through the ever-worsening mud, Meredith kicking mercilessly all the while. A few minutes later the horse and rider disappeared from view, but Olivia remained on the porch, the cold rain blowing straight into her as the wind shifted direction. She could not move, could not imagine turning around and going back inside the house and carrying on somehow as she did each and every day.

Never in her entire life had she hurt someone as she had just hurt this young woman who had done nothing more harmful than falling in love with Aaron. What in the world would happen now? What possible good could come of this horrible nightmare?

She could not think of an answer. She did not think one existed.

CHAPTER XVIII

There were answers, however, for everything, Olivia discovered. Sometimes those answers took a long time in coming, but come they did. Despite the months of despair, the overwhelming sadness that seemed to haunt her every day, there did at long last come a moment in time when things came right, when decisions were made that would affect Olivia's life in a positive way.

She would not have believed it, though, all through the long, torturous winter of '73–'74. A week after Meredith's stormy exit, the rains had turned to snow, snow that drifted downward in heavy clumps, drifting into banks higher than a horse's withers and packed up against the outer walls of the frame house so high that the view of the outdoors from the windows was completely obliterated. The days grew shorter and shorter until it seemed there were hardly any days of full light. The wind, the ever-present wind, howled across the white-blanketed plains, whistling around the eaves of the house like some strange, eerie music.

Olivia heard nothing more from David after Meredith's upset. Meredith herself never returned. Their silence could have been easily excused by the onslaught of terrible weather that affected everyone, but when at last the sun finally emerged in mid-February, there was still no communication from either. When the roads were passable, Olivia sent Cutter into town several times to gather the heavier supplies and staples that were needed for house and barn, and then finally she herself saddled up one day and rode into Hays. She spent much time at the general store, which was fairly picked over by others who had been in need of much the same necessities as she.

But she saw no one familiar. She stopped in the York House Hotel for a bite to eat before her trip back, hoping she would recognize someone of the old crowd she had come to know in her association with David. But, sadly, she was the only patron in the entire restaurant.

Riding homeward, she considered heading toward David's place, but something inside told her not to go. He would have contacted her if there were still an interest on his part, wouldn't he? And so she bypassed the turnoff that would have taken her to the road leading up to his estate. Though she knew it was the right thing to do, she felt a resurgence of the emptiness she'd battled all winter long. She hated feeling it! It only made her feel more the fool!

From the top of the last rise before the turnoff to her own private dirt road, she could see the distant, shadowed grove of cottonwoods, behind which stood the Talbott family's house. She could not pull her gaze away from it, could not stop herself from wondering how Meredith was doing, how she looked. She would be six months pregnant by now.

In late December she had received a letter from Morris Talbott. It was a brief, one-page letter, formal, yet to the point, and quite stern in tone. He and his wife now understood fully the cause of their daughter's illness, and had agreed to help her, with the stipulation that she never again associate with anyone in Olivia's family. It was a tragedy for all, he had written, explaining further in case she did not quite grasp his implication. Aaron's mental state was an affliction, he assumed, that could be passed on to the child his daughter was now carrying.

Olivia had realized immediately after reading the letter that her fate was sealed, if it had not already been so, as far as David was concerned. No longer would she be the nice American girl everyone in his circle had welcomed and fully accepted. Of course not . . . her brother was insane. Everyone knew it now; she had no doubt.

Aaron, of course, remained ignorant of the consequences of the sexual encounters he had engaged in with Meredith Talbott. Indeed, he had asked about her only once. He'd merely wanted to know if she was coming to visit them again. Olivia had said no, she didn't think so, and he had gone on with eating his breakfast. There was no expression of loss, certainly no emotional repercussion. In February Olivia had casually brought up Meredith's name to test his reaction, and had received a mere frown and a "Who?" for a response.

He had forgotten her totally.

On the first Saturday in March, after a week-long snowstorm, Cutter had managed to coax one of the mules into Hays and had brought back a newspaper, the first Olivia had seen in months. She'd expected it to be months old, but surprisingly, it had been printed just the day before. She'd sat down immediately and read it from cover to cover. It was a local paper, of course, but there were several articles about President Grant and the goings-on in Washington. These she read with avid interest, for it was far too seldom that one learned of the governmental affairs in the capital. But on the second to last page, a brief notice caught her eye. Slowly she read it, and when she finished, her hands lowered to her lap, her fingers releasing the newspaper, which slid off onto the floor.

Miss Meredith Talbott, the notice said, was to marry Mr. David Ellison on the fifteenth of March. Their betrothal had commenced on the first day of the year, and the couple had selected First Presbyterian Church for their nuptials. The ceremony would be a private one, and the couple planned a honeymoon of two months on the Atlantic Seaboard.

Olivia got up, cut out the article, and then tucked it inside a book, which she then placed in the drawer of her nightstand. Each and every night, for weeks, she pulled the book out, removed the small piece of paper, and reread the article. She wasn't quite certain when she stopped performing the obsessive ritual. Sometime in May she thought, though she wasn't quite certain what day. Somehow her brain had finally processed the information in that small article. At least she knew everything now, she told herself, though the hurt and pain were still there, burning a small hole into her very soul. She could not eat for a while, and combined with the extra work she was doing in the fields and barn with Aaron and Cutter, she began to lose weight. But though she felt no hunger, she did not experience a lessening of energy; indeed, she was up before dawn every day, preparing breakfast for herself and the men, and by midmorning, after her own chores, she was out in the fields lending a hand in the plowing and sowing. The melted snow of winter had left the sod easier to work, and Olivia had gone the route of many of the farmers in the area, resting her hopes on a good year. She followed along behind either Aaron or Cutter, dropping seeds of corn and wheat and cane. The rains came in time for all of the sowings, in proportionate amounts. Summer arrived early, but the crops grew high and healthy. Expectations among the settlers were of huge bumper crops.

Work was Olivia's respite from the heartache that gradually, inch by inch, was lessening. She had, by midsummer, worked out in her mind what had probably happened between the Talbott family and David. In his letter, Morris had indicated that he would help his daughter out. Obviously a man of such good standing in his own community would never abide the social shame of an unwed daughter living in his household, and so he had gone to his good friend, David Ellison. David, taking the noble stance, had agreed to help his friend by marrying Meredith. Rationally, Olivia saw that it was the best solution for Meredith.

But what of herself? What of her own feelings for David? They were simply the feelings of a fool, she reminded herself repeatedly. She'd best get on with her life. A life based on reality, not on schoolgirlish dreams of romantic love. How much had there been to begin with anyway?

On the last day of July she walked the rows of wheat and corn and cane, their long stalks high above her head. Everything looked in order, as Cutter had told her already, but still she had wanted to go out herself. She could think that day of but one thing: By now, perhaps today even, Meredith's baby would be born. Aaron's baby. Her own kin.

If only there were some way of knowing. But of course, there wasn't. She would have to wait, perhaps another two weeks, for the announcement to come out in the Hays *Gazette*. She kept walking, past the cultivated crops and into the adjacent pasture of thick, waist-high grass, mindless of the wind and heat, uttering a silent prayer for the young woman. And for the man who would be the father of her brother's child.

The first day of August was one that would be forever etched in every Kansan's memory. Everyone would have a story to tell about that day, but most would sound similar: descriptions of what had happened as evening drew near when on the horizon there had appeared an enormous cloud, resembling nothing so much as a snowstorm. Within minutes the cloud grew ever larger as it moved nearer, pressing an ominous, strange droning noise. Then, without warning, the cloud became alive, opened up completely. The sky itself began to rain down grasshoppers, the sound of them as they pelted everything in sight almost deafening.

No one could react in time for the onslaught, but even if it had been possible to do so, nothing could have reversed the devastating, almost immediate damage wreaked upon the land—upon all of them. For hours the pests rained and rained, down upon the fields of ripe, healthy crops, onto trees and bushes and livestock, into homes where they ravaged everything in sight: food, clothing, articles of all description. Wood, leather, cloth; it made no difference.

Several hours later the cloud had risen, shifted its route, and continued on, but many of the insects remained for days afterward. Olivia, like others, was too stunned for words. She had fought them off in vain until, when it was over, there was nothing left to do but fall down in a heap of total, debilitating exhaustion. For days she moved as in a trance; she cleaned from morning till night, and still the next day there was work to be done.

One week later she stood on her front porch, still sweeping up dead grasshoppers left behind. She paused and looked out across what had once been the most prosperous crops she'd ever raised. Now there was nothing but field after field of stubble. All was ruined, completely ruined. She swept some more and paused, reaching back to rub her aching neck. She hadn't slept normally for so long that she thought nothing would be more wonderful than to lie down right then and there and close her eyes. To just let it all go away. How much more of this could she bear?

At least Aaron was all right finally. He had reacted very badly to the pestilence, whipped into sheer panic when the insects covered him as he was struggling toward the house, invading his clothes, his nostrils, ears, and mouth. Olivia and Cutter had been in a similar predicament but were forced to deal with Aaron first. They'd gotten him into the house, sealed it off as best they could, and then Olivia had given him a few drops of laudanum. Mercifully, he'd dropped off to sleep, and they had been able to concentrate on hurrying back to see to the animals.

Cutter had returned from town just two days ago with the news that the depot was bustling. Boxes and crates were stacked everywhere, people gathered all around, waiting for the trains, which could not arrive soon enough. Faced with total losses now, many of the settlers gave up hope completely, deciding there was nothing to do but leave. Far and away, the majority of the voices he heard speaking, Cutter related, had British accents.

Olivia wasn't at all surprised. Reality, in its most brutal form, had finally taken hold of them. She wondered how many of those she had known last fall would still be here this coming autumn. Not many, she wagered.

One of the horses in the barn neighed loudly, and she looked up to see, cresting the bluff on the outskirts of her property, a familiar carriage traveling along the road leading up to the house. She froze. It was David Ellison's sleek brougham.

She turned to see if the men were around, and then quickly thought perhaps she should go inside the house. But that was ridiculous. She would not play the coward now. Certainly not now.

The carriage came to a stop just outside the small

picket fence Cutter had put up this year, and the Negro driver jumped down to the ground and hustled to the passenger door. He opened it, and a white-gloved hand stretched out to grab the pull, and then Meredith was gingerly climbing down the steps. She straightened her hat and pulled on the ends of her gloves as a young girl emerged to stand beside her. The girl then turned and reached inside the low-slung door for something, which she pulled slowly and cautiously into her arms. It was a white wicker basket cradle. The baby! Olivia thought, bringing one hand to her throat. But there was no sign of David, and as she waited, Meredith turned and saw her standing there, said something to the driver and the girl, took the basket, and then started walking up the pathway toward the porch.

Meredith climbed the steps and stood before Olivia, who could not remove her gaze from the wicker cradle.

"Hello, Olivia," Meredith said, her melodious voice strained, almost curt.

"Meredith," Olivia returned the greeting. "You look well." Indeed, she looked as beautiful as ever, though she had lost her fresh-faced innocence; in its place was a more mature, though somewhat sadder expression.

"Thank you." Meredith pulled back the tulle covering the basket and said, "This is your niece."

"A girl," Olivia whispered, her voice cracking. She reached down with one hand and tentatively touched the feather-soft skin, then a wisp of dark hair on the rounded head.

"Oh, she's beautiful!" Olivia looked up at Meredith, who seemed quite preoccupied with thoughts other than the babe she held. "What is her name?"

"What?"

"What is her name?"

"We've been calling her Sarah."

"Been calling her that? Is that her name?"

Meredith glanced back at the carriage, where the girl

and driver were still waiting, and nodded once. "Look, may I sit down?"

"Of course." Olivia offered her a chair and then took one next to her. "If you'd like, you can invite your help up here. I have refreshments and—"

"You don't have to be nice to me. I know you must hate me."

"I don't hate you, Meredith." Olivia sighed. "You did what you had to do."

"I did what my father said I had to do."

Olivia watched Meredith's face closely; she looked unhappy, very unhappy.

"I know you loved David. So if you loved him, you must hate me for taking him away."

Olivia digested this for a moment and then replied, "Meredith, David did not share my feelings. He never did. I don't begrudge you your husband. I am past that now." It had taken far longer than it should have to get to the point where she could say as much and mean it, but it was the truth.

"Well, I didn't come here to discuss him anyway. Only to discuss what he wants done. Quite frankly . . . what he wants done immediately."

Olivia, who had been gazing down at the sleeping babe, glanced up, a curious frown on her face. "What is that?"

Meredith hesitated a moment and then drew her shoulders up, her back suddenly as straight as a ramrod. "I would like you to take her. Rather . . . he would like it. And, of course, since we are going back to England, I cannot but agree that it would be a good idea for you to have the child." She lifted her chin slightly and gazed straight ahead. "I cannot live with the shame of it. I want to start my life anew. David is giving me the chance to do so, and therefore I must abide by his wishes."

It was a moment before Olivia could speak. "You want to give your own child to me?"

"She is your kin. Your niece. You told me once you had always wanted a child. Did you not?"

"Yes, I did, but . . ."

"But what? Are you refusing my offer? I must know if you don't, in order that we can take another route of action. We are leaving tomorrow."

"What other route of action?" Olivia's eyes widened. "Certainly you don't mean an orphanage?"

Meredith chewed one corner of her mouth for a moment. "It would be better if we could place her ourselves, but since we are leaving so soon, there isn't any time. . . ."

"You really mean all this, don't you?"

"I would not be here if I did not."

Olivia said calmly, "Do you not love her, Meredith?"

Meredith seemed to contemplate the question. "I do not know. I only know that if David cannot bear the thought of the child living with us, then I must do something. I am his wife."

"You have changed a great deal, Meredith."

Meredith raised her eyebrows and pursed her lips. "Yes, I suppose I have. Everyone changes. But . . . the truth is, I did not want children so soon in my life."

Olivia shook her head. "I don't believe you, Meredith. I think you simply didn't want my brother's child. You think that since something is wrong with his mind, then the same will hold true for his daughter. But that isn't so. Aaron's problems were not part of his natural makeup."

"All that may be well and true, but the fact remains that my husband does not believe it."

"And you don't think you could convince him of it?"

"No. I'm certain of it."

Both women were silent for a moment. Olivia looked

down at the baby and then up at Meredith. "Then my answer to you is yes. Of course I will take her."

Meredith hesitated for the briefest moment and then gave a decisive nod of her head. She stood up and went to the porch railing and called out to the girl at the carriage. "Bring it here, Becky."

Meredith turned then while her servant reached back inside the carriage, pulled out a large box, and gathered it in her arms. As she walked toward the house, Meredith turned and handed the basket to Olivia. Olivia held it firmly in her arms and gazed down at the baby again before replacing the protective tulle netting.

"Just put it there," Meredith ordered the young girl, who set the box down near the steps and then turned around and went back to the carriage.

"Well then," she said, pushing the seams of her gloves between each finger, "I suppose that is all. The box has all of her belongings. At least a year's supply that my mother purchased. Silly of her," she added, looking away.

"I don't really know what to say, Meredith," Olivia said tentatively. Her heart was breaking for the woman who stood before her. Though she herself was thrilled beyond belief to be holding the tiny baby in her arms, she could not imagine ever being so in thrall of a man that she would do what Meredith was doing now. But then, one could not always judge the actions of others based on one's own personal convictions.

"Except," she added, "that I will love her as my own. And I will tell her about you when she is old enough to understand."

Meredith's eyes darted swiftly back to Olivia's. "You don't need to do that."

Olivia didn't answer; she knew there was no use in explaining that she would do what she felt was the right thing, regardless of what Meredith said now.

"I will be going, then," Meredith said, moving toward the steps. "We have much to do before we leave."

Olivia followed her down the steps, waiting for Meredith to make a move to at least look at the baby one more time, to say good-bye to her. But Meredith hurried away from her, as if she could not bear to linger a moment longer. At the gate, she stopped, turned, and said, almost as an afterthought, "I do thank you, Olivia."

"You don't need to, Meredith. I hope your life will be happy."

Meredith gave the slightest shift of her gaze toward the basket, then nodded once and turned on her heel and hastened toward the carriage. Quickly she and the servant were handed up inside the vehicle, and the driver resumed his seat. Within less than a minute the carriage was headed back up the rise.

Just then, the baby awoke and began fussing. Olivia pulled the netting back and spoke softly. "Shhhh. It's all right, little Sarah. It's all right." The baby quietened. Then she looked back up, toward the top of the bluff; the carriage was gone. Only a puff of dust above the dusty road gave evidence that it had even passed by.

Olivia picked up the basket and went inside the house. She set it down on the couch and went back outside for the box, which she placed on the floor near one of the chairs. Then she sat down on the couch and gingerly lifted the baby, surprised at her feather-lightness. Cradling the baby girl's head with the palm of her hand, she maneuvered the child until she lay cuddled in her arms.

Slowly the baby began to blink, and then all at once her eyelids opened wide and she was staring directly into Olivia's own eyes. Olivia was stunned; it was as though she were staring into a mirror. Sarah's eyes were the same clear, grass-green color that she saw in her own hand mirror. Her eyes; her brother's eyes.

It was meant to be, she thought; everything she had done in her life until now had led to this one profound moment of happiness. It was as simple, and miraculous, as that. She lowered her head and lightly kissed the top of Sarah's head. "I'll love you forever, little one. Forever."

The baby was the most wonderful gift that Olivia had ever received in her life. She had loved before, that was certain, but it was doubtful she had ever loved anyone as fiercely as she did the beautiful baby she kept at her side almost every hour of the day.

But Olivia was not the only person affected by the presence of the noisy, cheerful infant. Aaron, after recovering from his initial surprise and incomprehension of the presence of the baby, took a shine to her that was unmatched by any other Olivia had ever observed in him. Cutter, too, seemed instantly in love with the child. He crafted so many pieces of baby furniture alone that Olivia soon was running out of space for it. Within the space of one day, all of their lives were changed. Meals were not always on time anymore, chores sometimes had to wait, and nights were often sleepless as Sarah went through various stages of colic and teething and just plain fussiness.

But none of them would have traded a moment of the discomfort she visited upon them. Indeed, Olivia and Cutter were known to get into more than a few arguments over the various treatments that were sometimes necessary. Aaron learned to help with the feedings and changings, and would often spend over an hour at night walking with Sarah cradled against his shoulder so that she would relax enough to sleep through the night.

On the morning of Sarah's first birthday, Olivia took one look at her scarlet cheeks and glassy eyes and was seized with fright. She picked her up, felt the limp little limbs and the fire-hot fever and panicked. She raced to the back door and screamed for Aaron and Cutter, and within three minutes they were all in the wagon and headed toward Hays. Cutter had put Rainy in harness, and the gelding seemed to sense the importance of the moment, for his head stretched out and his legs flew along the sides of the road where the ruts weren't so bad.

The doctor wasn't in; he'd been called out the previous night on an emergency, but his wife informed Olivia that he should be arriving shortly.

Cutter worked the tobacco in his mouth until it drove Olivia to distraction and she finally asked him to get rid of it. He did so immediately and, after coming back inside the small waiting room which was located on the side of the doctor's frame house, said, "Give her to me." Olivia shook her head but he insisted, "Naw, now come on. She needs Uncle Cutter here to shush her up." He took the crying baby in his wiry arms and started whistling the one and only tune Olivia had ever heard from him. She could replicate it, in fact, in her sleep, and normally it drove her to distraction to hear it more than three consecutive times, but today she didn't care. Sarah responded to the sound of Cutter's whistling as if it were something she'd been wanting to hear all along. Aaron, who sat stiffly in a chair, seemed visibly relieved when the baby stopped crying, even smiling and making faces at her whenever Cutter would pass back and forth in front of him.

Dr. Morgenstern was surprised to see the trio waiting for him, but after examining the infant he prescribed medicine and told them to take her home, bathe her in tepid water, and keep her calm. The horses and other livestock were lucky to be fed that day and the next, for each of them tended to little Sarah around the clock, until finally her fever broke and she came out of her illness almost forty-eight hours later. Aaron smiled and held the baby on his lap, helping to feed her bits of soft bread while Olivia fired up the stove to fix them all a decent meal. Cutter declared he was going to his quarters in the stable to uncork his favorite flask of corn brew. He'd felled an acre of trees before and hadn't felt as exhausted as he was right then and there.

That night, as Olivia lay in bed, she prayed for a good ten minutes, giving thanks for Sarah's recovery.

Unfortunately, sleeping through the night didn't happen for a good eighteen months after Sarah arrived—for any of them. When it did for the first time, Olivia awakened to sunshine peeking through her window, and her heart set up a powerful throbbing in her chest. Dear God, she thought, something must have happened. She panicked, jumping out of bed and over to the net-covered maple bed in which Sarah lay sleeping. Thumb in her mouth, her soft brown curls spread about her head, she looked nothing less than a beautiful, angelic creature.

For Sarah's second birthday, they had a party, just the four of them. After tea and cake, which Sarah managed to smear all over her newly sewn calico dress that Olivia had worked on for over a week, Aaron went with Cutter out back to the barn to fetch her present. Olivia sat Sarah down on the rocker next to her own, but she was having none of it. She bounded off the chair and into the front yard, where the hens were pecking away at leftover seed.

"Chicky, chicky," the toddler called out in a voice already deep and throaty, much like the beautiful, melodic tone of Meredith's.

Olivia, arms crossed beneath her bosom, shook her head and clucked her tongue as she watched her trying to catch one of the largest hens, which, of course, sent them all squawking and running. "Sarah, you little devil. Honey, come back over here."

"No, Mommy," she shouted back, a determined frown on her face. "Chicky, chicky. Come 'ere!"

Only upon seeing Aaron and Cutter did she stop what she was doing and race back up to where Olivia was.

"Pull off the sack, sugar," Cutter said, wiggling his eyebrows up and down.

Aaron nodded several times, then sat down on one of the rockers to watch.

Sarah yanked off the covering, and her mouth and eyes opened wide in the same moment. She clapped her hands together in front of her face and began exclaiming, "Horsey, horsey! Horsey, Mommy, horsey! See it? Horsey!"

Everyone was chuckling at the delight and excitement Sarah expressed for the small wood-carved rocking horse Cutter and Aaron had been laboring on for weeks, and Olivia leaned down and planted a big kiss on her daughter's cheek. "Happy birthday, sweetie. You really like it, don't you?"

"Oh, Mommy, my own horsey!" She began jumping up and down so hard and fast that the toe of one leather shoe snagged between two planks and she plunged to the floor. She started crying in earnest, but Aaron picked her up quickly and placed her astride the rocking horse. The tears were soon gone.

"I do believe she likes it, don'tcha think?" Cutter said, a most pleased expression on his weathered features.

Olivia nodded and, smiling, said, "There's no doubt of that."

Time seemed to accelerate as the next two years came and went. Sarah grew so quickly that it was all Olivia could do to keep her clothed, let alone keep up with the toddler's incredible amount of energy. She played as hard as she learned, and learn she certainly did. By the time she was three, she spoke as well as a five-year-old, and by the time her fourth birthday approached, she bombarded them all with incessant questions.

She wanted to know how things worked, why they did what they did, why the sky was blue, why the grass blew over sideways when it was windy, what caused the wind, what caused the rain, why did horses have four legs . . . when she could ride her own horse all by herself, of course. She never let up. But Olivia never grew tired of it all. She would often find herself lying in the middle of one of the hayfields, flat on her back, eyes closed, and trying to keep a straight face as Sarah stroked the tip of a grass stalk up and down her cheeks, over her forehead, and beneath her chin. All the while, of course, asking one question after another.

"Mommy?"

"Yes, Sarah-doll," Olivia would answer.

"I'm not a doll," Sarah would pout, her green eyes narrowing, her lips pursed together.

"Oh that's right, you're not a little doll. I forgot."

"Silly Mommy."

Olivia would sigh and shake her head slowly. "Silly me, that's right."

"Mommy?"

"Yes, Sarah-doll. Uh-oh, sorry, I mean Sarah."

"Mommy, I want to ask you something."

"I know, Sarah. You always want to ask me something. What would you like to know?"

"This is 'portant, Mommy." Sarah's brows were drawn together, and she stared intently at Olivia.

Olivia mirrored the seriousness in the little girl's expression, sat up a bit and said, "Yes. . . ?"

"Well, Mommy . . ." Sarah squirmed and then lifted her shoulders, took in a deep breath and asked, "How come no birds ever give milk? Like cows do. How come?"

It was all Olivia could do to suppress the laughter gurgling up inside her throat but she said as levelly as she could, "Well . . . honey, they aren't supposed to."

"Why not?"

"Hmmm, let's see. How do I explain this? The reason birds never give milk is . . . is . . . is because, well, because they don't have any milk to give!"

Sarah screwed up her face and looked off to the side, contemplating the answer she had just received. But Olivia suddenly pulled the little girl down on top of her and began tickling her furiously. Sarah's shrieks of laughter filled the air and Olivia taunted in a mock-serious tone, "Have any more questions, Sarah-doll?"

Now each day seemed absolutely beautiful, filled with promise. It didn't matter if she felt ill, tired, irritated. . . . She would not have traded one single minute of the past four years. Her love for Sarah was solid. She could not fathom life without her. To do so was simply unthinkable. Unimaginable.

CHAPTER XIX

LEAH'S pen had long since ceased moving. She had listened for the past half hour, completely absorbed in the story the woman in the rocking chair was relating. Now there was silence, and not only was Olivia staring unseeingly straight ahead, but she also.

Sounds filtered in from the open window: two blue-jays squawking at each other from the tree nearby, the chug-chug of a Model T as it traveled the street below, the faint creaking of the branches as a gentle wind removed the leaves and sent them fluttering through the air.

Olivia finally spoke, her voice faraway, still in the past. "She was my little one for four and a half years. That was all." Here her voice broke slightly and she lifted a hand to still her quivering chin. Then she became very matter-of-fact-sounding once again. Leah listened closely.

"Her mother came back, you see. Her real mother. Though of course, by then it was I who was her real mother. I had never imagined any such thing would happen. Ever. But it did. You see she—Meredith—had been widowed two years after she and David were married. When she remarried, her new husband decided to move her back to the States for a while. He could see no reason not to help her raise her only child, and so they came straight to Kansas.

"Well, she found me right where I was when she had left. Only this time it was all so different. Victoria was gone by then. Disappeared. Just like it had never been there. That was in, oh, seventy-eight or thereabouts. But we'd stayed put; things had gotten better, the crops were good for two straight years in a row, and my little Sarah was thriving. Aaron was, too. He loved her so, was so sweet to her. He was still much the same, but the baby—well, she took his mind off his thoughts, his fears, you see?"

Olivia smiled. "It was so heartening to see them together. Walking through the fields—he'd put her on his shoulders, and all you could see was her dark, curly head bobbing up and down, slow, then fast as he'd run with her through the grass. Her laugh would carry so. . . . Cutter and I used to shake our heads in amazement at the sound of it. It was so wonderful to see Aaron like that! So wonderful!

" 'Mommy,' Sarah would say, 'Mommy, where Awon?' If he was anywhere near, he would drop whatever he was doing and give her anything she wanted." Olivia sighed. "But she loved me, too. She really did. When she was around two and a half, I let her get in my bed." Olivia closed her eyes. "I can still feel her cuddled up in my arms, curled up next to me like a little spoon. She used to tell me before she went to bed and the first thing in the morning that she loved me."

Olivia's eyes opened, and her gaze lowered to the floor. "I thought she would always be with me. She was truly the most wonderful little girl. I loved her more than anything, or anyone." She shook her head slowly. "I thought the men who left me caused me great pain. It was nothing, *nothing* compared to the day when I lost her.''

Leah, who had drunk in every word of what Olivia was relating, every single detail, paid even closer attention now. Trying very hard to keep the nervousness out of her tone, she asked, ''What happened?''

''Oh, it was all quite simple, actually. Meredith arrived one day, just as she had arrived to bring her to me. But this time she brought her new husband with her. Very forceful character, he was. Polite but forceful. He explained that he had spoken with a lawyer, that I had no legal right to keep the child, and the mother wanted her back. Meredith was so changed, I hardly recognized her. She just stared right at the ground at her feet. Don't think she looked at me more than once or twice. Finally he told her to get back in the carriage. She did it, just like that. He then kept talking to me, breaking me down with insinuations that we could take care of it privately, without the aid of the sheriff, if I so wished. Many such statements. I was distraught beyond belief. I almost panicked, and then I thought, All right, I'll cooperate with them now. The last thing I wanted was a confrontation with the law. I didn't want them arriving and making a scene. There was no telling how the little one would take that. Nor Aaron. And, I figured, they would change their minds. They'd see she didn't want to go with them, and they'd just let her stay.

''But it didn't work out that way. He told me not to worry about her belongings—she wouldn't be needing them—just to get her and bring her along straightaway. Well . . . what can I say? It was the most painful thing I ever had to do in my whole life. She was in the hayfield with Aaron and Cutter; they had taken her for a ride in the back of the wagon. Naturally, she didn't want to come, but I persuaded her by telling her I had some sweets for her. She had a great sweet tooth, you see. She walked ahead of me down one of the paths and—this I've never forgotten—she turned around and with her big, green eyes lit up as bright as ever, shouted as loud as she could, 'You can't catch me, Mommy!' And then she was off, and I was running behind her, and when I caught her, we both fell down. It didn't hurt; the ground was grassy and soft. There we were in a field of grass, lying completely hidden in it. Just the two of us, the tall, sweet grass, and the blue sky above our heads. I held her in my arms for a long time, letting her tickle me with a bunch of wildflowers she'd picked. I thought if my life could just have ended right then, it would have been enough . . . a complete life.''

Olivia paused for a while. ''You know,'' she said, ''I haven't spoken to anyone about this before now. It's been—what?—some forty-two—forty-three years. That's a long time, wouldn't you say? It wouldn't seem that something that happened so long ago could still hurt so bad.'' She sighed heavily. ''I guess it's because I always felt the coward. On the one hand, I had no legal right to keep her; on the other, I loved her more than anything. And I just handed her over to them. They promised to write to me, let me know how she was doing. . . .'' Olivia shrugged, and the corners of her mouth turned downward. ''But they never did anything of the sort. Just disappeared. I think they must have left that very day on the train. I had no idea where to look, but I sure tried. Wrote letters to strangers in various city governments, thinking they might have some sort of way to get information for me—I mean, I knew the man's name and all. I figured he might be a prominent citizen somewhere. But nothing happened. Nothing at all.

''Well—It hurt so bad at first, I thought I was going to die. Lost so much weight, Cutter got scared and took me into town to see the doctor. He was a nice man, real nice. He knew what had happened—everyone did—and he just told me to go on and grieve about my little girl. Nice man. He understood. I really think he did.''

Olivia plucked at a loose thread on her shawl, and her face seemed suddenly to sag; she seemed diminished, defeated, as if she were living those days all over again. ''There's not much else to tell you, Mrs. Rice. My life went on; Aaron's didn't. Not for much longer. He took ill with lung fever the following winter and died before springtime. He never got over the little girl leaving. I never could explain it to him. He must have asked me every single day from the day she left when she was coming back. He thought, you see, like she did, that she was just going off with the nice lady and man for a ride. For a treat. Thought she was coming right back. I think it was better that he died so soon after. Couldn't stand to see him tortured like that.

''Well, Cutter stayed on, and we tried to keep up the farm, but neither of us had the heart for it anymore. One day I saw an ad in the Hays paper for a teaching job near Ellsworth. They accepted me right away, as they had no other applicants. I stayed a year. Didn't much like it; I was so tired of the isolation, the loneliness, so I decided to move on again. I sold the property near Victoria and then decided to move back east. Topeka was as far as I got. Started back teaching, went to college eventually to get my teacher's certificate, and taught until I couldn't go on anymore.'' She lifted her hands and held them in front of her. ''Until this cursed arthritis crippled my joints and I could no longer write—or even turn the pages of a book.''

Olivia looked up at the woman who had been listening in complete silence all this while. ''You're not writing. Sorry if I was boring you, but . . . that's about the extent of it. Not very exciting, I suppose."

Leah, her features pale and taut, began to shake her head slowly from side to side. "You said . . ." She swallowed, barely able to utter the words. "You said . . . about the grass . . ."

"Grass?"

"The grass you were running through. The tall grass where you fell down with the little girl. The little girl with the dark hair and green eyes."

"Sarah."

Leah nodded, swallowed again, feeling a hot sting in her eyes. "I have green eyes. I've always had dark hair." Her voice broke, and her lower lip trembled. Again she swallowed, feeling a single tear course its way down the side of her face and down onto her neck.

When she spoke, it was in a whisper. "I have something to tell you, Olivia. I am your Sarah. I am the little girl you held in the grass. Me."

The old woman seemed so stunned that she hesitated for a moment. But she had to go on . . . had to reveal the reason she had come here. After all these years of searching, she'd found her answer.

Leah began: "I've remembered you all my life. Though I didn't know for a long time what I was remembering. I used to have these dreams; dreams of grass, tall, wavy grass that completely surrounded me. And in these dreams I was always laughing, and I knew, I knew that someone else was making me laugh. It was just the happiest feeling in the whole world. But then I would wake up and I would realize there was no reason for the dream.

"I lived in London until I was twenty-two years old. My parents took me on trips, but never to any place where there was this grass that kept haunting my dreams."

Leah paused, took in a deep breath, and let it out slowly. The old woman was staring straight at her, her own green eyes widened and filled with incredulous wonder.

"I asked my mother for years," Leah went on, "if there was somewhere I had been as a toddler, perhaps, that would have accounted for that dream, but she always dismissed the notion, said it was silly to keep bringing it up over and over again.

"She died when I was twenty-five. My father died the next year. But on his deathbed he told me about my early years. Or some of it. He said I had lived with someone else until I was four—didn't say who, just that it was a blood relative of mine. And then he told me he wasn't my real father, that my real father had had a mental deficiency; that was the reason they'd never told me. They thought I would worry too much about it, think I would end up the same way." Leah's eyes narrowed as she recalled further. "He told me I was called Sarah before he became my father, and he and my mother changed my name to Leah. He was very close to death when he revealed all this, and sometimes he was almost incoherent. But I kept after him, badgering him really, waking him up, making him talk. It was mean, but I couldn't let him die before telling me everything. Just before he did die, I managed to get out of him that my father's first name was Aaron and that I had lived those early years somewhere in Kansas.

"I looked and looked after that, but came up with nothing. I even moved to Kansas to explore my past. Met my husband here, in fact. I drove him to distraction with my obsession. He kept thinking it would end. But it didn't. Then he heard about the Monroe project and encouraged me to get involved. To get my mind off things, I think was his purpose. He was tired of listening to me by then." Leah smiled. "But he did me the biggest favor in the whole world. As soon as I came across your name on the list of early pioneer women of Kansas, I knew this was the strongest possibility I had ever—or would ever probably—come across. You see, the nursing home here provided us with data on its most elderly patients. And on your record, it showed that you had had one sibling. Named Aaron.''

She stopped, swallowed, and blinked her green eyes at the old woman, who was as still as a statue. "I know I'm Sarah, Olivia." She smiled. "I always knew there was more to the dream, and now I remember it all. I remember my father—he was big, wasn't he, really tall, and he had lots of dark, dark hair. Didn't he? And I remember you. . . . I remember you very clearly now. You made me sweets, cookies and candies. I can still smell—''

She stopped suddenly, alarmed that Olivia had lowered her head, wasn't looking at her anymore. Then she saw the frail shoulders moving beneath the shawl, and she slowly got out of her chair. She crossed the space between herself and the woman she had once called "Mommy" and lowered herself to her knees before her. She placed her hands over Olivia's gnarled ones, squeezed them once, and then massaged them gently and repeatedly.

Olivia lifted her head, and then, slowly, her gaze. Her green eyes were clear and glistening with tears. "So long," she whispered. "Why did it have to be so long?"

Leah's voice was quiet, accepting. "I don't know why. We'll never have an answer to that." She added, "I missed you, Olivia. In my heart there was always something missing, and it was you."

Olivia's lips pressed firmly together and then lifted into a quivering smile.

And then, soothed by the peace that had eluded her for so very, very long, she answered, "But I was always there."

CHAPTER XX

Henry Rice pulled the Model T over to the side of the dirt road on the outskirts of Victoria and, after several residual sputters of the engine, opened the door and got out. With his wife's help, he assisted the elderly woman from the backseat, took her wooden walker with which she was able to traverse short distances, and handed it to his wife.

Olivia stared out from beneath the wide-brimmed hat Leah had bought her, temporarily blinded by the bright spring sunshine. The prairie here stretched before them in an undulating, unbroken line toward the horizon, the tall grass and the fields of corn and wheat waving beneath the invisible, soughing wind. It was the same, she thought, just the same. Didn't matter about the telegraph lines springing up here and there, didn't matter at all.

She turned to face Henry, Leah's kind, generous husband, also a man of substantial strength and girth, and gave a nod. Pride would not get in her way this day. "You ready?" he asked.

"Yes," she answered, watching as Leah set out ahead of them toward a path leading into the grass.

Henry lifted her, one arm behind her shoulder blades,

the other beneath her knees, and set off after his wife. When Leah stopped, he did so, too, then gingerly set Olivia on her feet. He turned then and said, "Take as long as you like." And then he started back down the path, his figure disappearing completely in a few moments.

Olivia took in a deep breath, closed her eyes, and felt Leah take her hand in hers. "Here, hold on to my arm," she said.

Carefully, with Leah to lean on, Olivia lowered herself to the ground right alongside her niece. The grass was all around them, completely camouflaging their presence from the rest of the world. Neither woman said a word; none were necessary. The bond they'd formed so many years ago was everlasting. Leah leaned to one side, plucked a few stray wildflowers, and then turned to Olivia. She raised her eyebrows, smiled, and then tickled the end of Olivia's nose with the fragrant blue petals.

Olivia smiled back, her heart swelling with satisfaction, with love . . . with completion. She tilted her head up and watched fleecy clouds drifting past in the azure sky. The world was still moving along, and with it . . . time.

But for Olivia, at long last, time *had* stopped. Right where she wanted it to.

About the Author

Nancy A. Hermann lives outside Houston, Texas, with her cardiologist husband and their two young adopted sons. She and her husband raise and show thoroughbred hunters and jumpers.

THE HOMESTEAD is Nancy Hermann's second novel for Ballantine Books, following OF SIMPLE DREAMS, the story of a young wife drawn into a community of Shakers. She is working on a third, set on the Texas frontier.

back inside the house and carrying on somehow as he did each and every day.